Mike Gayle has contributed to a variety of magazines including *FHM, Sunday Times Style* and *Cosmopolitan.* He is the author of eight bestselling novels. Visit Mike's website at www.mikegayle.co.uk

Praise for Mike Gayle and The *Importance of being a Bachelor*:

'This is Mike Gayle at his best – funny, charming, and life-affirming' *Daily Mail*

'Packed with drama, friendship, love and tragedy, this is a brilliant touching tale of what happens when real life catches up with us.' *Heat*

'What I love about Mike Gayle is the way he seamlessly blends humour and sensitivity – his books are always rip-roaringly funny, yet so humane too.' Freya North

'Mike Gayle creates real, ordinary people with real, ordinary lives who are so real and so believable that you mourn for them from the moment you finish reading.' Lisa Jewell

Also by Mike Gayle

My Legendary Girlfriend
Mr Commitment
Turning Thirty
Dinner for Two
His 'n' Hers
Brand New Friend
Wish You Were Here
Life and Soul of the Party

Non-fiction

The To-Do List

THE IMPORTANCE OF BEING A BACHELOR

MIKE GAYLE

HODDER

First published in Great Britain in 2010 by Hodder & Stoughton
An Hachette UK company

First published in paperback in 2011

1

A CIP catalogue record for this title is
available from the British Library

ISBN 978 0 340 91852 4 (B format)
978 1 444 7 2200 0 (A format)

Typeset in Benguiat by Hewer Text UK Ltd, Edinburgh
Printed and bound by Clays Ltd, St Ives plc

Hodder & Stoughton policy is to use papers that are natural, renewable
and recyclable products and made from wood grown in sustainable
forests. The logging and manufacturing processes are expected to
conform to the environmental regulations of the country of origin.

Hodder & Stoughton Ltd
338 Euston Road
London NW1 3BH

www.hodder.co.uk

Thus we never see the true state of our condition, till it is illustrated to us by its contraries; nor know how to value what we enjoy, but by the want of it.

Robinson Crusoe **Daniel Defoe**

To C. for everything

Acknowledgements

Thanks to Sue Fletcher, Swati Gamble and all at Hodder, Simon Trewin and all at United Agents, Phil Gayle, The Sunday Night Pub Club, Jackie Behan, The Board, Ron Davison, Danny Wallace, Chris McCabe and everyone who took the time to drop me a line this year. And thank you, above all, to C, for pretty much everything.

Part 1

'But are they happy?'

'Do you think we've done OK?'

It was just after six on a balmy Saturday night in June and sixty-eight-year-old pensioner and former GMPTE bus driver George Bachelor was settling down to watch his all-time favourite film that was just starting on Channel Five when Joan, his wife of nearly forty years, asked her question. George, who was more than a little bit concerned about missing the beginning of the film, considered the mug of tea in his left hand (strong and sweet just the way he liked it) and then the TV remote control in his right. George took great comfort in the fact that he knew the buttons on the remote control if not better than the back of his own hand then at least better than any hand belonging to any other member of his family. Since they had first bought their thirty-two inch Sony Bravia TV just over eight years ago George had spent a lot of time with its remote control and considered it possibly the single most useful tool that he owned. He often found himself remembering with disdain the days before TVs had remote controls. Obviously life had been simpler back then as there had only been a handful of channels but he recalled with perfect clarity just how much effort it sometimes took to summon up the will to leave the comfort of his chair (the very same chair in which he was sitting now) and rise to his feet (having endured the stresses and strains of a day at work on the buses) and turn over the channel at nine o'clock so that he could watch the news.

'Did you hear what I just said?'

George looked over at his wife. She appeared as though she was expecting some sort of reply but to what he couldn't begin to fathom. His hearing wasn't quite what it used to be plus he'd done all that thinking about tea and remote controls in between so the thread of whatever thought he might have had about whatever Joan had been going on about had long since been lost.

'Yes,' he said eventually. 'Of course I heard you.'

'So what do you think?'

George shrugged and turned off the sound on the TV. If he heard the dialogue he wouldn't be able to concentrate. 'I don't mind. Whatever you think is best is fine by me.'

'You weren't listening, were you?' said Joan.

'You're sat less than a yard away from me. Of course I was listening. I heard every single word you said.'

'So what did I say then?'

'How am I supposed to know?' said George, looking at the TV forlornly. He hated missing the beginnings of films and that included films of which he had previously seen the beginnings. It made him feel unsettled. 'You asked me a question and then started with a million and one questions about the first question followed by a lot of accusations about whether or not I was listening. I can't be expected to keep all that lot in my head can I?'

Joan sighed in the manner of a woman well versed in the art of communicating non-verbal displeasure. 'You were thinking about the film weren't you? It's only *Bridge On the River Kwai.*'

'Which is my favourite film.'

'Which you also happen to own on both videotape *and* on one of those DVD things too that came free with the Sunday paper.'

'It's not the same,' said George. 'I like films when they're on TV. They just seem better somehow.'

Joan said nothing and so George found himself feeling guilty. 'So what is it that you were asking?'

'If you thought that we'd done OK.'

'With what?'

'The boys of course: Adam, Luke and Russell.'

'I know who they are,' he said impatiently. 'You don't need to remind me of our children's names. What about them?'

'Do you think we've done OK with them. You know, done a good job of raising them to be decent young men.'

'What a thing to ask right at the beginning of *Bridge On the River Kwai*! What's brought all this on?'

'There was an item on the radio this morning while I was ironing. Jenni Murray was interviewing a lady who had written a book about the difficulties women face in raising sons and then they opened it up to the panel that they had in the studio. It was very interesting actually and it just got me thinking about what kind of job I'd done with the boys. I mean, look at them. All three of them are grown men and yet none of them are married.'

'It's different now,' explained George. 'Times have changed.'

'But are they happy?'

'How would I know?' shrugged George. 'They seem fine to me. Why don't you ask them tomorrow when they come for lunch?'

'Oh, you know what they're like. I can never get a straight answer out of any of them. I ask Adam why he's never brought anyone home to meet us and he just rolls his eyes like I'm some kind of lunatic. I mean it's not exactly a daft question, is it? He's never brought a single girl home! Then I ask Luke if he and Cassie have ever talked about making things official and he gives me the run-around saying that after last time "marriage just isn't on the agenda". And as for Russell, what am I supposed to think? The only girl he ever brings around here these days is that friend of his, Angie, and she's got a boyfriend! I don't understand it, do you, George? Why is a twenty-nine-year-old man spending so much time with a young woman who's in a relationship with someone else? It doesn't make any sense at all, does it?'

'I think she's a lovely girl,' said George, resigned to the fact that there was little or no chance of his being able to watch this film. 'He says they're friends. There's no harm in that, is there?'

'Well,' replied Joan. 'I don't think it's right.'

There was a long silence. George wondered if he could be bothered to put in the effort it would take to search out that free DVD Joan had been on about and recall his middle son's instructions on how to work the DVD player that he and Cassie had bought him for Christmas. He looked at his wife and then at the remote control. It might only take a minute or two to get into the film if Joan had actually finished with her questions for the evening.

'So, do you really think we've done OK with our boys?'

For the sake of a quiet life George considered the question carefully. 'I think we've done fine,' he said at last. 'They're just late developers, that's all.'

'Not exactly girlfriend material.'

At roughly the same time that George Bachelor found himself considering the question of his and his wife's ability to raise their children his eldest son, Adam Bachelor (bar owner, man about town and current holder of the title 'second best-looking bloke in Chorlton'), was standing at the crowded bar of Cheshire's exclusive Forest Hill Golf Club at the wedding reception of his friend Leo listening to his friend Jon proffering the following question: 'Which of us do you think will be the next to get hitched?'

As the laughter began and various theories were put forward Adam closed his eyes and yawned not just because he wasn't interested in getting into any debate that involved matrimony but also because right now all he wanted was to go to sleep. He was more used than most of his friends to the occasional late night, but the previous evening had been something of a marathon even for him.

Gathering together the boys for what was ostensibly Leo's second (and secret) stag do, Adam had led his friends into a night of monumental drinking that had taken in all their old haunts that still existed. The night had crawled to a conclusion some time after six that morning where, following breakfast at an all-night café in Rusholme, they had climbed into the back of the limousine that Adam had rented for the night and were dropped off at their own front doors before Adam finally allowed himself and the groom to be taken back to Adam's flat in Chorlton.

With eight hours to go before the actual wedding Adam and Leo assured themselves they would have plenty of time to recover from their evening of festivities. But when, sometime after seven, Leo's fiancée called Adam on his mobile with a long list of things that needed doing in his role as best man, Adam had to concede that he was well and truly up the creek. For the next seven hours he barely had a moment to himself as he ran around south Manchester undertaking all manner of errands before finally arriving back at his flat to pick up a suited, booted (and incredibly well rested) Leo and taking him to the church. And even though there had been times when he had wanted nothing more than to be sick or fall asleep (and on one occasion both at the same time) he had executed his duties like a true professional. He handed the rings to the groom at precisely the right moment, was charming to any elderly people passed to him for safe keeping, delivered a memorable and witty best-man speech and – when it looked like Joanna might get into a slanging match with one of the caterers over the fact that they had 'under-ordered' on the vegetarian main courses – he sorted that out too without even the slightest hint of bloodshed to offend the aforementioned meat-shy. All in all he had done a top job of being best man even if he said so himself.

'My money is definitely on Martin,' said Jon as Adam tuned back into the debate.

'No chance,' laughed Martin. 'Kay gave up all hope years ago, mate. For what it's worth my money is on Rich and Emma. He doesn't think we noticed but Emma's been sporting a big old rock on her left hand for a good few weeks now.'

'It's just a dress ring!' protested Rich. 'At least that's what she told me! Moving swiftly on, my money's on Del and Jen. The way Del's missus was talking up matrimony with Em over a chicken bhuna at mine last week makes me think he's got six to eight months tops!'

'No way!' said Del. 'No way at all. The way I see it is this: obviously discounting those of us that are already hitched, namely Fad, Leo of course and Dave, I reckon it'll be Rich and Emma first; me and Jen second; third Jon and Shelley; fourth Martin and Kay; and fifth Ade and Lorna.'

Adam looked at Del. 'What about me?'

Del looked confused. 'What do you mean what about you?'

'Exactly what I said: "What about me?" '

As one Adam's friends turned to him wearing the same expression of disbelief and confusion.

'What?' he said defensively. 'Why does one simple question cause you all to look at me like I'm a dog that's just walked into a bar on its hind legs and ordered a pint?'

'Probably because the likelihood of you getting married is about the same! Mate, with the best will in the world there are two chances of you getting married before any of us – no chance and slim chance. And do you know what? Slim's out of town.'

'What are you talking about?' said Adam as the boys all laughed at Jon's well-worn joke. 'Are you trying to tell me that Ade and Lorna – a woman who, let's not forget, once threw a carving knife at Ade's head – are more likely to get married than me?'

'Not that old one again,' interrupted Ade. 'First off, it was a long time ago; second, she missed; and third, she didn't really mean it. She was just a bit annoyed.'

'Ade, mate,' said Adam. 'She threw a knife. At. Your. Head. The fact that she's a rubbish aim is the only reason you're standing here tonight. When most women get angry they slam doors or smash china. They do not throw knives!' Adam turned back to Del. 'So as I was saying you'd give Ade better odds of getting married than me?'

Jon chipped in. 'How deluded are you? Of course Ade's got more chance of getting married than you have. For starters he's actually got a girlfriend.'

'And?' questioned Adam, unwilling to let small details like 'girlfriends' get in the way of him making his point.

'What do you mean "and"?' said Jon in his best withering tones. 'Have you lost the plot, mate? One of the prerequisites of getting married is that you have somebody to get married to, otherwise, well, you're just a bloke in a suit throwing a party for all your mates.'

'I'll have you know that if I actually wanted a girlfriend I could get a girlfriend just like that.' Adam proceeded to snap his fingers like a latter-day Paul Daniels as though he was about to conjure a girlfriend out of thin air.

'Mate,' said Del, placing a deliberately patronising hand on Adam's shoulders. 'We all know that you have a gift with the ladies. We all know that you can and indeed have pulled some of the most amazing women we could ever hope to see. But there's one thing we're sure of: you will not be getting married in this or in fact any other century.'

'And your reasoning is?'

Del shook his head in despair. 'Mate, are you really trying to say that you don't know?'

'If I did I wouldn't be asking the question, would I?'

'But you're not really going to make us spell it out for you, are you?' chipped in Fad. 'Surely you can't be that dense.'

'Well I must be, because I have no idea what any of you are on about. So come on. Take a moment out from your world of mirth to explain why out of all my oldest friends I am apparently the one least likely to take a walk down the aisle?'

The friends exchanged wary glances before staring contemplatively into their pints. Del then drew a deep breath, which Adam took as a signal that he had nominated himself the chief deliverer of home truths.

'Listen mate,' began Del, 'I just want to say that in no way do we see this as a deficiency in you. In fact it's the total opposite. We're completely envious of you. You're like . . . I don't know . . . the Fonz . . .'

'Or the bloke from *Cheers*,' said Fad.

'Or better still Warren Beatty in *Shampoo*,' added Rich.

'So what you're saying is I'm a womaniser?'

The boys all winced at Adam's use of such an old-fashioned pejorative word and shook their heads in unison.

'You're not a womaniser as such,' said Del diplomatically.

'What then?' asked Adam. 'I'm like the bloke out of *Cheers* only I'm not a womaniser . . . you're not saying anything really, are you?'

'The thing is,' said Del tentatively. 'It's not you. It's them.'

'Them who?'

'You know . . . the girls you go out with . . . or rather the *kind* of girls you go out with.'

'What's wrong with the kind of girls I go out with?'

'Well, not to put too fine a point on it, while the girls that you go out with are undoubtedly attractive and usually well turned out, none of them are exactly girlfriend material, are they?'

'"*Not exactly girlfriend material*"?' spluttered Adam. 'I don't even know what that means.'

'Just that. They're great to look at and all that but . . . they're not the kind of girls you want to grow old with, are they? Your problem is, mate, that you are quite plainly addicted to the wrong kind of girl.'

'Truly hopeless.'

While Adam Bachelor was debating the whys and wherefores of the women he dated with his friends over in Cheshire, back in south Manchester his youngest brother Russell (tall, thin, with a face that nine out of ten girls would describe as 'thoughtful') was turning down the volume on the TV before opening the two bottles of Grolsch sitting on the coffee table in front of him and handing one to his best friend, Angie. 'So come on then,' said Russell, leaning back in the sofa. 'What's going on?'

It had been over an hour since Russell had logged on to Facebook via his laptop to discover the message that 'Angie McMahon is no longer listed in a relationship.' Announcing to the world (or at the very least her one hundred and twenty-three Facebook friends) in such a dramatic fashion that she had split up with her boyfriend when her previous Facebook status update at ten the night before had read: 'Angie is . . . . loved up!' was, thought Russell, a very Angie thing to do and one of the many reasons that he liked having her in his life. Angie was always so random, so haphazard, so frequently lacking in any kind of sense of self-preservation that she was always fun to have around.

And while Angie's lesser friends were busy plastering her Facebook page with messages of condolence, Russell was the only one who had bothered to pick up his phone and call her in person. Angie had answered within three rings but her sobbing and gurgling had been so intense that Russell had barely been able to understand a word so in the end he had told her to jump in a taxi and make her way over to his place.

'It's over between me and Aaron,' said Angie, obviously struggling to stay in control.

'I know. Is it for real?'

Angie nodded and put her beer down on the table. 'It's as real as it gets. You know how things between me and him have been up and down for a while?'

Russell nodded.

'Well, this afternoon we had this massive heart-to-heart about where we were going and what we both wanted and all that and I suddenly realised we just weren't right together. Whatever it is that two people are supposed to have we didn't have it. I think we were just a bad habit that went on too long.'

'But you two have been together for ages.'

'Four years give or take.'

'I don't get it,' said Russell. 'I mean, I could understand if it was four weeks. After all, that's pretty much the standard time for things to run their course. But four years? That's ridiculous. Plus you live together. How are you going to be able to afford your flat on your own? You love that place and let's not forget how much you loathe living in shared houses. Remember last time you did it? You ended up in a girl fight over stolen yoghurt with the girl who lived across the hall!'

'Great. Thanks, Russ.' Angie started to cry again. 'That's just what I need right now: you telling me that I'm an idiot. Why stop there? I've got an iota or two of self confidence left so why don't you really go to town and point out that I've got a couple of spots breaking out?'

'Come on, Ange,' sighed Russell. 'You know that's not what I meant. It's a bit of a shock, that's all. Any time that I've seen you two together you've always seemed pretty OK to me. That's all I was trying to say. I wasn't having a go, mate. Honest.'

'OK,' she said and then put her head on his shoulder and carried on sobbing.

He felt as if Russell and Angie had been friends forever even though it was actually only six years. They first met when Russell returned to Manchester from a year of post-university travelling and, desperate to pay off his debts, had started working at BlueBar, his elder brother Adam's bar. Russell was more than a little attracted to her given that she ticked a lot of the boxes on his girlfriend requirements list. First, she liked to talk (Russell had dated enough cute but silent girls in his time whereas Angie could talk the back legs off a donkey), second he could talk to her (Russell had dated enough girls without sufficient personality) and finally she had a sense of humour (when she was on form Angie could make him laugh like no other human being on earth). As for looks, Russell wasn't too fussed as he had never been into girls who couldn't walk past a mirror without taking a glance at themselves. No, the kind of girls he liked were the kind that you didn't really know you liked until you started talking to them. Those were his favourites: the ones you had to actively seek out and discover for yourself. Angie was a perfect example of that type of girl. And he had sought her out for a carefully arranged but casually proposed drink on their day off only to discover over two pints of Stella that she, like all the good ones, had already been discovered. Over the next couple of years their friendship had flourished. Perhaps because they had never found themselves single at the same time, Russell convinced himself that if the opportunity ever arose, sparks would be sure to fly but when that happened a month before she started seeing Aaron it was something of an anticlimax. Instead of feeling extra flirtatious Russell just felt really awkward and Angie obviously likewise. 'It's like we missed our window of opportunity,' Russell later explained to Adam. 'Ange and I are mates now. Anything else would be just plain weird.'

Russell sat silently cradling Angie in his arms on the sofa for over an hour before he felt able to suggest that it might be a good idea to get them both another beer. While he was up and in the kitchen he ordered a Chinese set meal for two to be delivered to the house and made a mug of tea just in case Angie wasn't in the mood for Grolsch. Returning to the room he set the drinks on the table and turned on the TV. It being Saturday night there was nothing on but talent shows and big films and Russell was about to switch off when Angie made a comment about one of the celebrity contestants, which was the first time in an hour that she had spoken about anything other than Aaron. The comforting nature of reality TV appeared to relax her and by the time the Chinese food had arrived, been unpacked and consumed she seemed a lot more like her old self.

'I really am sorry about ruining your evening,' she said, setting her empty plate down in front of her. 'You must think I'm a right nutter going on about Aaron like this.'

'No chance,' replied Russell. 'We're mates, aren't we? That's what mates do. They look out for one another.'

Angie picked up her beer and sighed, 'I suppose.'

'What does that mean?'

'It's just that when it comes to us it's always you looking out for me rather than me looking out for you. I thought friendship was supposed to be a two-way street.'

'It is,' said Russell. 'You're always looking out for me. You just don't do it in such obvious ways, that's all.'

'Can't agree with you there. I mean look at the evidence: I've been sitting here for a couple of hours now and it's all been me, me, me. Think about it, Russ.

I haven't asked you a single question about your own life.'

'Well go on then,' laughed Russell. 'What's stopping you?'

Angie rubbed her hands with mock glee. 'OK then, how's work?'

'It's all right,' said Russell. 'Nothing to write home about but it'll do.'

'Next question: how are your folks?'

'They're cool. I'm having lunch at theirs tomorrow as per usual.'

'That's good to hear,' said Angie. 'I like a boy who is good to his old mum and dad. Next question: how are you getting on with your plans to go travelling next summer?'

Russell shrugged. 'Haven't done a thing about it.'

'Nothing?'

'Not saved a single penny. In fact I'm more broke this month than I was last.'

'But you promised me you were going to start saving this month.'

'I know. I know. I just had a couple of big bills, that's all.'

'Right,' said Angie, 'finally here's the question that I always like to ask even though I know you'll hate me because it reminds you of how loose your tongue gets when you've had a few. Anyway, here goes: how's being in love with your middle brother's girlfriend going?'

'Hopeless,' sighed Russell. 'Truly hopeless.'

'That's not even a word!'

While Russell was lamenting the fact that he was in love with someone he shouldn't be in love with, his middle brother Luke (average in both height and outlook on life but handsome in a teddy-bear-ish sort of way) was (even though he was unaware of it) staring very hard across the candlelit table at his girlfriend.

'Are you OK?' asked Cassie.

'Why wouldn't I be?'

'No reason, it's just that you were looking at me a bit strangely, as though that mackerel starter you just wolfed down was in the process of letting you know that it didn't agree with you.'

'Nope, it was great. Fantastic even. Possibly the best starter I've ever had.'

'What's up then?'

Luke shook his head. 'Nothing . . . it doesn't matter.' He picked up the half-filled red-wine glass in front of him and raised it to eye level. 'Let's make a toast. To me and you and the last eighteen months of us-ness.'

'Us-ness? That's not even a word!'

A cheesy smile spread across Luke's face like he

had just won a hundred pounds on a scratch card. 'Isn't it? Well it is now!'

Luke wanted the earth to open up and swallow him whole. What was wrong with him? Why was he acting like an overgrown schoolgirl? As Cassie began telling him about an earlier conversation that she'd had with her sister, Luke tried to work out what was going on inside his brain and came to the conclusion that he was grateful. Not just ordinary everyday grateful but rather a big-grin-on-your-face, chest-puffed-out, walking-on-air kind of grateful. Appreciating the things that you have rather than the things that you want to have is not a particularly male trait and Luke was well aware of this. In general men aren't given to moments of needless reflection. If things were going OK you might occasionally want to give yourself a mental thumbs-up sign, or spend a moment too long grinning at yourself in the mirror, or even occasionally close your eyes and raise a right hand for a symbolic high five. What you didn't do was sit in a swanky city-centre Spanish restaurant on a Saturday night trembling with emotion as you stared at your girlfriend of eighteen months wondering what on earth you had done to be this lucky.

'I love you, you know,' said Cassie, raising her glass for Luke to clink. 'I love you more than anything in the world.'

'I love you too,' said Luke.

There was a silence. Luke wondered if he ought to have offered more than a simple 'I love you' in return.

Women liked it when you started getting into stuff a bit more deeply, didn't they? They liked it when you said more than the bare minimum. He thought about telling her how grateful he was having her in his life. He thought about telling her about the difference that she made to his day, the thrill he still felt whenever he walked down the street holding her hand knowing that every guy who saw them together would know that he was her boyfriend. He thought about all this and more but of course he didn't say any of it because the words just wouldn't come. He'd never been great with words, at least not in a smooth way like his older brother Adam or in a sensitive this-is-how-I'm feeling way like his kid brother Russell. Even at work, when he was one hundred per cent in his own element and all he had to do was present the outlines of his contribution to a big engineering project, it still felt as though every word was a boulder that he had had to cough up from the depths of his belly. If he reacted like that outlining engineering reports then how was he supposed to be when it came to talking about love?

'Eighteen months,' said Cassie. 'It doesn't feel anything like eighteen months does it?'

'More like two.'

'That's so sweet of you.'

Luke shrugged. He felt deceitful for giving Cassie the impression that that was the best he could do. There was more. Lots more. And it wanted to emerge, to be free and out in the open right now. In his thirty-four years alive he had only had this feeling once before and that had ended in disaster. Perhaps that was why he was trying to hang on to the words:he was desperately trying to keep history from repeating itself.

'What can you remember about our first date?' asked Cassie.

'Everything.' Luke was deliberately succinct. 'How about you?'

'Oi Bachelor!' laughed Cassie. 'I see what you're doing! I want the detail, mister. I want to know everything that you remember. And I mean everything!'

It had been an ordinary Friday night eighteen months earlier and Luke had been drinking in a town bar with some workmates. The bar was throbbing with pent-up 'it's-the-weekend' energy and seating was at a premium. People began to peel off to go home or get some food and soon Luke soon found himself on one side of a table on his own. Just as he had been planning to call it a day he'd received a text from Russell, asking whether he could borrow his car for a couple of hours to run some errands. Luke had replied that was fine as long as Russell remembered to put in petrol this time otherwise he would be forced to give him a severe beating and he had just been about to press send when he sensed that he was no longer alone and had looked up to see Cassie standing over him asking if the seats opposite were taken.

Luke had been so thrown by the sight of this amazing woman that he forgot to answer her question and just stared. He managed to regain his composure long enough to invite her to sit down. As Luke realised he no longer wanted to go home, he typed a new text message to his brother: '£100 and car for a week if get down to the Ha Ha Bar Room in 30.' Luke pressed send and looked up at Cassie: 'I'm just waiting for a friend,' he said. 'Looks like he's running late.'

'And do you remember how all we did that night was talk?' laughed Cassie as she joined in with the story. 'We just talked and talked and talked and talked. I'd never met anyone like you in my entire life.'

'My favourite moment was when Russ turned up.' Luke grinned. 'He looked a right mess. There he was in a bar full of suits like some kind of overgrown student.'

'He didn't!' protested Cassie.'He looked really cool.'

'No, he looked like an idiot. The kind of daft fashion victim that populates record shops – which was in fact where he was working at the time – and who could have ruined my chances of getting the phone number of the young thing I was giving the full-on Bachelor treatment to!'

'But making out you didn't even know him was a bit cruel!'

'It would've been more cruel to have spoken to him because if he had ruined things between you and me I would've had no choice but to take him outside and pummel him. Anyway, he got his hundred quid and my car and he still managed to return it without any bloody petrol!'

They both smiled as they recalled the events of that night. This is what happiness feels like, thought Luke.

The feeling that some people spend their whole lives looking for and never find.

He sneaked an unsteady hand across the table, nearly knocking over Cassie's wine in the process, and lifted up her fingers until they were intertwined with his own.

'Listen,' he said, 'I've had something on my mind ever since we sat down tonight and I've been trying to find a way to express it but I keep hitting a brick wall. I wish you could just climb into my head and know what I feel without me having to say. How great would that be? Not having to put stuff into words?'

'I do know,' said Cassie. 'I really do.'

'Well do you know that right now if I had a ring I would ask you to marry me?'

Cassie nodded. 'And did you know that ring or no ring were you to ask me the answer would be yes?'

'In that case I'm asking you to marry me,' said Luke.

'And in that case I'm saying yes.'

'Filed away on my SIM card.'

It was the morning of the following day, a Sunday, and a barefoot Adam was standing on his front doorstep waving to the minicab driver currently pulled up over his front drive.

'She'll be with you in a minute, mate!' he called as the driver wound down his window. 'She's just getting her things together.'

The minicab driver nodded and Adam returned indoors, picked up the mug of tea from the table in the hallway and took a sip. She made good tea. Nice and strong. No sugar. Not too much milk. He swished it around his mouth a bit as though it was mouthwash and was about to swallow when she appeared at the top of the stairs.

'This is a nightmare,' she said. 'I can't seem to find my other shoe.'

'Have you checked the bedroom?'

She nodded. 'And the bathroom. You couldn't be a love and check downstairs for me?'

Heading into the kitchen Adam dropped a couple of slices of bread into the toaster and gave the room a quick scan before heading to the living room. He spotted the missing footwear – a gold high-heeled sandal – almost immediately as it was sitting on top of the coffee table in the middle of the room. He picked it up, smiled as he recalled the manner in which it had been abandoned and then called out that he had found it.

'You're a life saver!' She slipped on the shoe like a latter-day Cinderella and smoothed down the creases of her gold lamé minidress. 'Right then, I'd better be off.' She put her arms round his waist, kissed him and gave him a cheeky wink. 'So, you've got my number?'

Adam nodded. 'Filed away on my SIM card.'

'Good.' She kissed him again. 'Don't wait too long to text me.'

'Make a lady wait? Wouldn't dream of it.'

The girl picked up her expensive-looking designer bag from the sofa and left the room. Adam followed, picking up his tea on the way.

Adam stood on the doorstep and watched as she tottered down the drive and into the back of a silver Toyota Corolla. As the car pulled off Adam offered a final wave and then closed his eyes, turned his face towards the morning sun and savoured the sensation of the warmth on his face. This is the last time, he told himself, the very last time.

In essence, he reasoned as he returned inside and closed his front door, it had been his friends' fault. All that talk of him being the least likely person to get hitched had provoked a lot of soul-searching when he should simply have been enjoying himself at the wedding. In truth Adam was actually quite worried that his friends were right. He had indeed spent too long chasing the wrong kind of girl and in the process had turned his whole life into one big fat men's magazine cliché. After all here he was, a devastatingly good-looking, solvent, single man in his mid-thirties who also happened to be the owner of one of the coolest bars in south Manchester. The kinds of women he liked were indeed ones that most mere mortals couldn't get within a few feet of without being tackled to the ground by security guards. And going out with them meant that he was part of an exclusive club featuring premier league football players, top name DJs and the odd younger member of the cast of *Coronation Street*. Really, it didn't get any more exclusive than that. As for the women themselves Adam's libido had a kind of mental checklist that it constantly and unconsciously referred to. Great face? Check. Long legs? Check. Tanned (fake or otherwise, he wasn't fussy)? Check. Ridiculously tight minidress that showed off every asset? Check and bingo! In short Adam liked his women to be as flashy, sexually attractive and downright head-turning as it was humanly possible to be.

Now granted that Ameee (she had insisted that it was spelled with three 'e's) wasn't up to Adam's usual standard but as he had stood at the bar with his mates searching his soul and wondering exactly when his life had become this superficial he found himself making eye contact with an amazing-looking blonde in a spangly gold minidress who had the longest tanned legs he had seen in quite a while. Presented with the dilemma of confirming his friends' prejudices or refuting them

Adam went on to automatic pilot. He walked over to the girl, dazzled her with his best sales talk and just after midnight hopped into the back of a cab with her. The rest had been depressingly inevitable.

Adam plucked his long since popped-up toast out of the toaster, slapped a large wedge of butter on each slice and headed back into the living room. For a while he sat on the edge of the sofa, intermittently chewing his toast and slurping his tea, while he stared at the fireplace thinking about everything and nothing until an idea suddenly presented itself. Adam began searching the room first for some paper (in the end he had to settle for the back of the envelope that his latest gas bill had arrived in) and then for a pen (in fact a stubby IKEA pencil that he found down the side of the sofa) and then began writing. At the top of his envelope he wrote the following:

THINGS I SHOULD BE LOOKING FOR IN THE RIGHT KIND OF WOMAN

1. Must have read at least one book in the previous month.
2. Must be no prettier than a solid eight out of ten.
3. Must not consider sleeping with me until after first date.
4. Must have a career of some kind (this excludes ALL models and actresses).
5. Must want to start a family.
6. Must be able to cook without use of microwave.
7. Must be able to hold a conversation.

8. Would be nice if she had a sense of humour (though not compulsory).
9. Must not have been sick through overindulgence in the last three years.
10. Must occasionally like doing cultural stuff.
11. Must be over thirty (preferably over thirty-five).
12. Would ideally be a non-cat owner (but given item eleven am prepared to be flexible on this one).
13. Must not be currently seeing a therapist.
14. Must not possess more than a moderate belief in complementary medicine . . .
15. Or astrology.
16. Must like me.

Adam looked over the list. This was it. This was brilliant. Everything that he wanted in the right kind of woman together with the perfect method of weeding out the wrong kind. Just to double-check his list's brilliance Adam decided to score Ameee with the three 'e's against it and was pleased to discover that she would have scored a very poor three out of sixteen and been sent packing. Adam then did the same for his last three conquests (a one-time glamour model, the ex-girlfriend of a former Liverpool defender, and a former *Big Brother* contestant) and was delighted to see that they too would have been weeded out.

Maybe the boys were right: maybe he should have done away with this kind of girl a long time ago. Without further challenge to his synapses he closed his eyes and promptly fell asleep.

'Twenty minutes after Luke met her.'

Mid-morning on Sunday found Russell in the kitchen of his shared house in Chorlton pouring a huge mountain of Coco Pops into his bowl. Returning the cereal packet to the cupboard he was about to bend over the counter and hoover up a number of stray Coco Pops with his lips when his mobile phone buzzed. The message was from Angie: 'Thanks for talking me off the ledge and feeding me lager! Love you! A xxx'. Russell smiled and was about to return to his Coco Pops when his phone buzzed again: 'PS. I hope you're not having Coco Pops for breakfast again! Those things will kill you!' Russell kept his eyes fixed on the screen in the knowledge that when Angie was in this kind of mood the texts tended to come in threes. Sure enough, a third message arrived: 'PPS. And whatever you do don't spend all morning mooning over Cassie!!!! That's an order!!!'

At the very sight of Cassie's name Russell felt his frame sink under the weight of remorse. Remorse for being in love with his brother's girlfriend and even worse for having shared this knowledge with another human being. Heading to the living room Russell settled down in front of his Sunday newspaper and found himself distracted from both cereal and newspaper by the question of why he'd ever told Angie about Cassie in the first place. For starters admitting to fancying your brother's girlfriend was more than a bit weird. Normal people, didn't do that kind of thing unless they were the sort who appeared on daytime TV talk shows and he was certainly not that kind of person. Second, having told Angie, there could be no untelling which meant that even if one day he was to get over his secret crush on Cassie there would always be at least one person in the world who knew what kind of freak he really was. Finally, despite his reassurances last night, it was completely true that their relationship had always been something of a one-way street. Angie would unburden herself of whatever was on her mind while Russell would listen and nod in the appropriate gaps in the conversation before offering Angie such nuggets of wisdom as he could lay his hands on. That was how it was supposed to work and that was how he had always liked it. And yet Russell had, in a moment of weakness, in a pub, on an evening when they had both imbibed more than a fair bit of alcohol, willingly told her everything about his feelings for Cassie. The reason was simple: it is one of the fundamental truths of human nature that there's only so much keeping of a secret a person can do before it comes out of its own accord. Russell had been aware for some time that he was reaching maximum secret-keeping capacity so it came down to a choice of either telling Angie his true feelings about Cassie and learning to live with the consequences or telling Cassie about his true feelings, thereby ensuring that neither she nor his brother Luke ever spoke to him again. So basically it was tell his best friend or end up being cast out by his family. It wasn't a decision that took him a long time to make.

A few weeks later on one of his regular Friday nights out with Angie, the moment of truth arrived in the form of a slightly drunken rant from Angie very similar to the one that he had heard last night.

'You do realise that this isn't fair.'

'What isn't fair?' asked Russell.

'This,' replied Angie, gesturing to the space between them. 'You and me sitting here now doing what we always do. I spend the night bitching on about the stuff that's wrong with my life and you get to come out with the words of wisdom that make it all right again. I hate it. It should be more equal. You know, a bit more give and take.'

'Fine,' said Russell.

'Excuse me?' Angie was obviously taken aback by this deviation from the usual script.

'Fine, I'll tell you about something that's going on in my life where I could do with a bit of advice.'

'Really?'

'Really.'

'So go on then,' said Angie. 'It's not about you and that girl at work?'

'No.'

'You're not going to tell me you're dying are you? That would put a real dampener on the evening.'

'Thanks,' laughed Russell. 'It's good to know that my untimely passing would mean so much to you.'

'What is it? What's the big problem?'

'It's me,' he began awkwardly. 'I'm the big problem . . . I think I'm in love with Cassie.'

Angie had pulled a horrified face and put her hands up to her mouth as though she was watching a car crash. 'You mean Cassie, Luke's stick insect of a girlfriend?'

'Yup,' replied Russell looking sheepish.

Angie smiled. 'I didn't even know she was your type. I thought you liked them a bit chunky like me. Is this something new?'

'Nope. I think I've loved her since the day I met her.'

'And that was when exactly?'

'About half an hour after Luke met her.'

'And you really do love her?'

'Insofar as you can love someone without them loving you back, I'd say yeah.'

Angie had reached across the table and held Russell's hands. 'I don't know what to say.'

'There isn't much to say really.'

'How did it happen?'

'I guess it's just one of those things.' He proceeded to tell the story of how he had been out in the Jockey with some mates when he'd got the text from Luke.

Although he had guessed that the text was designed to help his brother out with a member of the opposite sex Russell had imagined that the girl in question must be the kind of average-looking office worker who wouldn't hold even the slightest bit of interest for him and so he had been more than a little bit surprised to find that Luke was in fact in conversation with a girl with a cute face, and great style. The fact that she was so held in Luke's gravitational pull as to barely give him the time of day was neither here nor there. As far as he was concerned there must have been some kind of tear in the time space continuum so frequently referred to in sci-fi programmes that had resulted in his future girlfriend being handed to the wrong Bachelor brother and Luke pretending that he didn't know him simply rubbed salt into the wound.

A week later when Russell discovered that Luke was going on a second date with Cassie he found himself hoping for one of two things: for his brother to get bored of Cassie as quickly as humanly possible or for a miracle. He was out of luck on both counts as it turned out that Cassie was as clever as she was beautiful and even he could see that there was no way Luke was going to let her go. Russell had no choice but to stand by the wayside while Cassie and his brother fell in love. When they eventually moved in together (roughly six months after first meeting) Russell hoped he would finally be able to move on but it had never happened.

'So that's why you turned down that girl with the overplucked eyebrows who was sniffing around you at Liane's party last month?'

Russell nodded.

'And why you didn't make a move on that girl at work who's always trying to get you to go to the cinema with her.'

He nodded again.

'And I'm guessing that explains why you turned down my friend Katie when we all went out for my birthday even though she is obviously not the kind of girl who ever gets turned down by anyone?'

'Don't get me wrong,' laughed Russell. 'It's not like I'm a monk or anything. I did consider it.'

'But you didn't do anything.'

'I wanted to but I couldn't. It would have felt too weird. Like I was cheating on Cassie.'

'But you weren't going out with Cassie!'

'I know.'

There was a long pause. Then Angie said: 'You know you can't carry on like this, don't you?'

'I know,' said Russell. 'I've got to sort myself out. I've got to make a change.'

Nothing did change though. In fact things stayed exactly the same.

'He's been here half an hour if that and not lifted a finger!'

It was midday and Adam was standing in the hallway of 44 Woodford Road soaking up all the familiar sights, sounds and smells. This was the best thing about his parents' home: the fact that nothing changed. The wallpaper which his mum was always threatening to rip down because it looked so dated; the family phone book with the fake telephone dial on the front cover that sat on what was always known as 'the telephone stool'; the dark wooden wall clock that ticked so loudly it sounded like the noise was actually coming from inside your head; the one and only official Bachelor family portrait (taken two days shy of Adam's tenth birthday) featuring a middle-aged-looking Mum and Dad in their smartest outfits with the boys positioned in front of them in descending order; to Adam's eyes all of these items represented the very essence of the Bachelor family home.

There was something special about this place that kept drawing the three brothers back to the extent that they were now that most rare of filial formations: a family where none of its members lived further than twenty minutes away from the other.

Adam headed to the kitchen to find the comfortingly familiar sight of his mum standing by the sink shaking the water off a colander full of new potatoes. He walked over and gave her a big squeeze from behind followed by a peck on the cheek. 'And how's the most beautiful woman in all the world on this bright and sunny summer afternoon?'

'You've decided to come then?' reprimanded Mum, unimpressed by his charm. 'When was it I called you? Wednesday? And you didn't get back to me.'

Adam flashed his best butter-wouldn't-melt grin. 'I was busy, Mum. You know how it is when things get busy down at the bar. But you should also know that if it's Sunday and there's food on the table I'll be here.' He picked up a recently washed strawberry from a dish on the counter and dropped it into his mouth before she could smack his hand away. 'Anyway,' he said cheerily, 'how come I don't get any points for being the first one of your strapping young sons to be here?'

'Well there's plenty to do,' she said, pushing Adam away from her in a no-nonsense fashion. 'The table needs setting and the glasses need getting out of the cupboard and giving a good clean. I don't want Cassie thinking that Luke doesn't come from a good family.'

Adam considered pointing out that Cassie had been coming to the Bachelors' for Sunday dinner for long enough now that any thoughts she might have on whether or not the Bachelors were a good family would have long since crystallised, but he chose to bite his tongue.

'I'm on the case, Mum,' said Adam, opening up the drawer where the 'good' cutlery lived. 'Where's Dad?'

'Where do you think?'

'Why do you always answer a question with a question?'

'Why do you always ask questions that you already know the answer to?'

'Because that's my role in the family. I ask questions to which I already know the answer, Luke's your man for fixing stuff and Russ . . . well, Russ is just Russ, isn't he?' Adam peered through the kitchen window and spied Dad mowing the back lawn. Spotting an opportunity to leave the setting of the table to one of his less wily siblings Adam closed the cutlery drawer and announced that he really ought to go and say hello to his dad. Mum just shook her head and carried on with the potatoes.

'All right, son?' said Dad, turning off the lawn mower as Adam approached. 'Is it lunchtime already? I haven't got my watch on.'

Adam placed an affectionate hand on his father's shoulder. 'Nah, Dad, it's not lunchtime yet. I'm just early.' Adam paused to take in his father's gardening outfit: a blue shirt with the sleeves folded up, brown corduroy trousers and wellington boots. It was the same gardening outfit that he had been wearing for as long as Adam could remember and he was touched by his dad's constancy. Adam looked around at the lawn admiringly. 'How's the gardening going, Pop? Looks like you're doing a cracking job on it.'

'I'm not sure I've got the energy for it these days. I don't mind so much when it's warm like this but give me a single drop of rain or have it a bit too cold and do you know what? I lose all interest.'

'You should get Russ down here doing all the donkey work. It's the least he can do after you paid his way through university. Three years multiplied by however much you used to send him every month? That's got to be worth a bit of weeding surely?'

'I'm fine with the gardening, thank you very much. And as far as I'm concerned Russell's education was worth every penny. It's not too late for you, you know. What are you? Thirty-six? Thirty-seven? Still plenty of time to get a degree.'

'I'm fine without one, thanks. I've got the bar; I've no use for a degree. And for future reference, Dad, I'm thirty-eight.'

'Time certainly is flying,' said George. 'I know you're thirty-eight, son. How could I forget? The day you were born was one of the proudest days of my life.'

The two men stood talking for a good twenty minutes or so before George indicated that he wanted to finish off the garden before lunch. Back inside the house Adam was instructed to wash his hands but before he reached the sink Cassie and Luke appeared in the kitchen and within seconds the room was filled with raucous laughter.

'So you've finally turned up,' said Adam. 'Some of us have been helping out with the preparations for quite some time, I'll have you know.'

'Don't listen to him, Luke,' said Mum, batting Adam across the back of his head with her hand. 'He's been here half an hour if that and not lifted a finger!'

'Did you see that act of child cruelty, Cass!' said Adam rubbing the back of his head. 'A mother beating her poor son just for pointing out the truth?'

'I'm sure she had her reasons,' said Cassie. 'Anyway you, where's my hug?'

Adam gave her a big squeeze. He had always liked Cassie. His favourite way to describe her to people who had never met her was: 'She's like a real proper girlie but without all the nonsense that goes with it', and people knew exactly what he meant. As far as Adam was concerned Cassie was one of the best things that had ever happened to his brother and despite his mum's best efforts to treat her like a guest he considered Cassie to be a fully paid-up member of the Bachelors in all but name.

As Luke chatted to their mum Adam caught up with Cassie's news about work and life and found himself mulling over his friend's comments from the night before about 'the right kind of girl'. Cassie was definitely the right kind of girl, the kind you'd want to spend your life with if you were that way inclined and yet Adam couldn't really see himself with someone like Cassie. Perhaps finding the right kind of girl was going to be a lot harder than he'd initially thought.

Adam was about to ask his mum what time she was expecting Russell when he felt the weight of a large body leaping on to his back. He spun round to find Russell attempting to get him in a headlock. Within seconds the whole kitchen was in uproar with three grown men play-fighting like the big kids they were, as had been a part of their routine ever since they were small. Their mother was bellowing at the top of her voice, 'Enough is enough!', while their dad stood in the doorway chuckling at the look of dismay on Cassie's face.

Wrestling over and mowing complete, the Bachelor men took their places at the table while Mum and Cassie (having refused all offers of assistance) started bringing in the food: plates of roast beef, roast potatoes, boiled potatoes, sweet potatoes, rice and peas, carrots, cauliflower and home-made gravy. Adam smiled. It was June; possibly one of the hottest days of the year. But as far as his mum was concerned Sundays just weren't Sundays without a roast.

With all the food on the table Cassie took her seat next to Luke and Mum began serving up. Luke stood up and cleared his throat.

'Mum,' he said quietly, 'can you just put down the potatoes for a second.'

'Why? What are you after?'

'Nothing.'

'Then why are you asking me to put the potatoes down?'

'Because I've got some news.'

'What news?'

'Sit down and I'll tell you.'

His mum did exactly as she was asked and, pausing only to throw a smile in Cassie's direction, Luke started talking: 'Cassie and I, we're—'

Luke didn't get to finish his sentence. Mum had already sprung to her feet and was throwing her arms round a bewildered Cassie and within a matter of moments the whole family was up on their feet congratulating Luke and Cassie on the best bit of Bachelor family news of the year.

'Hope, love, family.
Those are the important things.'

'Anyone fancy another brew?' asked Luke.

It was late in the afternoon and Luke was still on a high. Normally he and Cassie would have long since left his parents' and gone home but this particular afternoon was different. Although Russell had gone (something to do with a crisis he was having at work), Adam (who was usually out of the door around the time the washing-up began) had stayed and Luke had had no choice but to endure his brother's regaling Cassie with embarrassing stories from their youth. Now they were all packed into the living room with *Antiques Roadshow* on in the background and talking and laughing animatedly. Today really was something special. Today was Christmas Day and New Year's Eve wrapped into one.

'What's going on?' teased Adam. 'Has someone kidnapped my middle brother and replaced him with a Teasmaid? Lukey boy has never made tea in his entire life. I'm not even sure he'd know how without looking it up on the Internet.'

'Ha! Ha! Very funny!' replied Luke. 'I'll have you

know that I actually make a damn fine cup of tea for my Cassie every single day.'

The family looked at Cassie in disbelief. 'Is it true,' asked Adam. 'Does Boy Wonder here really bring you tea every day in bed?'

'Every morning without fail,' said Cassie, winking at Luke. 'He's completely and utterly under my thumb!'

Luke's mum stood up decisively. 'You boys and your teasing, when will you ever stop?' She turned to Luke. 'Come on son, you count up the hands and I'll give you a hand putting the kettle on.'

Luke knew what that meant. Mum had been asking questions about the wedding all afternoon and this offer of tea-making assistance was her opportunity to ask a few more questions away from prying eyes. Luke counted up the hands: two teas, two coffees and a whatever his mum was having. He made his way to the kitchen to face his grilling and found his mum at the kitchen counter setting out the 'only for best' teacups.

'I'll get the milk out, shall I?'

'No, son, you leave it,' she replied. 'I'll get it when I'm ready.'

There was a long silence.

'So are you pleased then?' he asked. 'You know, about me and Cassie?'

'I'm thrilled,' she replied. 'Cassie is a wonderful girl. And she really loves you, you know. You only have to look at her to see that.'

'I know, Mum. She's the best thing that's ever happened to me.'

Joan smiled. 'I don't think I could have picked a better girl for you.' She looked down at the empty teacups. He could tell straight away that she was thinking about Megan, his daughter from his first marriage whom he no longer saw.

Of all his family the one person who knew how he felt not having Megan in his life was his mum. He put his arms round her as she began to cry. 'I know you miss her, Mum,' he said. 'I miss her too. I miss her more and more each day. The only thing that keeps me going is that one day she'll be old enough to come and find me. And she will come, Mum, she'll come and find me and we'll talk and we'll get rid of all the years of poison that her mum's filled her with and we'll start something fresh and new. What do you think about that then, Mum?'

'I think it's lovely,' she said. 'You've got to have hope, haven't you? That's what life's all about: hope, love, family. Those are the important things.'

Luke was as uncomfortable with strong emotions as any of his brothers. Did his mum want to ask more questions? Should he give her another hug? Should he just leave her to get on with making the tea? Luke took the last option as it was the one he knew would benefit himself the most.

Back in the living room, there had been a change of pace. The TV was off and Adam and Cassie were either side of his dad on the sofa. Luke looked over Cassie's shoulder to see that they were flicking through his parents' wedding album.

'I haven't seen that thing for years,' he said. The wedding album was one of those childhood objects that had acquired a near-mythical status. He could count on one hand the number of times he had seen it and yet he could recall it with perfect clarity: a cream padded album with a built-in wind-up musical chime, pages and pages of photographs of his young parents protected from dust and grime by the most delicate tissue paper. The last time Luke had looked at that album was for an essay he had to write when he was thirteen about his family's personal history. He only spent an evening or two on it whereas most people had spent a week and was therefore not the least bit surprised by his 'D' grade and his English teacher's comment that he had not only let himself down but his family too.

'Your dad has been telling us some great stories about his and your mum's wedding day. Did you know that your mum was over twenty minutes late arriving at the church? The hairdresser overslept and your mum refused to leave the house without her hair done so they had no choice but to wait.'

'Is that true, Dad?'

George nodded. 'I was stood at the back of the church looking at my watch like a damn fool. Everyone thought she had done a runner. Still, she turned up in the end.' He gave Cassie a cheeky wink. 'I always knew she would.'

'And,' continued Cassie, 'did you also know that your Auntie Rose wasn't meant to be your mum's maid of honour?'

'I didn't even know that Mum had a maid of honour,' replied Luke.

'Well she did,' replied Cassie. 'It was meant to be your mum's best friend Janet but she never turned up on the day and by the time your mum and dad went back to work the following week she'd moved and no one's seen her since.'

'You make it sound like a murder mystery,' laughed Luke.

'Maybe it is.'

'Any other factoids about my parents' wedding that you'd like to impart?'

'Only the best one.'

'Which is?'

'Not only did your mum and dad get married the same month that we're planning to get married but guess what?'

Luke thought for a moment. It could be anything. 'Is it that they got married on the same day that we're planning to get hitched?'

'Nice try but that's not it.'

'OK . . . how about . . . I don't know . . . their first dance is the same song that you want to be our first dance?'

Cassie shook her head.

'I officially give up. What's the big secret then?'

'Next year is their fortieth wedding anniversary! Isn't that amazing? Your mum and dad have been married forty years! I asked your dad what the secret was but he just shrugged and said, "I'm blowed if I know." '

Luke looked at Adam. It wasn't the least bit surprising that neither he nor Luke knew that their parents' fortieth wedding anniversary was coming up. They could barely muster the energy to remember each other's birthdays without severe prompting from their mum; adding a parental wedding anniversary to the mix was a step too far. 'Is that right, Dad? Are you and Mum really celebrating forty years together next year?'

'What's that?' Luke's mum was in the room carrying a tray laden with tea and coffee.

'Dad was saying it's your fortieth wedding anniversary next year.'

'Been counting the days have you, George?' she laughed. 'There's no time off for good behaviour.'

'So how are you going to celebrate, Joan?' asked Cassie. 'Something nice?'

'George and I don't like to make a fuss,' said Mum. 'It's not our thing really.'

'You can't not celebrate a fortieth wedding!' Cassie was genuinely shocked. 'It's not right. Luke, tell your mum that she can't ignore her wedding anniversary.'

'Honestly, Cassie,' interjected Dad. 'It really isn't our thing.'

Cassie turned to Adam. 'Well, aren't you going to say anything?'

'Nah,' said Adam. 'It's not really our kind of thing either. What you've got to learn about us Bachelors, Cass, is that we don't like to make a fuss.'

'I wouldn't go that far,' said Mum. 'Cassie does have a point. Forty years is a long time.'

'Exactly,' enthused Cassie. 'It's a massive achievement in this day and age, Joan, and I think it would be a shame to just let it slide like that.'

Luke watched his mum warming to the idea of a celebration. 'What kind of thing were you thinking?'

'Oh, nothing too showy,' replied Cassie. 'A small party. Some nice food, family, friends, just the people you love and care about most. It won't be a big deal. And you won't have to lift a finger. The boys and I will organise the lot for you.'

Luke saw his mum look to his dad for approval as he had seen her do a million times before. Not exactly an act of deference (she always did whatever she wanted to do anyway) but not exactly not either. 'What do you think, George?'

'I'm happy if you're happy,' he replied.

'Then we'll do it,' she said, clapping her hands. 'We'll do it!'

'It'll be my good deed for the day.'

Adam was lying in bed wondering where his life was going. Since committing himself to his project to find the right kind of girl over a month ago he had been on over a dozen disastrous dates without a shred of success. Of late he had persuaded his friend Jon's girlfriend Shelley to let him take her friend Farah for lunch; three days later he had found himself on an unofficial blind date with his bar manager's sister Linda, and a week after that he went out with Ellen, his friend Martin's sister who had just returned to Manchester after living in Spain. Each one of his dates had been cursed with the same affliction: they were all nice enough as people but as potential girlfriends there just wasn't any spark or chemistry at all. Try as he might he couldn't fake the slightest interest in their careers, hobbies, outdoor pursuits, countless godchildren and cats (especially their cats).

But if that wasn't enough (and Adam felt that it was, thank you very much), now that he had officially sworn off dating the wrong kinds of girls it was as if they were all determined to keep him from the straight and narrow. Wherever he went, whether for an innocent midweek drink with a mate, catching up with his paperwork in a coffee bar or even (as happened on one occasion) buying toothpaste in Superdrug, young girls with beautiful faces and bodies to die for were making eyes at him. But whereas the old Adam would have coaxed them into releasing their phone numbers within a few minutes this new Adam had to bite his lip and head in the direction of the nearest cold shower.

Now, not only had he not had a date with a potential right kind of girl for over a week but he also had nothing lined up for the future either. He reasoned that the best thing he could do to cheer himself up on a Saturday morning would be to take himself over to Beech Road, find a nice café and treat himself to a slap-up English breakfast. Then he would head to Marks and Spencer on the High Street to hang around their 'Meal for One' chill cabinet in the hope of sourcing a few potential right-kind-of-girl dates.

Quickly getting dressed, he made his way out of the house and ducked into his local newsagent's to pick up a *Daily Mail* and the latest issue of *Men's Health*. Whiling away his time in the longish queue at the till Adam recalled various snippets of his conversation from his last right-kind-of-girl date (had she really confessed that she called home from work twice a day to leave a message for her cats on the answerphone?) and was oblivious of his surroundings until he looked up to see that the queue appeared to have stalled because the woman directly in front of him was searching around for change to pay for the copy of the *Guardian* in her hand. Tutting under his breath Adam reached into his pocket and pulled out a two-pound coin.

'Here,' he said, handing her the coin. 'Take it.'

'I really couldn't,' said the woman, rummaging around the pockets of her vast handbag.

'Go on,' said Adam. 'It'll be my good deed for the day.'

She looked up and smiled. 'Thank you. I really don't know how I could have left the house without—'

She stopped.

'Adam Baxter!'

'It's Bachelor,' he replied. 'Adam Bachelor and you're . . .' He momentarily scanned her mental image through his brain cells. A girl. A girl from school. A bit of a brainbox. Not particularly exciting. May well have teased her about wearing braces. That was it.

'You're Stephanie Holmes!'

The last time he had seen Steph Holmes was probably on the day of his final English O level paper. She had been sitting at a desk a few seats in front of him and he remembered being impressed at the speed with which she had opened up the exam paper and started writing. She was easily the smartest girl in the school and was bound for greatness while he was, as the various teachers who wrote his numerous school reports never tired of saying, 'very intelligent but inherently lazy'.

'It's got to be at least twenty years,' said Adam, marvelling how the time had flown.

'Oh, don't say that! It means we're both really old and I don't think I'm ready for that. Look, let's agree it's been more like fifteen and we'll say no more about it.'

Adam paid for his things and they walked towards the door of the shop. 'So what have you done with your decade and a half?'

'Where to begin? After school my mum sent me to a private sixth-form college, after that I went to Oxford, after Oxford I went travelling for a while but I had to return early because my mum fell ill – it was just me and her you see – and then after she passed away I ended up moving to the US to work for a bank in New York. Then I moved to a bank in Tokyo, then I moved to another bank in Tokyo, then I decided I had had enough of both Tokyo and banking and moved back to Manchester and bought a house on Wilton Road and started working for a women's shelter that a friend of mine set up in Stretford.'

Although she had attempted to gloss over it quickly Adam felt he ought at least to acknowledge the fact of Steph's mum's death but then he remembered that they were in the middle of the newsagent's. This was neither the time nor the place. Instead he went for a much lighter topic. 'Which number Wilton Road are you?'

'Two eighty-three, why?'

'Two eighty-three! I'm mates with your neighbours Jon and Shelley. They live at two eighty one!'

'Small world.' Steph smiled.

'I can't believe you've done all that in fifteen years! You must never have stopped.'

'Maybe I should apply for early retirement. Anyway, how about you? What have you been up to since school?'

'Nothing that impressive,' replied Adam. 'Left school, did a bit of this and that, moved around for a bit, came back to Manchester, did a bit more of this and that and now I run my own bar on Wilbraham Road. You probably know it, BlueBar?'

'That's yours? Oh yes, I know it. Never been in it, mind. It all looks just a little bit too trendy for my liking. If I go out at all these days it's more likely to be for a meal. Still, you must be doing really well to have your own bar. Well done you.'

There was a long pause, most of which was Adam's fault because he was engrossed in thoughts about Steph. She clearly wasn't his old type. And she wore glasses. Adam had only ever been out with one other woman who wore glasses and she hadn't actually needed them: they were part of a sexy buttoned-up secretary look that had been popular at the time. Those glasses had been a prop, something to be removed in order to elicit the 'Why Miss Jones, you're gorgeous' response whereas Adam could tell that without her glasses, Steph would be struggling to find him. Still, in general at least she fitted the right kind-of-girl label and given that he had nothing better on he was prepared to give her a go if only to keep himself in practice. He checked her left hand. There was no ring in sight. He wondered if he should ask more questions but in the end decided he would be better off just jumping in with both feet.

'Look, I don't suppose you fancy going for a coffee do you?'

Steph pulled a face. 'I'd love to, it's just that—'

'Go on,' he interrupted, flashing her his best smile. 'You know you want to. One coffee, maybe a small pastry and then I promise that you can get on your merry way. In fact you won't even have to talk to me. If I get boring you can just whip out your newspaper and I won't complain. Go on, what do you say?'

'You're not going to take no for an answer are you?'

Adam grinned and shook his head. She was putty in his hands.

'Fine,' she relented. 'Let's go for a coffee. But I really can't be too long.'

'One day it really will be all right.'

As Adam was going for coffee with Steph, Luke was lying in bed eyeing the remains of a long-digested coffee and croissant breakfast as he dozed in Cassie's arms.

'We should get up and do something,' said Cassie, yawning. 'At this rate the whole day will be over before we've got out of bed.'

'I know,' said Luke, 'but it's so nice and we've both had pretty manic weeks so can't we stay here a little longer and just be?'

'You'd love that, wouldn't you? If it was up to you we'd spend all day in bed.'

'And all night and the day after too.'

Cassie's smile faded as though something serious had come to mind. 'I know this isn't really the time or the place . . . but are you going to tell Jayne about our plans to get married?'

Luke sighed and sat up. Was it really impossible for women to be happy about anything for more than ten minutes at a time? Would their lives fall apart if they weren't in constant search of the next obstacle? 'She wouldn't want to know,' he said briskly. 'I doubt that she would care one way or the other. She's probably remarried herself for all I know.'

'And what about Megan?'

'What about Megan?'

'Surely she deserves to know that her dad's getting married again?'

'Of course. Don't you think I'd be with her right now telling her to her face if I could?' Luke put his head in his hands and Cassie leaned across and kissed his temple.

'It'll be all right,' she said. 'One day it really will be all right.'

The story of Luke and Jayne was a depressingly familiar one, or at least that's what Luke's solicitor told him when they initially tried to find a way for Luke to gain access to his daughter. Whenever Luke looked back at that first meeting with Jayne he was struck by how random life was. Everything would have been completely different had he not bothered going down early to his housemate's get-together at the Crown and Garter in Ealing and instead spent, as he had intended, the better part of the evening at home cramming for his Master's in construction management. Jayne, it turned out, had planned to leave his housemate's celebration at just after nine. Luke hadn't planned to get there until well after ten. If they had both stuck to their plans then their future might never have happened. Maybe Jayne would have got together with one of Luke's other housemates or maybe Luke would have asked out the girl at work with whom he had been sharing awkward smiles in the lifts for weeks. Still, just after eight as Jayne was fending off the advances of one of Luke's mates Luke walked into the pub, bought a drink, found his friends and casual introductions were made. Luke grabbed a spare stool and placed it in the only space available left: next to Jayne.

Given the significant odds against it, maybe there had been something inevitable about their meeting. Luke didn't believe in stars or destiny or any of that mumbo-jumbo but he couldn't help believing that the two of them had been deliberately brought together because the moment he sat down next to her he felt as though a piece of himself that he'd never even known was missing had clicked into place. How was it possible to have so much in common with a random stranger? Was it an accident? Was it fate? Luke didn't know but Jayne obviously felt the same because the moment they left the pub and were out of sight of their friends her fingertips had reached out for his own.

A year on the magic had all but disappeared, replaced by the mundanity of life – which neither of them were really prepared for. Living in an overpriced rented flat in the wrong part of Hackney, Luke liked to believe that they both knew their time together was coming to an end. Far from being perfectly matched it seemed that the only thing they had in common was the ability to bring out the worst in each other. Rows would follow rows, tempered only by brief bouts of making up before the cycle would begin all over again.

In the September of their second year together Jayne fell pregnant and everything changed. Determined to try and interpret their new circumstances as proof of the genuine nature of their feelings for each other they put all their effort into papering over as many cracks as they could find in a vain attempt to rescue their relationship. Within a few months they had moved up to Manchester and the year after Megan was born they got married in a register office in Jayne's home town of Bath. All the Bachelors came down from Manchester for the big event; Luke's dad made a joke in his speech about how he had always feared that all three of his boys would end up being 'Bachelors by nature as well as by name'; and Luke concluded his moment in the spotlight with his own words of wisdom: 'Some people spend a lifetime looking for the right person to love and still never find them. I'm just thankful that having found Jayne so quickly I'll be lucky enough to spend my lifetime loving her.'

It barely took a year before things fell apart. Luke got seconded to a building project back in London which meant he had to live in a hotel from Monday to Thursday; Jayne's control issues became more and more exaggerated and eventually she refused to allow Luke's parents to take care of their granddaughter for more than a single hour a week despite the fact that she was desperately in need of assistance. Finally, one afternoon in the summer that Megan turned four, Luke returned home to find a note from Jayne telling him she was leaving him for good and taking their daughter with her. Guessing that they'd gone to her parents' house Luke got back into his car and drove to Bath only to be told by his father-in-law in no uncertain terms that Jayne didn't want to see him. From there things went from bad to worse and Luke found himself bouncing from lawyers' offices to family law courts and back again in a bid to see the daughter he was missing so much. After weeks of toing and froing access was established. Luke would drive to Bath on a Friday, pick up Megan, take her back home to Manchester and have her back in Bath for just after seven on the Sunday.

It wasn't perfect. He could see that his little girl didn't understand what was going on but there was nothing he could do other than to squeeze her hand and tell her everything was going to be all right. But it wasn't. Things became increasingly bitter between Luke and Jayne as divorce proceedings began but even so Luke wasn't prepared for the bombshell that Jayne dropped next: she was moving with her recently retired parents to France to start a new life. Luke tried everything to make her stay. He reasoned with her, pleaded with her and finally resorted to the kind of angry legal letters that only made matters worse, but to no avail. Jayne left and took his daughter with her. Flying from London to Brittany every other weekend, staying in impersonal hotels time after time, all took its toll on Luke's already fragile state of mind but he carried on for the sake of his daughter. And then it started. One week he'd turn up to collect Megan and the house would be empty; the following week he'd be told that Megan had come down with a cold and was too ill to see him. On and on it went, excuse after excuse until the one time he turned up unexpectedly and virtually forced his way inside Megan had been so distressed that she had sobbed inconsolably from the moment he arrived to the moment he left. And though he loved her more than life itself Luke knew he couldn't do that to her again and so he never did. Lost and alone at the age of thirty-one, it was all Luke could do not to fall apart. Then one day a few years later he chanced upon Cassie, the girl who would change his life, and suddenly he found hope where there had been none. But the mystery of what had caused Jayne to turn against him in that cruel way had always remained.

'Not a clue.'

It was the following Monday evening. Russell was staring blankly at his section of the fridge looking for inspiration when his mobile phone rang. He expected it to be Angie with updates on the latest news that her ex-boyfriend Aaron was finally getting round to moving out of her flat but when he casually looked at the screen, it was all he could do not to drop the phone.

Cassie calling. That was what the screen was saying. *Cassie calling*. It had been over a month since Russell had heard about her and Luke's engagement. It had really hurt. Being surrounded by all of his family congratulating the happy couple while inside he felt nothing but rage and self-loathing. Excusing himself straight after the meal under the guise of having a crisis on at work Russell had made his way over to Angie's and told her everything. 'This is it, Russ,' she had said. 'This is your chance to move on. Cassie's got her man and she's gone for good but now you're free, don't you see? You can grab your life back and do something really special with it. You have to move on, Russ, you have to.'

Russell agreed wholeheartedly. It was time to move on. It was time to get a life. He had spent too long wanting something that he was never going to have. His brother's happiness was about to set him free and so he had avoided the Bachelor Sunday lunch in a bid to rid Cassie from his system.

'Hi, Russ, it's me.'

Russell tried to regulate his breathing. 'Hi, Cass, how are you doing?'

'I'm really good, babe. Work has been a bit of a bind but that's only to be expected. If work isn't a bind then it isn't really work, is it? How about you? I feel like I haven't seen you in weeks. Where have you been hiding yourself?

'Oh, you know how it is,' said Russell. 'Things have just been a bit mad. I've had to work on a couple of Sundays and then Mum was saying that you and Luke were away this Sunday. Did you go anywhere nice?'

'It was absolutely amazing. Luke booked the two of us into a luxury spa hotel just outside Cheltenham for two whole nights! All we did all weekend was eat, sleep and get massaged.'

Russell swallowed at the mental image of Cassie lying semi-naked on a massage table and tried to blink it out of existence but it wouldn't budge. It was as though the image was burned on to the inside of his retina.

'So, is this just sort of a catch-up call? Only if it is, could I call you back some time as I'm sort of running late for a thing.'

'Oh, I'm so sorry, Russ,' replied Cassie. 'There's me gassing on and making you late.' She sighed. 'What's happened to us, Russ? I miss the days when you used to drop by unannounced with a bottle of wine and we'd spend the night yakking about nothing. You do know that you're my favourite brother-in-law-to-be, don't you? I mean, Adam's lovely but you're the real cutie of the Bachelor clan.'

Russell was lost for words. 'I . . . umm . . . I . . . er . . .'

'I've embarrassed you, haven't I? A girl shows a bit of affection and you're straight back into your fortress of solitude! Well, before you spontaneously combust I'm going to take my leave but I want you to promise me that you'll come round and see us for a proper catch-up, plus we can talk over some ideas I've got for your mum and dad's fortieth. How does tomorrow sound?'

'I can't,' said Russell. 'I've got a work thing on that I can't miss.'

'OK, well I've got a double Pilates lesson on Wednesday but I'm not sure I can be bothered so how about then?'

'Wednesday's pretty busy too.'

'OK, Thursday?'

'It's five-a-side Thursday night.'

'That's with the same lot that Luke used to play with? That's sorted then, isn't it? It's only on from eight until nine. You could come round to mine straight afterwards, have a shower and I'll make us something to eat. You'll be doing me a huge favour as I could really do with the company.'

'What do you mean, company?' asked Russell. 'Won't Luke be there?'

'Chance would be a fine thing,' sighed Cassie. 'He's away all week in London on some course or other so, yes, you will be keeping me company. You'd better sharpen up your conversational skills pronto!'

Russell mulled over his sister-in-law-to-be's proposition and felt sick. He wanted to say no. He needed to say no. But knowing that there would now be no way of getting out of it without him coming across as a nutter he found himself saying: 'That sounds great. See you Thursday night,' while simultaneously hoping that somehow in between now and then he might get run over by a car.

Three days later at ten minutes after nine Russell found himself standing on Luke and Cassie's doorstep ringing the bell.

'At last!' said Cassie as she opened the door. 'For a minute there I thought you'd bailed on me.'

She was wearing a red and white checked shirt over a green vest top, skinny jeans and flip-flops. Her jet-black hair was piled on top of her head in a haphazard fashion. This was the off-duty Cassie and strictly for people with whom she felt comfortable. It was by far and away Russell's favourite version of her and she could not have looked any more adorable, which meant his attempts to get over her were doomed to defeat. 'Come here and give me one of those hugs of yours,' she said.

He put his arms round her, conscious of the slenderness of her frame and the warmth of her breath on the nape of his neck. This was bliss. A perfect moment in an otherwise nightmare day that had seen him arrive late for work, drip coronation chicken dressing down the front of his suit and lose his bank card. Suddenly none of it mattered any more. He closed his eyes, instinctively dug his nose a little deeper into her hair and inhaled. Is this what life was like for Luke? Was he forever walking round on a cloud of happiness?

'Right then,' said Cassie, patting Russell on the back and pulling away. The embrace was clearly over. 'Are you hungry?'

He shrugged. 'I suppose I could eat something.'

'Good. I'll knock us up some pasta, you go and take a shower and I'll see you in a bit.'

Half an hour later, showered and dressed, Russell returned downstairs to the smell of pasta primavera, which they ate sitting on the sofa, an old Alton Ellis album playing in the background. As they worked their way through two bottles of super-chilled Pinot Grigio the conversation flowed so seamlessly that it was impossible to tell where one topic ended and another began. Amongst the million and one subjects covered were wedding plans and the perils of becoming one of the Bachelors; Russell's mum and dad's fortieth and how amazing it was to have first-hand evidence that love can last forty years; and then finally, somewhere around midnight, having worked their way though a tub of Ben and Jerry's the conversation turned to Russell himself, and specifically the question of his love life.

'So come on then, Russ, what's going on with you? It's ages since you've brought a young lady along to the Bachelor Sunday dinner.'

'And that's not likely to change any time soon.'

'How come? A good-looking boy like you should have the girls queuing for miles! What about that Angie who came with you a few times? Are you two definitely just good mates or is she a project in progress?'

'Definitely just mates, believe me, nothing's going to happen there.'

Cassie refused to let the subject go. 'So what are you saying? There's no one? What a waste of a decent bloke. I'm definitely bringing you out next time I meet up with all of my friends. They would love you to bits! I could see a couple of them ditching husbands for you!'

'There's no need to do that, honestly,' said Russell quickly. 'I'm fine.' He paused, desperate to unburden himself but unsure of how far to go. 'Look, there is sort of someone special.'

Cassie clapped her hands in glee. 'See! I knew it! Who? Anyone I know?'

Russell shook his head quickly, realising he should never have had that sixth glass of wine. 'No, you don't know her, but yes I do really like her.'

'Really like or love? I bet you love her, don't you? You're way more romantic than either of your brothers.'

Cassie looked into Russell's eyes. 'I can see it right there. You love her. Who is she?'

Russell felt his mouth go dry. 'I can't tell you. I haven't told anybody. Anyway it's pointless because she's already got a boyfriend and she's madly in love with him.'

'And does she know how you feel?'

'Not a clue.'

'Are you sure? Because when it comes to love us girls have got the best detection skills in the world.'

'I promise you she doesn't have the faintest clue. Otherwise she'd never act the way that she does around me.'

'And how's that?'

'I dunno, sort of flirty but without knowing it. I think she's just one of those incredibly tactile people.'

'And what's she like as a person?'

'Amazing. That's the best word I can think of to describe her. She's amazing and funny, sweet, warm-hearted, generous too. She's everything that I'm looking for in a girl.'

'So why don't you just tell her? You never know, she might be feeling that way too and just be too scared to tell you.'

'I can't,' sighed Russell, suddenly feeling very sober. 'It's never going to happen so I might as well just keep it to myself.'

'Will you just listen to yourself?'

Adam was had one eye on MTV but mostly he was thinking about Steph.

It had been nearly a week since Steph had allowed him to take her for a coffee after their encounter in his local newsagent's and yet she was still very much on his mind. Adam frequently found himself thinking generally about what she might be doing or saying at any particular moment; occasionally these thoughts were tempered by cogitations on what she might be wearing when she was saying or doing the various things that he imagined. This evening however Adam had excelled himself and was debating what she might be thinking about when she was wearing what he imagined she was wearing when she was saying or doing the various things that he imagined she might be doing or saying. Adam couldn't remember the last time he had felt this way about a girl. Admittedly he had been keen on girls before but in a more acquisitive way, not in this precise manner where he felt breathless and giddy about them, willingly allowing them to occupy various corners of his mind when they weren't actually there standing in front of him.

How good had their 'coffee date' been? Amazing. Initially they talked about their various jobs but then the conversation had flitted this way and that from school days to current affairs and from current affairs through to the current plight of Man City (which was a surprise) but for Adam the real eureka moment, the tipping point at which this ceased to be a battle to make a theoretical change of heart and when he actually thought seriously about kissing Steph in the way that he might have kissed a hot-looking girl in a very short skirt, was when she told him she really had to go and he realised they had been talking for an hour and that Steph possessed something he had never encountered before in a date prior to this moment: a personality. From that moment forward he was officially smitten.

Groaning at the thought that he was suffering from an overdose of oestrogen, Adam decided to take action. Reasoning that even the right kind of girls observed the 'wait three days before re-establishing contact' rule, Adam had opted to add an extra couple of days into the mix just to make it clear that he was a busy man with a busy life, and now there was nothing stopping him from making the call.

He dialled Steph's number and waited. Steph's phone rang out for half a minute or so before clicking on to voicemail. Adam didn't really do voicemail on the grounds that it was seriously uncool but it would be far less cool for Steph to see his number as a missed call and draw the conclusion that he was the sort of person who worried about leaving voicemail messages because they were uncool.

'Hi Steph, it's me Adam . . . y'know . . . Bachelor . . . from your school days . . . y'know just in case you know any other Adams and you're finding this message confusing. Anyway I just wanted to say that I really enjoyed that coffee the other day and would love to catch up with you again when you're free some time. Hope all is good with you. Let's speak soon. Oh . . . do you like tapas? I'm pretty sure everyone does. Anyway if you do there's a new tapas place just opened on Wilbraham Road that had a great review in *City List* if you fancy that . . . and no offence if you're not a tapas fiend . . . after all each to their own, right? Anyway . . . this is turning into a bit of an epic message . . . I'm worried that this thing is going to run out of space . . . Anyway . . . whatever . . . hopefully I'll see you soon . . . oh, by the way this is . . . was . . . Adam . . . as in Adam Bachelor from school. Bye.'

As Adam pressed the end call button on his phone and placed it carefully on the table he pushed his chair back to make space for himself to get down on his knees, curl up into a ball and with fists clenched let out a loud groan that was sixty per cent gut-wrenching embarrassment, forty per cent pure anguish. How could a universe exist in which a man as impossibly cool as he was could leave an answerphone message of such buttock-clenching awfulness? Had he entered a parallel universe where the laws of normal human interaction didn't apply? Didn't the people of this parallel world know who he was? That he had a plaque on his mantelpiece bearing the inscription 'the second best-looking bloke in Chorlton'? Didn't they know that he was definitely not the kind of bloke who left rambling voicemail messages? What was wrong with this world? And more importantly, what was wrong with him?

Adam got to his feet and stared at his phone as though it might ring at any second. When it didn't he went to the loo but in the process of washing his hands he imagined that he heard his mobile and rushed downstairs with wet hands only to discover that it was just his imagination. As he was about to leave the room for something to eat his phone actually did ring but it turned out to be a cold caller trying to sell him new kitchen units.

Annoyed and more than a little agitated Adam went in search of food and once again found himself thinking about Steph and what she might be doing/thinking/saying. He created a scenario where Steph (little realising that her life was about to change) was microwaving her evening meal while looking forward to an hour or so of work to fill her empty evenings before settling down for a glass of wine or two while she watched repeats of *Sex and the City*. He imagined the look of delight on her face when she retrieved his message, heard his voice and realised (probably for the first time) that her life was about to change for ever.

The phone rang.

Dashing back into the living room Adam grabbed the phone and looked at the screen. There it was: Steph's name.

'Steph! How are you? I'm glad you've called back.'

A short pause. 'Really? Er . . . thanks.'

'So how have you been?' asked Adam, trying to temper his earlier enthusiasm.

'Good, thanks. How about yourself?'

'Great,' said Adam breezily.

There was a silence.

'Listen, Adam . . .' began Steph, 'it really was lovely to bump into you the other day—'

'I know,' interrupted Adam. 'It was really good, wasn't it?'

'Still, I think what I'm trying to say is that even though it's always nice to bump into people that you went to school with there's not always a need to take things further, if you know what I mean.'

'Further?'

'Yes, further.'

'I don't understand,' said Adam. 'Are you saying that you don't want to meet up?'

'That's exactly what I'm saying,' replied Steph. 'I just don't think it would be a good idea.'

'Because . . . you've got a boyfriend?'

'Erm . . . well no, actually. As it happens I'm single but . . .'

Adam was incredulous. 'I don't get it. You're saying that you're single but you don't want to go out for a drink with me? How does that even make sense?

It wasn't just me, was it? The two of us did have a moment the other day when we went for coffee, didn't we?'

There was a long silence. Adam knew he ought to let this go but he couldn't. 'Look, just so that we're both clear: you do realise that I'm asking you out on a date?'

'Oh, Adam,' sighed Steph. 'Do we really have to do this?'

'Yes,' replied Adam, 'yes we do. Because I've got a terrible feeling that you've not fully grasped the fact that *I'm asking you out.*'

'Will you listen to yourself? Anyone would think that you've never been turned down for a date the way you're acting. But as clarity seems to be something of an issue for you: one, no we did not have a moment the other day; two, I only agreed to have coffee with you because I thought it was the easiest way to get rid of you; three, you seem to have forgotten the small fact that you made my life hell when we were at school; and four, even if points one, two and three weren't true I still wouldn't go out with you because one thing that was abundantly clear in the short time that I spent with you in the newsagent's and talking over badly made, overpriced coffee, is this: you, Adam Bachelor, are completely and utterly the wrong kind of guy for me.

'You think I've let you down.'

The following weekend Luke and Cassie were on the motorway in Luke's Honda singing at the top of their voices to 'Total Eclipse of the Heart'.

They had driven up to Harrogate on the Friday night to spend time with Cassie's family. Desperate to make the best of the weather on their arrival Cassie's dad had fired up the barbecue and they had all enjoyed an alfresco meal featuring chops and burgers and salads of every description in what remained of the dying sun. The following morning had seen the arrival of Cassie's sister Rebecca, her husband Tom and their two kids; the entire family had decamped to Valley Gardens. A brass band had been playing which the kids had adored and when they stopped to take a break everyone headed over to the already overrun kids' playground. Cassie took Poppy on the swings and Luke pushed Lucie on the roundabout. Whenever the kids got bored they just swapped activities, moving from the climbing frame to the slide and from the slide to the roundabout. The kids never stopped smiling the whole time they were there. At lunchtime the family headed en masse to an upmarket pizza restaurant on Albert Street and were joined by two of Cassie's aunties and a now eighteen-year-old cousin who Cassie hadn't seen since he started secondary school. Not only were the Shergolds by far the biggest group in the restaurant but they were also the most raucous, with Cassie's dad regaling the table with boisterous anecdotes about his time in the navy. It was some time after four as the kids' batteries began to wear down and people started to make their excuses that Luke and Cassie finally said their goodbyes before heading back out towards the M62. Luke slipped on a compilation CD that he had made specifically for the journey. It was full of stuff he knew they would both love singing along to and was a hit from the first track onwards as they both gave their all in tuneless harmony to every song from 'Sympathy for the Devil' to 'Billie Jean'. Half an hour from the outskirts of Manchester (and directly after Bonnie Tyler) Cassie had turned off the music and they had segued into the kind of light-hearted conversation that was their staple: daft observations about the places they were passing through, jokes about the day they had enjoyed, gentle teasing about each other's foibles and then, seemingly out of nowhere, Cassie turned to Luke and said: 'I want us to start a family.'

'You want us to do what?'

'I said I want us to start a family.' She clarified her position. 'I don't mean right now. I mean after we're married. Very soon after we're married. I want us to have kids.'

'What brought this on?'

Cassie didn't reply and Luke knew the reason. No matter how even his voice, the question had sounded like an accusation. To all intents and purposes it had been. Luke kept his mouth shut, willing the subject to just go away. Maybe she didn't really mean it. Maybe she was saying the words out loud to hear what they sounded like. He thought how much fun they had been having and how carefree they had been. He wanted that feeling back. He didn't want it to disappear and be replaced by reality.

Luke prided himself on the fact that he had been honest with Cassie from the start. If it hadn't been on their second date then it was definitely by the time of their third that he'd said: 'I think there's something you should know about me. I never, ever want to have more children and I'm never going to change my mind about it. I can't do it. I won't go through all that again. I'm sorry if that sounds harsh but it's the way it is.'

At the time Cassie had said that she understood. She knew all about Jayne and Megan and the hurt that Luke had endured but even so she had listened patiently as Luke had recounted relevant parts of the story. The love he had for his daughter, the hurt that his ex-wife had inflicted, the tears shed every year by his mum around the time of Megan's birthday. He was firm in his intention. No matter what happened in the future, no matter how deeply they fell in love, he wasn't going back there. Not now, not ever.

'Why does this feel like I'm letting you down?' asked Cassie. Her eyes were fixed on the road ahead. 'Why does this feel like it's all my fault?'

Luke didn't utter the words but his immediate

thoughts were there all the same: 'Probably because you *are* letting me down,' came the internal voice. 'Probably because this *is* actually all your fault.'

Time and time again Luke had gone against his deepest instincts for self-preservation in order to revisit the subject and allay his fears that Cassie might have simply been telling him what he wanted to hear. On their six-month anniversary he took her for a weekend in Prague and raised it as they waited to board the flight back home. Her response had been to laugh and tell him that she knew the rules: 'No babies!' and then she had kissed him passionately, oblivious of the passengers who surrounded them. Months later when the first of Cassie's group of friends became pregnant Luke had asked if she was having second thoughts as they stood in Mamas and Papas in the Trafford Centre searching out a set of lilac baby blankets and she had assured him it was nothing of the kind. The last time had been a little under six months ago when Cassie had come to him in tears, clearly suffering from a case of pre-thirtieth-birthday blues. 'What would make things right for you?' he had asked, well aware that the reply could be one that he wouldn't like. 'The words: "I will always love you," plus a simple kiss would do right now.' Luke's sense of relief had been immense and without a moment's hesitation he had told her that he would always love her.

Luke glanced over at Cassie; he thought she might be crying.

'Are you OK?' he asked. 'Look, before, what I said. I shouldn't have said it. It was wrong of me.'

'Not really,' said Cassie keeping her eyes fixed to the road ahead. 'That's what you think, isn't it? That I've let you down.'

'No, no, of course not.'

'You've never left me in any doubt as to your position on this. You've always said it would never change.'

'So why bring it up now?'

'Because I love you.'

'And you didn't before?'

'Of course I did.'

'Then what are you saying?'

'I'm saying that this is different. I'm saying I love you with everything I have to give and more. And when you love someone like that, you want to see that love made flesh. That's what kids are, aren't they? They're two people put together. Why wouldn't I want that for us? Why wouldn't I want to bring someone into the world who's made of our love? I know how much you've hurt at times. I've been there with you and wiped away the tears, but Luke, you can't let the past rule the future. I'm not Jayne and I never will be. I'd sooner hurt myself than hurt you like she did so you don't need to protect yourself from getting hurt any more because I'm here and I love you and nothing bad is ever going to happen to you again.'

Back in Chorlton Cassie helped Luke unload the car but once the job was done she disappeared to the bathroom, locked the door behind her and ran a hot bath. It was an hour before she emerged and then she went straight to their room and closed the door behind her.

When Luke (who had spent most of his hour alone waiting for Cassie to emerge so that they could call a truce) heard the bedroom door close he froze. He wanted to go up and see Cassie. He wanted to say, 'Look, I'm sorry, babe. You're right, I'm wrong, of course we should start a family,' but the words just weren't in him. Nothing Cassie had said to him had changed his feelings about having children and though he was aware that the situation had the potential to snowball into something more lethal than a simple tiff, there wasn't a thing he could do to stop it. He took a deep breath, made his way upstairs and knocking on the bedroom door (why he wasn't quite sure) he entered the bedroom to find Cassie sitting on the edge of the bed in her pyjamas doing her hair.

'Are you hungry? I was thinking of doing fish fingers and chips or something.'

'No thanks.'

'So are you going to bed then?'

'I'm tired. It's been a long day.'

'I thought we were going to watch that DVD you borrowed from your mate.'

'You watch it if you want to,' said Cassie, picking up the brush beside her.

Luke had had enough. 'So this is how you want to leave things? This is so typical.'

'Do you know what really hurts?' said Cassie, seemingly oblivious to Luke's accusation. 'That you couldn't even find it in yourself to say that you'd think about it.'

'Is that what you want?'

'Of course it's what I want!'

Luke couldn't believe it. She might as well ask him to lie to her face. What was the point of agreeing to think about something when he was one hundred per cent sure that he wouldn't change his mind? Wasn't that just offering hope when there was none? Wasn't that just dishonesty dressed up as pragmatism? But because this *was* what Cassie wanted to hear, he said (mostly because he loved her and partly because he just wanted this to be over), 'Then fine. If it's what you want I'll think about it.'

'You know I don't dance.'

The following Friday night, Russell and Angie were sitting in a bar on Thomas Street for their usual hey-it's-the-weekend-let's-drink-ourselves-silly meet-up. The bar was more packed than usual but fortunately for the pair as soon as they had stepped through the doors a large group of students sitting on the worn leather sofas in the corner stood up and before they had even put on their jackets Angie had slipped in behind them, handed Russell a crumpled ten-pound note and ordered him to get her a double vodka and Red Bull by fair means or foul. Now they were firmly ensconced in their favourite spot.

For the most part they talked about two items currently highest of Angie's list of things that were bothering her. The first was the fact that now Aaron had moved out of the flat it would only be a matter of a few months before she couldn't afford to carry on living there. Russell had suggested that perhaps she should go into a house share but Angie had looked at him in a withering fashion as though he had suggested that she take up part-time prostitution. Next Angie had brought up Aaron again, this time in relation to the recent news that he had apparently been seen by a mutual friend in the company of another (female) mutual friend with Angie declaring that 'the fat bitch can have him for all I care; it's the sneaking about that really gets under my skin.' Russell didn't bother challenging this because it would only annoy her.

When they had exhausted Aaron-related topics Angie firmly set down her glass and demanded to know what was ailing Russell.

'Who says there's something ailing me?' said Russell, taking a long sip from his pint by way of diversion.

'I do,' laughed Angie. 'First off you've barely said a word all night and what's more you've called me three times this week to check I'm coming out tonight. Not even my mother calls me that often.'

'OK, there is sort of something going on but I know you're going to go mad at me . . . I've finally decided to tell Cassie how I feel about her.'

Angie's eyes widened. 'You've what? I thought you were all sworn off Cassie since your brother and her decided to get hitched?'

'I thought I was over her.'

'So what happened?'

'Everything.' Russell could see that Angie was already losing patience. 'It's not easy, you know. I really was serious about moving on. Even I could see there was no point now that they're engaged. But just when I thought I was rid of her for good she invited me round to hers and I couldn't say no, and Luke wasn't there and she was looking all cute and vulnerable in that way she does and . . .'

'You're not trying to tell me something happened?'

Russell shook his head. 'Not in the way that you mean. It's just that . . . I don't know . . .'

'You're back in love with her?'

'It's pathetic isn't it?'

'I think the word you're looking for is spineless.'

'That's a bit harsh.'

'I'm just telling it the way I see it: nice bloke falls in love with wrong girl is fine. Nice bloke falls in love with wrong girl and is given a cast-iron reason to fall out of love and yet still remains in love with wrong girl is . . . spineless. You don't want me to sugar-coat this for you do you? Because I'm sure that I don't need to remind you I'm *not* that kind of friend.'

'At this rate you won't be any kind of friend at all,' complained Russell. 'Sometimes I don't know what gets into you.'

'Fine,' she snapped, shooting him a look of hurt and fury. 'Whatever.' She headed in the direction of the downstairs toilets.

Russell leaned back in the sofa and finished off his pint. Angie was right. What was he doing even thinking of telling Cassie about his feelings? He made his way to the bar and, after ten minutes of being ignored by an over-coiffured barman, ordered another round and returned to the sofa where a glowering Angie was now back.

'For you,' he said, sliding over a fresh vodka and Red

Bull by way of a peace offering. 'Because I love you, you old slag.'

'Is it a double?'

Russell nodded and Angie threw of look of mock disdain in Russell's direction. 'In that case I suppose you're forgiven.'

They drank more than usual in a bid to make good their pact to avoid any conversation related to Cassie or Aaron, and when Angie received a text inviting her to meet up with some of her friends at a club in town, she put the proposition to Russell.

'But I don't dance,' said Russell. 'And I hate nightclubs.'

Angie rolled her eyes. 'One: you don't have to dance, and two: given the fact that I've forgiven you for this whole Cassie thing that you've got going on the least you can do to keep me sweet is to ignore the fact that you hate nightclubs. All I'm asking is that you come along with me and keep me from doing anything stupid.'

'So doing something stupid is definitely on the cards then?'

'Have you seen how much I've had to drink? I'll probably do something stupid and then something really stupid on top of that just for effect.'

They arrived at the club on Princess Street just after midnight and within seconds Russell was wishing he had caught a taxi home. It wasn't just that the club was filled with students and that their very presence seemed to render every item of clothing he was wearing immediately unfashionable. No, what bothered Russell were all the couples dotted about the place rampantly getting off with each other. Did they need to do this in such an open arena? Couldn't any of them wait until they got home? Did none of them possess a sufficient sense of decorum to conclude that this kind of thing might be better done in private?

'They're just being kids,' reasoned Angie. 'Don't you remember what it felt like?'

'Nah, mate, not like that.'

'You sound like an old man.'

'Maybe that's because I am,' shouted Russell over the music. 'I don't understand what we're doing. We're practically a decade older than most of the kids in here. It feels like we're a couple of creepy weirdos crashing their party or something.'

Angie stared at Russell.

'What?'

'Are you really going to tell Cassie how you feel about her?'

Russell shrugged.

'What do you think she's going to say when you tell her?'

He shrugged again. 'I don't think that's really the point of the exercise.'

'So what is?'

'Who knows? To unburden myself I suppose. To stop feeling like I always bottle everything up. I'm sick of keeping in all these things that I want to say . . . that I feel I need to say. I'm not expecting she'll say them back. I'm not that naive.'

'And your brother?'

'What about him?'

'What will he do when she tells him?'

'Probably punch my lights out. Luke's temper's never been as bad as Adam's but even he's got his limits.'

'You are insane, do you know that?'

'I know. It'll be a suicide mission, though knowing my luck I'll live to regret it. But sometimes the only thing is to be true to yourself, isn't it?'

Russell turned to walk towards the bar to get them another drink but he felt Angie tug on his arm.

'Come and have a dance,' she said. 'I love this song.'

Russell groaned. 'I told you I don't dance.'

'I know you don't dance for you. But you never said that you wouldn't dance for me.' She tugged his arm again. 'Please! Pretty please! Russ, I love this song. Please don't spoil this for me.'

'OK, OK,' sighed Russell, allowing Angie's hand to slide down his arm to his hand. 'Lead the way.' And that's exactly what she did. She excused her way through dancing groups and couples right to the centre of the dance floor and began moving in time to the music, eyes closed, her hands firmly clutching Russell's and singing along with the words with such conviction that it was almost as though the words were her own and coming directly from her heart. Russell allowed himself to loosen up and began dancing too.

He closed his eyes in a bid to feel slightly less self-conscious and for a moment or two he was lost in the music and probably would have remained there had something odd not happened. Angie put her arms round him, her face buried in his chest and he found himself wrapping his arms round her, pulling her body close into his own. A moment or two in this new position passed and then Russell found himself lowering his head towards Angie's and was pleased to see her meeting him halfway. This was a joint decision, a moment of mutuality, a brief acknowledgement that things would never be the same between them ever again, a tacit agreement that this new state of affairs was all right. But at the forefront of Russell's mind was the idea that this was the answer to all his problems: with one swift action he could rid himself of Cassie once and for all.

So he kissed her.

'You'll wake the baby!'

It was just after eight the following evening and Adam was standing in front of his bedroom mirror undertaking the time-honoured four-dab aftershave splash as part of his preparations for a big night out when his home phone rang.

Picking it up from its cradle on his bedside table he carefully admired his reflection in the mirror. In a crisp white designer shirt, jeans and a pair of tan leather brogues (all of them brand new) he really did look good enough to eat.

'Hello?'

'Hello, Adam, it's me,' said his mum quietly.

Adam sat down on his bed, immediately on edge. Mum was supposed to be in Leeds visiting her sister Rose. Mum never called when she went to stay with Aunt Rose because they always had such a good time. Plus his mum's voice sounded wrong. Strained somehow.

'Hi Mum, are you OK? You don't sound like yourself.'

'Oh, I'm fine,' she said, sniffing slightly. 'I'm just feeling a little under the weather, that's all.'

'Is it a cold or something?'

'Probably.'

'You should see a doctor.'

'You can't go to the doctor's for a cold, Adam! That's not how I brought you up. You don't clog up Dr Evensham's surgery with that kind of thing, do you?'

'Of course not.' He wished he'd kept his mouth shut. 'I was just thinking about you, that's all.'

There was a silence. Adam couldn't work out what was going on. As well as never calling from Auntie Rose's Mum never called for a chat. One of the golden rules Mrs Bachelor had instituted for her sons was that all chat-based telephone conversations should originate from her offspring. 'I'm not going to be chasing after you with expensive telephone calls just to find out how you are,' she had told Adam the day he left home. And she never had either. She'd call under the guise of delivering important information ('Don't forget that the clocks go back tonight!'); she'd call in order to recruit Adam to pass on messages to his brothers ('And the next time you speak to that middle brother of yours make sure you tell him to call me straight away!'); and occasionally she'd even call to ask him to explain some matter of technology that was eluding both her and Dad ('So, Adam, this email business? Where exactly do you buy the stamps?') but the one thing she never did was ring without a purpose. And yet here she was at the end of the line saying absolutely nothing. Possibly it was her cold. Colds could indeed do that sort of thing to people but Adam was pretty sure that his mum was not in any way shape or form 'people'.

'Are you sure you're OK, Mum?'

'Yes, yes, I'm fine . . .'

'How's Aunt Rose?'

'She's good and sends her love.'

'Have you spoken to Dad yet?'

'Not tonight.'

'How come?'

'I didn't want to bother him.'

There was another long silence. Adam looked at his watch and wondered how long this would go on for.

'Look, Mum, I was sort of just on my way out . . .'

'Oh, of course,' she replied. 'Yes, sorry, you get on.'

'I'll see you tomorrow though.'

'Yes, yes of course.'

'Love you, Mum.'

'Yes, dear, love you too.'

An hour and a short cab ride later Adam was sipping a Grey Goose vodka and tonic at the Silver Arcade Bar at the Armada Hotel (aka the number one Premier League footballers' hangout). His presence there was purely based on the golden rule of big nights out in the North-West: the best-looking girls in Manchester are always be found in the vicinity of the best-looking (and richest) men in Manchester and there really wasn't a better place he could be in order to make his point.

There were girls everywhere. And not just regular pretty girls either but ludicrously hot-looking girls in shimmery tops and short skirts with perfectly tanned legs. These were to a woman the Wrong Kinds of Girls but he didn't care about any of that any more. Although it had taken him the best part of a week to process Steph's rejection (which had involved him wandering glowering around south Manchester with only the blackest of black moods to keep him company) he now considered himself well and truly over the event and had chosen to celebrate in the only way he knew how: by going all out to pull the most wrong of all wrong types of girl that he could possibly pull on a Saturday night in the one place that he knew would be thronging with them. The Meals for One chill cabinet in M & S this was not. And so after a couple of circuits of the bar to measure up the talent he finally decided on a tall, frizzy-haired girl with deep brown eyes wearing a purple top and barely-there miniskirt who looked as though she had just stepped out of the final frame of a hip-hop video on MTV.

The girl was called Dee and as it turned out wasn't even from Manchester. She was actually from Essex but was up in the North-West for the weekend working as a promotions girl for a leading sports car manufacturer at the motor show being held at Manchester Central. Within ten minutes Adam came to the conclusion that not only was Dee vain and superficial to the point of caricature but she wasn't all that bright either. But Adam didn't care. All he cared about as he left the bar with Dee and some of her equally glamorous mates and ushered them past the queues to the VIP entrances of three different bars and two different clubs, was the fact she made it clear that the only way she could have thought he was any cooler would have been for him to have levitated right in front of her.

Seeing her friends off in a cab just after five, Adam took Dee to one last club (just so that he could introduce her to a couple of the younger members of the cast of *Hollyoaks*) before heading back home to Chorlton.

'So do you live here on your own?' asked Dee as the taxi pulled up outside his house and Adam paid the cab driver.

'Yeah,' replied Adam. 'I know it's a little big for just me but I like my space.'

Dee kissed Adam full on the lips and led him up to his front door where they kissed again.

'We really should do this indoors,' murmured Adam, reaching inside his jacket for his key, 'the last thing I need is the neighbours complaining again!'

Dee sniggered like a naughty schoolgirl as Adam opened the door enabling the two of them to collapse giggling into the hallway.

'Shhhhh!' Dee adopted a comedy Mancunian accent. 'You'll wake the baby!'

'Listen, babe, why don't you go put some music on in the front room while I'll go and see if I can find some glasses for this champagne you made me buy.'

He kissed her again, a long slow kiss, and then brandishing the bottle of ludicrously overpriced champagne he headed for the kitchen. He was still rooting around in the cupboard when there was an ear-piercing scream from the living room.

Adam was there within seconds and was completely

gobsmacked by what he saw: a horrified-looking Dee facing his horrified-looking dad who was standing in the middle of the living room wearing only a plain white T-shirt and boxer shorts.

'I thought you lived alone?' said Dee.

'I do,' stammered Adam. He looked at his dad and the duvet lying on the sofa behind him. 'Dad, what are you doing here?'

'I needed somewhere to stay, son.'

'What do you mean? Why would you need somewhere to stay? You've got a house.'

Dad looked at Dee, his face the picture of embarrassment. 'I'm sorry, love.'

'You nearly gave me a heart attack,' said Dee.

'You and me both,' he said, sitting down on the sofa.

Adam couldn't stand this small talk any more. 'Dad! Come on! You're in my living room in your boxer shorts . . . what's wrong? Why aren't you at home?'

His dad looked at the floor. 'I didn't want you to find out like this. I didn't want you to find out like this at all.'

'Find out what?'

'It's me and your mum.' He met Adam's gaze full on. 'I don't really know how to say this so I'll just come out with it. I'm sorry, son, I've left her.'

Part 2

'Just say it.'

Adam cracked his left eyelid open, yawned and cast his gaze in the direction of the bedside clock which told him was it was quarter to one in the afternoon. Squeezing his open eye shut, he turned over and tried to go back to sleep. Given the strange and disturbing nature of the dreams that he had been having all night (something to do with his dad, a screaming girl and a very nasty surprise) this was probably a mistake. Something was wrong, he could feel it deep in his bones. But what was it? He snaked out an arm out from underneath the warmth of his duvet and stretched out his legs; he opened his left eye, quickly followed by his right and saw the problem right in front of him: the other side of the bed was empty. How could that possibly be true? Surely his throbbing head was evidence that he had been on a big night out? And what kind of big night out could possibly result in him waking up alone in bed? Adam pondered the problem and decided the scenario was so unlikely that there could only be one answer: she had already got up and was currently doing something sexy like making breakfast for the two of them wearing nothing but his shirt. What did she look like? He had no idea. But she would be a cracker. He climbed out of bed, flung on his towelling dressing gown, and made his way gingerly downstairs. He was all ready to feast his eyes upon the cornucopia of delights that were no doubt waiting for him when the kitchen door opened and there in front of him with a bowl of cereal in his hands and wearing a shapeless plain white T-shirt and blue boxer shorts and very little else was his dad. Suddenly it all came back to him. His dad. A girl. And an awful lot of screaming. No, it hadn't been a dream at all. It had been real. Very real. His parents' forty-year marriage was over.

Half an hour later having showered, shaved and left half a dozen messages for each of his brothers Adam made his way back down to the kitchen to restart his morning.

'All right, Dad?' he said to his father who was standing at the sink washing up his cereal bowl. Adam glanced down at the dishwasher that he was pretty sure his dad knew existed and sighed. 'Sorry about just turning round like that and heading back upstairs. I think I was still half asleep and well . . . you sort of took me by surprise. Anyway, did you sleep OK?'

'I slept fine, son.' He shook the soap suds from his hands into the sink, then paused and looked at Adam as if awaiting some kind of news or admonishment from his son. Adam felt there was nothing to say until his dad had at the very least had a cup of tea.

'Fancy a brew?'

'Definitely. And some toast wouldn't go amiss. I had some of your bran flakes but I can't say that they really agree with me.'

'One tea and toast coming up,' said Adam. 'Just make yourself comfortable in the front room and I'll bring it in to you.'

'Are you sure?' asked Dad. 'I don't want to be any trouble.'

Adam felt his heart melt for his dad who had done so many wonderful things for his son in his lifetime and now thought that a request for a cup of tea and toast must somehow constitute 'trouble'.

'It's no trouble, Dad, honestly. No trouble at all.'

Adam filled the kettle and wondered again what was happening in his life. He focused mainly on the over-the-top reaction of Dee-the-promotions-girl at coming face to face with his dad in his living room. It would almost be funny if it a) hadn't happened to him and b) he didn't feel that right now his life was falling apart.

What could be going on in the mind of a sixty-eight-year-old man, a few months shy of his fortieth wedding anniversary, to make him decide to give it all up so that he could be on his own? It didn't make any sense. Much as Adam liked his space, even he could see that one of the upsides of marriage was that you didn't have to grow old and die alone. So this step that his dad had taken this close to seventy, well, he just couldn't take it seriously. Maybe it was some kind of delayed mid-life crisis? Was it more of a wobble in confidence than an out-and-out statement of intent? Adam couldn't imagine how his dad would last ten minutes alone, never mind ten days, without Mum.

The water for the tea came to the boil signalling to Adam that it was time to do the toast. He got out a loaf of white bread and dropped two slices into the toaster. He was just about to reach across for a plate when the phone on the kitchen counter rang.

'Hello, Adam?'

It was Luke.

'Where have you been?'

'It's a long story. I switched my phone off last night and forgot all about it.'

'You and Russ, you're both useless,' snapped Adam. 'What's the point in having mobile phones if no one can get hold of you?'

'What's the problem? Is everything OK? No one's ill are they?'

'No, no one's ill.' Adam paused, thinking of how to say what needed to be said. 'Look, mate, I can't go into it on the phone. I just need you to get over to mine, OK? And bring Russ with you.'

An hour later Adam opened the door to his brothers. 'Finally!' he said, scowling in their direction. 'I thought you pair were never going to turn up. Come in.'

'What's the big deal?' Russell was clearly annoyed that Adam had invoked his right (by virtue of being the first born and the most physically imposing) to talk to his brothers like they were a pair of errant schoolkids.

'I'd tell you but you'd never believe me. Just follow me and be prepared to have your minds blown.'

Exchanging puzzled glances Luke and Russell followed Adam into the front room where their dad was sitting uncomfortably on Adam's slouchy low-level grey sofa staring up at the motor-racing on the huge flatscreen TV.

'All right, Dad?' Luke was confused. 'What are you doing here?'

Dad looked guiltily at Adam. 'I thought you were going to tell them?'

Adam shook his head. 'You must be joking. You can't tell this kind of news second-hand, Dad – I heard it directly from you and I still don't believe it. No, Dad, this has to come from you and you alone.'

'It's not Mum is it?' asked Russell. 'She's OK, isn't she?'

'You're mother's fine,' replied Dad. 'There's nothing wrong with her at all.'

'OK,' said Luke, struggling to remain calm 'this is ridiculous. We've established that Mum's fine, and as far as I can see you're fine too, Dad, and I'm pretty sure that me, Russ and Ad are all hunky-dory, so just put me and Russ out of our misery, will you? It doesn't matter who, but will one of you explain what it is that's going on because you're both freaking me out with all this.'

Dad stood up from the sofa to put himself on a level with his sons. 'Look,' he said, addressing Luke, 'what you've got to understand is that this situation . . .' He paused and looked over at Russell to include him too.

'Well, the thing is it's really difficult for all of us. There aren't any rights and wrongs. There's just . . . I don't know . . . lots of shades of grey.'

Adam could see that Luke was getting impatient. Dad, usually one of the most straight-talking people in the history of the world, was suddenly talking in the fluffy touchy-feely manner of a daytime talk show host. If ever there was a red alert signal this was it. Men were the problem with this situation, thought Adam. Here they were, four grown men standing in a room trying desperately to communicate with each other and failing miserably.

'Look, Dad,' said Luke. 'Whatever it is you've got to say just say it, OK?'

'Very well then.' He took a deep breath and told them everything.

'Why don't we all just calm down for a second?'

Russell didn't know where to look, or even what kind of expression should be on his face. His father's news had rendered him well and truly speechless. Plucking up the courage to meet the gaze of the other members of his family in the room, he registered that his father looked weary; Luke looked like he was about to explode in rage; and Adam looked like all he wanted was to go back to bed and pretend this day had never happened.

Russell barely understood his dad's explanation. In fact it was as though Dad didn't really understand it himself even though he was at the centre of it. But the long and the short of it seemed to be that he had left Mum. Having a lot of time on his hands since his retirement five years ago Dad had apparently started to think about his life and begun to wonder how it might have been different if he had never married and had children. All this wondering might have ended up nowhere but a few weeks ago he had bumped into Roger, an old friend from his time on the buses, and they had gone for a drink together and over a couple of pints of stout George had learned that Roger had just split up with his wife Marion after forty-four years together. Roger professed to be having the time of his life now that he was single and that was it. The seed was planted in the boys' father's head and it started to germinate. It was possible to start again. It was possible to live the life that you always wanted to live: a life free of commitments and compromises; a life where he could just do his own thing. Over the following weeks he packed and unpacked a suitcase several times and even got as far as calling for a taxi but always changed his mind at the last minute. Then last night with Joan spending the night away at Aunt Rose's in Leeds he had packed his suitcase, placed a letter that had taken him all day to write on the telephone seat in the hallway and called a taxi to take him over to Adam's. He explained his choice of destination thus: 'Luke's got Cassie, Russell shares his house with strangers so Adam's really was my only option.' On hearing the minicab beep its horn outside the house he had removed the spare keys to Adam's house from the living-room drawer, taken one last look around the house, locked the door behind him and headed over to Adam's house secure in the knowledge that Adam being Adam would most likely be out until the early hours. George had taken the duvet from the bed in the spare room and settled down on the sofa to wait for his eldest son's arrival home. At roughly six a.m. Adam had arrived home with a young lady who Dad had never seen before and said young lady had entered the living room to discover Dad in his boxer shorts.

She had screamed. The rest, as they say, is history. Now all he wanted was for Joan to keep the house and everything in it and allow him to find a place of his own to rent and try his best to be happy.

Russell looked up at his dad. 'I don't understand.' George looked confused. 'I don't understand what you've just said, Dad,' he clarified.

George looked at the ground. 'Don't get me wrong, boys, it's not like I don't love your mother. I do. I really do. She's a great woman and has done an outstanding job of raising you three boys into the fine men you are today.'

Luke spat a terse and dismissive 'But?' in Dad's direction.

George refused to acknowledge the hostility in Luke voice. 'There is always a "but" with these situations isn't there? And the "but" here is me. It's not your mother's fault and it's certainly not you boys' fault either. If there's anyone at all to blame it's me. This is all my fault.'

'Well you're not wrong there,' snapped Luke. He walked towards the window as if he couldn't trust himself to be in too close proximity to his father. 'Of course it's not Mum's fault and why would any of us think it's our fault? It's got nothing to do with us at all. I don't even know what you're thinking. None of this is making any sense.' Russell watched Luke's face and felt a tight ball of tension in his stomach. The suggestion that Luke was about to make hadn't even crossed his mind until this moment and even the thought of it made him feel sick.

'There isn't anyone else involved, is there?' asked Luke.

'Of course not,' replied their dad, genuinely horrified at the question. 'What kind of man do you take me for?'

'I don't know, Dad,' replied Luke, 'with this news you're making it hard for me to tell.'

'Look boys, I know you're angry—'

'Angry doesn't even begin to describe it, Dad!' interrupted Luke. 'It's like we don't even know you. How can you just stand there and tell us that after the best part of forty years of marriage you've had enough and you're off? How did you think we were going to react? Did you think we'd congratulate you? Well done there, Pops, for smashing up the family unit?'

Luke's anger was rising. Something needed to be done to bring the temperature of the room down a few degrees before things got said that they would all regret. Russell glanced over to Adam in the hope that he might step up and do the big brother thing but he clearly wasn't about to. Maybe Adam, having had time to deal with his reactions, was simply standing back and giving himself and Luke the opportunity to get fully up to speed.

'Look,' Russell was surprised by the forcefulness of his own voice used in the presence of a group of people with whom he was rarely if ever forceful, 'why don't we all just calm down. I understand this must be really difficult for you, Dad,' continued Russell in his role as peacemaker, 'but I'm still having a lot of trouble getting my head round this so if Luke and I both promise to keep our mouths shut, will you tell exactly what's happened?'

Everyone nodded and Dad explained everything again only this time more slowly and with a lot more detail.

'OK Dad,' said Adam, aware that his brothers were looking at him with a 'So what now?' expression. 'Now we've got to sort out the way forward. First thing we need to know is what time Mum's getting back.'

'I'm not sure,' said Dad. 'Maybe you should go over there now and make sure she's all right. She'll need all the support she can get.'

'Too right,' snapped Luke in his father's direction. 'In fact I'm getting out of here right now. Just being in the same room with you is driving me insane.'

'Luke, wait!' commanded Adam. 'Just wait, OK? And then we'll all go. Look, Dad, with the best will in the world I really can't take the idea of you and Mum splitting up seriously. I don't know what's going on with you but I've got a strong feeling that you're going to regret this once Mum finds out. So here's what going to happen: you'll stay here, me, Luke and Russ will go over to yours and get rid of the letter, we'll tell Mum you felt ill last night, stayed at mine and that you're fast asleep now. Then once you've had a couple of hours to yourself we'll pick you up and take you back home, OK?'

'You're talking as though you haven't heard a word I've said!' shouted Dad. He took a moment to compose himself. 'I know it's hard for you boys but it really is over between your mum and me and I'm not going back. So just leave the letter where it is and let things proceed the way they were meant to.'

'Not a chance!' snapped Luke. 'Maybe we can't make you stay if you don't want to, but I'm not going to let you split up with a woman you've been with for forty years by letter!'

Dad didn't say a word. He sat down on the sofa and hung his head in his hands.

'Luke's right, Dad,' said Russell. 'You can't just walk out on Mum like that.'

Still no word.

'They're both right,' said Adam. 'This is no way for things to end. So you're doing what you think you've got to do, but we're doing exactly the same.'

'Do you think I'm stupid?'

As Luke's car pulled into Mum and Dad's road Adam was thinking how odd it had been to hear his father talk about his emotions like that. Adam had never seen such an explicit emotional outburst from his father in his life. Not when his grandad Tom died, not when Uncle Al died, not even when at the age of fifteen Adam had had to break the news that Luke had been knocked down by a car outside school. These were all times when the whole family had been in tears and yet their dad had never shared a single shred of what was going on inside his head. Instead he took action; he made arrangements and got things organised and remained calm and focused throughout. Even though they were polar opposites Adam had always admired his father's lack of emotion because that meant there was at least one member of the family he didn't have to worry about. Maybe it was an eldest child thing; the fear that goes hand in hand with knowing that his brothers were always looking to him for leadership. Yet while as a child (and later as a teenager) Adam worried about every member of his family (his mum especially) whenever they left the home without him, he never, ever worried about his dad because he knew Dad could look after himself.

'Maybe we should have called Mum on her mobile and told her that we'd pick her up,' said Russell as the car came to a halt outside his parents' house. 'You know, just to be on the safe side.'

'Have you tried talking to Mum on her mobile?' scoffed Adam. 'First of all it's a miracle if she answers it at all and secondly she can never hear anything you say so you end up bellowing into your phone like some kind of nutter. Anyway, you know what trains are like. She's probably running late.'

'Oh yeah?' said Luke, who was still very much in glowering mode. 'Then how come I can see her in the front bedroom opening the curtains?'

Adam leaned across his brother and peered out of the passenger window up at the house. He was right. Their mum was indeed opening the upstairs curtains.

'Don't panic,' he said. 'You know what Mum's like when she gets back from being away it's always shoes off, kettle on and make a brew so chances are she's breezed past the letter on her way upstairs to give the house one of her famous "good airings" even if she's only been away overnight. Let's just keep calm, grab the letter and make this as quick and as painless as possible. Because do you know what? I'm shattered and after I've finished patching up our parents' marriage the first thing I'm going to do is head home, climb into bed and try to forget this day has ever happened.' He paused and took a deep breath. 'Right then, let's go.'

The boys climbed out of the car, made their way up the front path and paused while Adam used his set of keys to open the door. They could see their mum's overnight bag sitting in the middle of the carpet but there was no sign of the letter. They began frantically searching around the hallway in the hope that it had accidentally fallen off the stool but to no avail. Adam was just about to suggest that they split up and check over the house when he became aware that they were no longer alone: his mum was standing at the top of the stairs watching them.

'Mum,' said Adam guiltily. 'You're home.'

'Of course I'm home,' she replied tersely. 'There's my bag and shoes right in front of you.'

'Yes, yes, of course,' said Adam. His mum came downstairs and he gave her a kiss with Luke and Russell following suit.

'So what are you all doing here?'

'Nothing,' replied Adam casually. 'We were just passing on our way to a thing in town so we thought we'd drop in and say hello.'

Russell stepped forward. 'Did you have a good trip?'

'It was fine.'

'And the taxi ride over here was OK?'

'It was all fine.'

'I know,' suggested Adam, determined to move her out of the current hallway search zone. 'Why don't you put your feet up and we'll put your stuff away for you?' He tried to usher his mum into the living room but she refused to budge.

'Do you think I'm stupid?'

Adam was confused. Although his mum had always been a big fan of rhetorical questions he couldn't work out what had provoked this one. 'I never said anything of the sort, Mum,' he said cagily. 'I was just suggesting that you have a rest. Since when was that a crime?'

'Adam,' she said fixing him with her most stern look, 'do I look like an idiot to you?' She didn't wait for his response. 'Then don't treat me like one.' Then she made her way into the kitchen.

Adam exchanged perplexed glances with his brothers and followed. She was in the process of filling the kettle but as the boys entered the room she carefully turned off the tap, set down the kettle on the kitchen counter and faced them.

'This is about your father, isn't it?'

'What do you mean?' bluffed Adam.

A look of utter exasperation flooded her face. 'Adam,' she said carefully. 'What did I tell you less than a minute ago about treating me like an idiot?'

Adam decided the game was up. 'You mean you've already seen the letter?'

'What letter?'

'The letter from Dad?'

'What letter from Dad?'

Adam's brain was about to explode. 'Are you saying that you haven't seen the letter Dad wrote to you?'

'I've just told you that,' snapped his mum impatiently. 'Have you got something wrong with your ears?'

'I don't understand,' said Adam. 'If you haven't seen the letter then what do you think we're here about?'

'Your father of course.'

Adam rubbed his throbbing temples. 'So you already know Dad is at mine?'

'Is that where he went? Doesn't surprise me.'

'Mum, look, I don't know what you know or what you think you know and I hate being the one to tell you but it's like this . . .' He felt sick. This was no way for a woman of his mum's age to hear news like this.

'I came in last night from a night out to find Dad sleeping on the sofa at mine. Apparently he wrote you a letter telling you that he was leaving you and we're here because we were hoping that we could get rid of the letter before you could read it.' Adam put his arms round his mum and hugged her tightly. 'I'm sorry, Mum.'

She pushed Adam away. 'So where is this letter?'

'I don't know. Haven't you got it?'

'No, and do you know why that is? Then let me enlighten you: you can't find the letter because there was no letter and there was no letter because your father didn't leave me . . . I threw him out. Now if you don't mind, boys, I'd like some time on my own.' Her expression indicated that she would brook no further questioning. 'Don't just stand there!' she snapped like she used to when they were all kids, 'Move! And whatever you do,' she added as her fury reaching maximum velocity, 'don't slam the front door on your way out!'

'I eat out a lot.'

'None of this is making any sense,' said Adam, staring into his pint. 'Dad's claiming he's left Mum; Mum's counter-claiming that she kicked him out; and I've got a horrible feeling that they're both lying through their back teeth.'

It was mid-afternoon and Adam and his brothers were sitting in BlueBar trying make sense of the weirdest couple of hours in the Bachelor family's history.

It was incredible that their mother had thought she could get away with dropping a bombshell like 'it was me who kicked your father out' and expect them to accept the situation without any further clarification, but there had been no getting through to her. Adam and his brothers had bombarded her with questions but she had simply refused to engage and had made herself a cup of tea which she took into the living room. Switching on the TV as if she hadn't a care in the world she had flicked through the cable stations to TCM and made it clear through her body language that she had every intention of following the plot of *Rio Bravo*. For ten whole minutes she kept up this charade until finally she said in a voice that made it clear she was only going to say it once: 'I want you to leave, boys. Right now. This is between me and your father and nobody else.' Realising they were smacking their heads against a brick wall, they headed to BlueBar for a drink and the opportunity to regroup.

'I agree,' said Luke in reponse to Adam's statement. 'Dad's story about the letter didn't stack up because there was no letter. But I can't understand why he would make up something like that.'

'Maybe it's true that Mum kicked him out and he was trying to save face,' suggested Russell. 'Maybe all that stuff about the marriage being over and wanting to be free to do his own thing was actually what Mum said to him when she asked him to pack his bags.'

'There's no way Mum kicked Dad out because she wanted a last chance to sow her wild oats or whatever,' said Luke firmly. 'First off, Mum's just not like that and second off, you know as well as I do that Mum's mantra has always been that the Bachelors don't air their dirty laundry in public. If Mum really has kicked him out the neighbours will be all over it within the week! Now for her to put herself up for that kind of public scrutiny, there has to be a more solid reason than "I fancy a bit more time to do my crocheting" or whatever.'

Adam agreed, especially given how much she disapproved of people 'living over the brush'. All any of Adam's reprobate friends had to do to go up in her estimation was to get hitched; it didn't seem likely that she would give up on forty years of marriage without a fight.

'So what do you think happened?' he asked.

'I don't know, do I?' sighed Luke. 'But my guess is that the answer to this mess lies with Dad, not Mum. Mum looks to me like someone reacting to circumstances outside her control.'

Adam looked over at Russell. 'And what do you think?'

'I think I need another drink.'

As Adam stood at the bar and ordered two pints of Peroni and a Coke for Luke he spotted Rob and Ashley, a couple of old regulars, and chatted to them for a while, glad of the distraction.

Drinks in hand, Adam turned to head back towards his brothers but then froze as he glimpsed out of the corner of his eye, sitting amongst a group of thirtysomethings at a table covered in tapas, was Steph. Adam nearly said something but then he saw that it wasn't Steph at all, just a someone who looked like her. The Steph-a-like was wearing a black top and jeans and even though there were half a dozen better looking girls in her vicinity Adam couldn't take his eyes off her. The Steph-a-like was talking animatedly to a tall, clean-cut guy who was obviously her boyfriend. Adam found himself wondering what his Steph, the real Steph, was doing right now and for a moment or two he actually missed her. Then he brutally pushed all thoughts of Steph from his mind and headed back to his brothers.

Back home an hour later, Adam faced a dilemma. Although he had agreed to undertake further questioning of his dad he was well aware that if his mum was the queen of stubbornness then his dad was undoubtedly the king; it was highly unlikely that he would get any information until his father was ready to give it up of his own accord. At the same time, if Adam even popped his head in to say a simple hello, his dad would undoubtedly ask him a million and one questions about his mum and brothers and who said what to whom and why, and Adam wasn't up to playing messenger boy. No, he would leave his dad to his own devices for a while longer. He was heading quietly up to his bedroom when the door to the front room opened and his dad stepped out.

'Dad,' said Adam guiltily. 'I was just . . .' His voice trailed off. He still found it impossible to lie to his dad. He came back down the stairs. 'Have you eaten?'

'I'm not really all that hungry. I had some more toast earlier, then I had a rummage in your cupboards and helped myself to a can of tomato soup. You're not a big fan of food shopping are you? There was barely anything in the cupboards.'

'I eat out a lot,' explained Adam.

Dad nodded but his face made it clear that this was definitely an alien concept.

'I could murder another cup of tea though.'

'One cup of tea coming up,' said Adam with forced cheeriness.

Adam put on the kettle, grabbed a couple of slices of wholemeal bread and dropped them into the toaster, then leaned back against the kitchen counter and tried to work out exactly how he was feeling about everything that had happened. There was something about his dad's manner that smacked of guilt. And yet, self-created as these problems no doubt were, his dad seemed somehow diminished, older and more vulnerable than he'd ever seen him. Adam wanted to lecture his father about bucking his ideas up and sorting things out, but even more, he wanted to sit down with his old man and tell him not to worry, everything was going to be OK.

'King-sized or normal?'

'So what have you got to say for yourself?'

Russell looked blankly at Jeanette Nicholls, his middle-aged and needlessly aggressive boss, and briefly pondered a response. Of course she didn't really want an answer. All she wanted was to make him feel small. And even if she had wanted a response, she wouldn't have accepted that the reason he had messed up on the figures he was working on was because, in the last seven days alone, not only he had got off with his best friend and then not heard a word from her since, but he had also learned that the nigh-on forty-year marriage of his parents had come to a very dramatic and upsetting conclusion.

'You do realise,' continued Jeanette, 'that if I'd let these figures through without checking them it would have cost us the tender?'

Russell (well versed in being reprimanded by Jeanette) noted that the change of tone and inflection meant she had stopped being rhetorical and wanted some kind of acknowledgement that he wasn't – mentally speaking – jabbing his fingers in his ears and screaming 'La, la, la!' at the top of his voice and was indeed listening.

'Yes, Jeanette,' he said sombrely. 'I completely understand. It was totally and utterly my fault and you have my assurance that it won't happen again.'

'I should hope not!' snapped Jeanette. 'I haven't got the time or the resources to be constantly checking and double-checking your work. This isn't the student union, Russell, you're at work now and all your actions have consequences. I'll be making an official note of everything that I've said to you this morning for the record and passing it on to Human Resources. Is there anything that you'd like to add in your defence?'

Despite being more than a little irked by Jeanette's 'student union' comment (exactly how old did she think he was?) Russell kept quiet. This was his second reprimand (the first had been after a trip to Glastonbury festival the previous summer that had resulted in him going AWOL for a week) and he was determined to stick this job out after Angie had pointed out that in the time she had known him he had had at least fifteen different jobs (everything from a bank teller through to trainee park-keeper).

'Right then,' said Jeanette, holding eye contact just long enough for Russell to feel it necessary to look away, 'I'm sure you've got work to be getting on with, haven't you?'

Russell offered Jeanette a barely perceptible nod and left the room, closing the door firmly behind him. He grabbed his jacket and headed in the direction of the exit.

'Are you doing a shop run, Russ?' asked Debbie on reception. 'Because if you are I'm gagging for a Twix.'

Russell considered the question. It had been his intention to walk out the door, take an early lunch break and have a long hard think about his future but now that Debbie was asking him about shop runs and confectionery he realised there was no point in hiding his head in the sand every time things got tough. This messy stuff – parents splitting up, mates getting off with each other, being in love with people you shouldn't be and now cocking up the figures – was simply the stuff of life.

Russell looked at Debbie. 'King-sized or normal?'

'Normal.' She immediately corrected herself. 'No, king-sized . . . I'm quite hungry.' She thought again. 'I'll tell you what, Russ, why don't you just surprise me?'

Russell felt his mood change for the better. 'I might do that. Don't get your hopes up but I reckon a pack of salt and vinegar might be coming your way too.'

Twenty minutes later, having had enough time out of his airless workplace to feel almost like a regular human being again Russell returned to the office, dropped off an ordinary Twix plus a packet of crisps and a can of Fruit Twist Fanta with Debbie and decided that the best thing he could possibly do was keep his head down and hope for the best.

Waking up his computer to check his online diary against Jeanette's, Russell was about to book as many meetings with outside agencies as he possibly could to coincide with times he knew Jeanette would be in the office when his mobile phone vibrated gently. Russell was so cheered when he saw that it was a message from Angie, he almost let out an audible whoop of joy.

Even though it had been over a week Russell still found it hard to believe that he and Angie had actually snogged. And it had been a snog rather than a kiss. A huge, big, open-mouthed snog tantamount to a battle of sucking, licking, darting and probing. He hadn't been able to get enough of her. And she hadn't been able to get enough of him. All through the kiss his brain had been so aware of the momentous nature of the occasion that he had felt himself trying to seize snippets of the experience and permanently record them. He had wanted to remember for ever the taste of her mouth, the sensation of her chest pressing against his own, the softness of her skin against his fingertips. It had been an amazing moment: two friends standing in the middle of a packed nightclub dance floor, limbs and lips locked together while everyone around them danced along to 'Leave Before the Lights Come On'.

The moment the song came to a close and the DJ played an upbeat dance track that heralded a change of personnel on the dance floor everything was lost. Their hands separated, the self-consciousness returned and Angie's friends who had been on the other side of the club and had missed the whole event suddenly appeared from nowhere and swept her away. And while they all stood gossiping about some girl who had just turned up with a guy in tow who apparently wasn't her boyfriend, Russell had stood at the edge of the huddle wondering what exactly had just occurred and why. He didn't give it long with the thinking and the mulling (three, maybe four minutes tops) before coming to the conclusion that it had been a mistake of colossal proportions.

Whispering in Angie's ear that he was just going to the loo Russell did a hundred-and-eighty-degree turn, grabbed his work bag from the cloakroom and made his way home secure in the knowledge it would be at least a few hours before he would have to face the music. The moment never came. Angie didn't call or text and even though he carefully monitored her Facebook status update over the days that followed there wasn't even the faintest allusion to what had happened.

Russell eyed his phone suspiciously as though it was Angie incarnate. He checked the message. She was asking if he was 'still' up for their usual Friday night drink. Was this a loaded question? Was this her way of asking what was going on between them? Russell wasn't sure. What he really wanted was for someone to make the decision for him. For all he cared a complete stranger could flip a coin, draw straws or even play a few rounds of Rock, Paper, Scissors. As long as it wasn't down to him because this was simply too big to involve someone as flaky as him in the process.

That was why he had left the nightclub without telling Angie he was going.

That was why he hadn't called Angie the morning after the kiss.

That was why right at this moment he wanted to throw his phone away and move to Brazil.

He took a deep breath and then typed his reply: 'Can't make it tonight, mate. Have got something on. But let's do it next week for sure.' Double-checking the message for spelling mistakes and accuracy he pressed send and switched off his phone.

'It was you, only you.'

Russell looked up at his mum as she rose to her feet during the ad break. 'I'm going to make myself another cup of tea,' she said. 'And you need to go home now, son. That's an order!'

It was just after eight and Russell had been in the front room at his parents' house since just after six that evening having invited himself round late in the afternoon. Armed with a bottle of wine he had arrived straight from his nightmare day at work and had been thoroughly heartened by the fact that his mum had pulled out all the stops just for him: chicken and ham pie, broccoli and new potatoes followed by apple crumble and ice cream. The simple but satisfying meal had allowed Russell to forget his troubles and just be. He didn't say a word about his dad and his mum allowed him to get away with the response 'It was OK,' to the question 'How was work today?' Thus he had a small respite from the idea that he was letting Angie down badly.

Now though, having sat through a constant stream of consumer shows, soap operas and nature programmes his mum was finally turfing him out and he would have to face the music alone, which was why he was planning on heading straight home, cracking open the bottle of wine that he had brought for his mum (which she had declined for reasons of indifference) and getting as drunk and maudlin as humanly possible.

'Are you sure?' he asked as his mum hovered in the doorway absent-mindedly watching an advert for a local sofa warehouse. 'Because I can stay longer if you want me to.'

'Absolutely,' she replied. 'All I really want to do is have a bath, get into bed and settle down with the Catherine Cookson I started last night.'

Russell left the room to get his shoes, jacket and work bag and returned moments later to kiss his mum goodbye.

'So you'll call me if you need anything?'

'Of course I will.'

'Promise?'

'Cross my heart.' She looked as though she was about to kiss him on the cheek but obviously had something on her mind. 'Russell,' she began. 'About this Sunday lunch. Do you and your brothers mind if we give it a miss? I was thinking that I might just go to the mid-morning service at church and not bother with the usual rigmarole.'

Russell wondered if she was going to unburden herself of the mystery of why Dad was no longer at home but when the gap that he left in the conversation was filled with silence he eventually assured her that it would be fine with them all.

Outside it was still light although the weather had turned for the worse and the temperature was more like that of late November. Russell turned on his phone. There were a couple of text messages from his housemates but nothing at all from Angie. He took her lack of communication as a bad sign because Angie never needed much of an excuse to communicate with anyone about anything. She must be on the warpath. What form her displeasure would take was anyone's guess; in the past Russell had witnessed everything from Angie punching in the face a guy who made one suggestive comment too many right through to her refusing to speak to an ex-housemate for six months because she'd borrowed Angie's favourite top without asking. Shuddering at the thought of whatever punishment awaited him he zipped up his jacket, plugged the headphones of his iPod into his ears and started for home.

The song 'We Will Become Silhouettes' was coming to a close and Russell was feeling more than a little bit depressed as he turned into his road. He felt bad. Really bad. He should never have sent Angie that text. What had he been thinking? How could lying to her about being busy make things any better between them? As he crossed the road he was considering calling her and confessing all but then he saw a familiar figure sitting on the wall and knew that he was officially too late to beg for mercy.

'How long have you been here?' he asked, taking

off his headphones and bundling them into his bag as Angie did exactly the same.

'About an hour.'

'Didn't you get my text?'

'Of course I got it,' she said tersely. She kicked a stone at her feet. 'Look, let's just get a drink, OK?'

'Yeah, of course, anywhere in particular in mind?'

'I don't care,' she shrugged. 'I just don't want to do this here.'

Russell noted Angie's unequivocal use of the words 'do this' as though there was no doubt in her mind that 'this' would indeed get 'done'.

He suggested a bar on Manchester Road that his housemates had been raving about earlier in the week. Angie didn't say anything and so Russell considered offering her an alternative venue as though it was his choice of bar and not the situation between them that was the problem but then he thought better of it. Instead he just started walking up the road in the hope that Angie would do the same.

Aware of the awkwardness that lay ahead Russell launched into a monologue about the Mongolian beers that were served in the bar, pretty much regurgitating word for word what his housemates had told him. When he had exhausted that topic he went on to tell her all about his week at work, concluding with his run-in with Jeanette. Angie still refused to bite. Finally, he threw himself into a marathon of monologues encompassing everything from a newspaper article about a new weight-loss wonder drug through to gossip about a mutual friend until they were finally at their destination.

'So here we are,' announced Russell, shoe-horning a note of jollity into his voice in the hope that it might coax Angie out of her mood. 'Looks pretty busy but I reckon we should be able to get a seat.'

He moved aside to let Angie walk in first but she didn't move.

'I can't do this, Russell,' she said, looking down at her feet. 'I thought I could but I can't so I'm going home.'

As she headed back down the road Russell felt as though he had lost all control of his limbs. His best friend in the whole world was walking away from him. He had to do something. He had to say something. Because if he didn't there was a strong chance he would never see Angie again.

He yelled her name at the top of his lungs and as she turned round he finally unfroze and ran until he was standing right in front of her.

'Ange.'

She didn't say a word.

'I'm sorry.'

She still didn't speak.

'Look, I don't understand what you want from me,' he pleaded, feeling himself flood with indignation given that she had been as willing a participant in the kiss as he had been. 'I really don't understand! What is it you want me to say? How scared I am that I've ruined everything between us? How all week I've been missing you like mad because my mum and dad have split up and you were the only person in the world I wanted to talk to? You don't get it, do you? You're everything to me. Everything. I feel like I ruined it all for a stupid kiss.'

'You're wrong,' said Angie. 'You're about as wrong as you could ever be. It wasn't a stupid kiss, Russ. It was the best kiss of my life because if this is the moment that we're finally going to say all the things that need to be said then you ought to know that I love you, Russ. I really bloody love you. I always have done and I always will.'

'That's what difficult is, Dad.'

At the very moment that Russell was being presented with Angie's surprising and overwhelming declaration of love, Luke was slouched on the sofa at home half watching a Sky news bulletin on TV while he waited for Cassie to get home from her spin class so that they could order an Indian takeaway and settle down in front of the TV for the night in the hope of unwinding from the disastrous week they had both had.

Luke hadn't spoken to either of his parents since the visit to his mum's house had revealed that contrary to his dad's banging on about 'needing his freedom' like he was south Manchester's answer to Nelson Mandela it had actually been Mum who had kicked him out. Part of the reason was that his workload had reached a critical mass and he'd had to sleep in Travelodges as far apart as Exeter and Peterborough for three nights in a row in preparation for a variety of site meetings. But mostly it was because he wanted to stick his head in the sand and pretend that the whole thing wasn't happening.

Luke picked up the remote control and flicked over to a comedy panel show on Channel Four. He was about to reach for the menu for the Raja Indian takeaway when the phone rang. Luke's first instinct was to let it go to voicemail but after two or three rings his resolution crumbled and he picked up the cordless receiver and jammed it up to his ear.

'Hello?'

'Luke, it's me,' said his Dad. 'Have you got a minute?'

Luke felt his whole frame sink. He could hear the sound of Cassie opening the front door. 'Yeah, I've got a minute,' he sighed. 'What's up?'

Dad said, 'How are you?'

'I'm fine.'

There was pause. 'Look, I understand this is difficult for all of you boys but I—'

Luke cut him off. 'No, Dad,' he snapped, 'you don't understand. You don't know anything at all about me, or about Russ or Adam because if you did, you and Mum wouldn't be doing this.'

'Look, son, it's—'

'It's what? Difficult? No, Dad, I'll tell you what's difficult. Difficult is watching something that you thought was completely solid fall apart. That's what difficult is. I still don't understand what's going on here. You're saying one thing and Mum is saying another. And I'm getting to the stage where I'm not even sure I care any more. So unless you've called to tell me you're heading back home to sort out this mess I don't want to hear anything you've got to say.'

'Luke, it's complicated, OK. This thing with your mother and me, well it's going to take time and—'

Luke had had enough. 'Do you know what? I can't do this right now. I'm sorry but you've caught me at a really bad time. I have to go. Let's talk some other time, OK?'

Luke put the phone down just as Cassie entered the room, kissed him and sat down next to him.

'Who was that?'

'Dad.'

'Is he OK?'

Luke shrugged. 'I don't know. I wasn't particularly nice to him.'

Cassie took his hand. 'I'm sure this will all get sorted soon, Luke,' she said, squeezing his hand tightly. 'They've been together too long for it to be all over.'

'Do you think?'

'I know.'

Luke picked up the menu from the coffee table and handed it to her. 'Hungry?'

'Starving.'

'Good. Death by chicken bhuna it is then.'

Later that night, having watched TV, demolished their takeaway and worked their way through a half-dozen bottles of Budweiser each, they made their way upstairs and fell into each other's arms underneath the duvet.

'That has got to be the single best night that I've had this week.' Luke kissed the top of Cassie head. 'We should both book a week off work and do this every single night until our arteries harden and our blood turns the colour of curry.'

'You'd love that, wouldn't you? You don't care that in the space of a couple of hours you've helped me to ruin all the good results of a ninety-minute spin class, do you?' She rested her head against Luke's chest and then fell silent. Luke thought she might have fallen asleep but when he looked down at her face her eyes were open and she clearly had something on her mind.

'What is it?'

Cassie sat up and pulled the duvet up around her. 'I know you must have a lot on your mind with everything that's going on with your parents,' she said, avoiding all eye contact. 'And I know you must think I've got the worst timing in the world but I can't keep this in any more. I need to talk about us.' She corrected herself. '*We* need to talk about us.'

Luke studied her face. She was looking away from him, her eyes glued to the end of the bed. His heart went out to her. She had been an absolute rock over this thing with his mum and dad. And now she was looking for help to get the conversation started which he had promised her they would have about their future. About children. No woman wants the man she loves to have to be forced at gunpoint into agreeing to become the father of her children. It should be a freewill offering. Obviously there were women in the world who didn't mind making direct demands; who had the self-belief required to make life-changing decisions not just for themselves but for others who lacked their clarity of vision. But Cassie wasn't one of them. Luke could see how much she wanted this to be a joint decision. The slightest hint of doubt on his part; the slightest sense that this wasn't a decision made by two equals and everything would be permanently tainted. And even though he was tempted to slip into avoidance-through-conflict mode, he had a duty to make this as painless as possible for Cassie.

'You're right,' he said, reaching out to touch her hand. 'We do need to talk, because I promised you that I would think about it and I'm sorry I didn't bring the subject up before now but the truth of the matter is I just haven't had the time.'

'Oh,' said Cassie in a small voice.

'You know work has been mad and then there's this thing with my parents . . . But how about this? How about we set a date right and even if we hear that the world is going to end the following day we will definitely talk about it.'

'When?'

'How about this time next week?'

Cassie pulled herself tightly into his chest. 'If that's OK with you?'

'It'll be fine,' said Luke, reaching over to his bedside table to turn off the light, plunging them into the darkness of the night. 'It'll all be absolutely fine, I promise.'

'Are we really happy for them?'

A week later, Luke and Cassie were sitting in their back room about to have The Talk. Earlier they had been out for a meal in town at a restaurant that all their friends had been talking about for weeks that they had both tried (and failed) to enjoy. The problem hadn't been the food or the company but rather the timing. The deadline was over. A decision was going to have to be made. And with only one of them knowing for sure which way the conversation would go it was hard not to feel like a prisoner on death row partaking of a final meal.

'So here we are,' began Cassie nervously. 'I can't believe we're really going to talk about this.'

'I know,' sighed Luke. 'My stomach is all tied up in knots.'

'Mine too,' said Cassie. 'I almost sent you a text today suggesting that we call the whole thing off. I hate having this hanging over our heads. It's ridiculous. We're getting married next year. We should be celebrating us and everything we've achieved and instead I feel like I've ruined everything.'

'You haven't ruined anything, babe,' reassured Luke. 'It would've been much worse if you hadn't said anything. This is just one of those things that pops up every now and again even in the best of relationships and the fact that we're talking about it shows that we're going about things the right way.'

'OK then, I'm ready. I'm absolutely ready.'

Since their conversation Luke had thought and thought about whether he was willing to start a family with Cassie. All week he had applied his best analytical skills to building cases both for and against until finally, on the night before his self-imposed deadline, he left his hotel in Exeter, found a quiet wood-panelled pub in the city centre and determined not to leave until he had come to a conclusion.

He had bought himself a pint of bitter, found a nearby table, sat himself down, taken a few sips from the glass then reached inside his jacket pocket for his single most treasured possession: a photograph of his daughter, Megan, taken shortly after her fourth birthday.

The photo showed Megan (all curly black hair, teeth and smiles) standing in the garden of the house that he and Jayne had first bought when they moved to Manchester. It had been summer and Megan had been wearing a green and white stripy T-shirt and the red plastic sunglasses that Russell had given to her. She had fallen in love with those sunglasses and had insisted on wearing them everywhere regardless of whether they were indoors or out or whether it was daytime or night. Her face captured the essence of everything that makes children so life-affirming; a single moment of happiness. Her smile was so huge and her eyes so full of life that it was as though she was beaming happiness from her every pore. Whenever Luke looked at this photo he had no choice but to smile too and he knew that others felt the same; he had seen it happen too many times for it not to be an objective fact. Even his solicitor, a man not given to needless sentimentality, had cracked a grin when Luke first showed him the photo.

It went everywhere with him. Yet every time he took it out he knew he was lying to himself and to Megan too. In the four years since the photograph had been taken she was bound to have changed. She would no longer be his chubby-cheeked angel. She would be older and wiser, perhaps already seeking her own little forms of independence. The girl in the photograph who was his hope and his mainstay no longer existed apart from in photographs and home video footage and yet here he was pretending that one day she might come home. Could he really bring another child into the world when he had done so badly by the first? Was it possible for him to start a second family with Cassie without feeling as though he had abandoned his first? These questions had clarified his position.

'I can't do it,' he said quietly. 'Cass. I can't.'

There was a long silence. Cassie let go of his hand. He tried to read her face but it was inscrutable.

'I know you must be disappointed,' he began. 'I know you must think it's unfair but—'

'My sister's pregnant again,' said Cassie, talking over

him. 'She called me at work yesterday morning to tell me. It's going to be a June baby apparently.'

Luke's instinct for self-preservation told him to say nothing but his conscience wouldn't allow the silence to continue.

'We should send her and Mark a bottle of champagne or something to celebrate,' he said quietly, aware that his innocent comment was about to be torn to shreds.

'Should we?' said Cassie. 'Are we really happy for them?' Tears started to roll down her cheeks. 'I'm not sure I am because when she told me the news I cried. And they weren't tears of joy, Luke, they were tears of jealousy. I was so jealous of her. My own sister. I was so completely and utterly jealous that all I felt was rage.'

Imagining what would drive Cassie to feel jealous of a sister she loved more than life itself brought home to Luke just how much she wanted children. This wasn't a whim, or a yielding to peer pressure, but a real want, a desire that had become central to her being.

'Look,' began Luke. 'I know you must feel like I don't love you enough. Or that I don't trust you enough. Or even that I don't care how you feel. But that's not true. I love you with my whole heart and I'd trust you with my life, Cass, I would. And I do appreciate what having a kid must mean to you. You love your family more than anything. You love my family like they're your own. Family means everything to you just as it does to me. And it's because family means so much to me that I'm sitting here telling you all this. If I started a family with you it would feel like I was giving up on Megan, the family that I've left behind, and I just can't do that to her.'

'But it doesn't have to be that way!' Cassie stood up, trying to wipe the tears from her face. 'I'm not asking you to give up on Megan. I'm asking you to start a family with me.'

'I know, I know. But if I start a family with you, to me it would be exactly like giving up on Megan! She'll be nearly eight now, you know. Can you imagine how it must feel to be eight and not have a dad around? She must feel that I don't love her. She must feel like I didn't care about her at all! And how could I ever prove her wrong if I start all over again with someone new? How could I ever look her in the eye and tell her that she meant the world to me when I've been playing happy families somewhere else? I won't do that to her, Cass. I can't.'

'Where's the logic in that?'

In the dim light of his bedroom Adam could just make out the outline of a man leaning over him. The man was saying something but through the drunken fog of confusion clouding his brain, Adam couldn't quite work out what. He glanced over at the clock on his bedside table: it was seven thirty a.m. The man slowly came into focus as though Adam was looking through the lens of a camera. It was his dad. He was holding a tray of food: a plate of sausages, bacon, fried eggs, and tinned tomatoes with a mug of tea next to it. The volume suddenly kicked in. Dad was saying: 'I thought you might fancy a spot of breakfast. I'll leave it down here, shall I?' Adam looked at his dad, at the food and at the clock again. He attempted a quick calculation, subtracting the time that he had gone to bed having stayed up late watching DVDs (three thirty-five a.m.) away from the current time (seven thirty-one a.m.) and after several stalled attempts worked out that he had been asleep for approximately three hours and fifty-six minutes in total. He looked at his dad again. His face was like that of a child: open and eager to please. Adam uttered a gruff 'Cheers!' in his dad's direction which appeared to do the job: Dad grinned from ear to ear, put the tray down on the floor, then left the room closing the door behind him and returning Adam to a world of darkness and mild nausea.

Having his dad as a house guest for this past month had been pretty much the stuff of nightmares. Within days Dad had abandoned any illusion of formality and transformed himself from father figure to housemate. With a swiftness that took Adam by surprise Dad's twenty-year-old (formerly royal blue now pale grey) bath towel became a permanent fixture in the bathroom; meals of the 'meat and two veg' variety kept making an appearance in Adam's fridge with handwritten notes attached to them ('microwave for two minutes and thirty seconds'); and, most alarmingly, Dad (who had at one point seemed genuinely scared of Adam's vast array of remote controls) had taken up permanent residence in front of his widescreen TV. Of course Adam loved his dad. Of course he didn't want anything bad to happen to him and of course he wanted him to feel at home, but he didn't seem to be making any plans to patch things up with his mum or move into a place of his own. In fact he appeared to be bedding in for the long haul and now Adam wanted his old life back and he wanted it back now.

When he finally rose some time after midday he felt bad about not eating the breakfast that he had stepped over on his way out of the room and guilty that his dad had had to spend another day alone and so still only wearing his boxers he wandered into the living room for a chat.

'Hey Dad, how's your day been?'

'I've been thinking about our arrangement here,' said Dad, ignoring Adam's question. 'I must insist on paying my way.'

'Er . . .' Adam was confused.

'I wouldn't want people saying I'm freeloading.'

'I'm not saying you're freeloading, Dad.'

'I know you're not,' snapped Dad. 'What I'm saying is this: it doesn't look good. I'm your dad. If anyone should be looking after anyone it should be me looking after you. Never let it be said that George Bachelor doesn't pay his way.'

If Dad was referring to himself in the third person, there would be little point in standing in his way.

'Of course you pay your way, Dad. That's not an issue. Now tell me what it was exactly that you had in mind?'

'Well I was thinking just before you came in that you and I ought to go shopping.'

'Shopping?'

'Yes, shopping for food. You do eat, don't you?'

'Not really.'

'When do you normally do your weekly shop?'

'I don't really do a weekly shop, Dad. I sort of buy stuff when I need it.'

Dad shook his head in disbelief as if Adam had revealed that he liked to spend his spare time setting fire to ten-pound notes.

'That's no way to do shopping, son. No way at all. Next you'll be telling me that you buy your milk from the newsagent's round the corner.'

'I do,' said Adam. 'It's easier that way.'

'Easier? Easier? I bet you any money that it's at least ten to fifteen pence more expensive in there than in the supermarket! You young people, none of you have got the common sense you were born with.' With great difficulty (given the low nature of the sofa) Dad stood up and gave Adam a look indicating that he was ready for action. 'Come on then, get your coat.'

'Why am I going to need my coat?'

'Because I'm taking you shopping.'

While Adam had shopped in the big Somerfield on Wilbraham Road plenty of times before, one thing he had never done (mainly because he was usually still in bed fast asleep) was go shopping in the big Somerfield on Wilbraham Road at one o'clock on a Saturday afternoon. For some reason it appeared that this was the exact time when everybody from good-for-nothing students to overburdened young mums decided that they needed a couple of things to tide them over for the weekend and descended on the store en masse. Adam had never seen the store so packed. It was like being at a rock concert without any of the benefits of actually being at a rock concert. Adam suggested several times that they turn back and try shopping some other time but his dad had looked so disappointed that he felt he had no choice but to carry on.

Fifteen minutes, a frantic search for a pound coin and several dodgy trolleys later they were in the pasta and tinned vegetable aisle discussing tinned carrots.

'Will you eat them?' Dad asked.

Adam looked at the tin of Somerfield's own-brand tinned carrots unable to hide his look of disgust. 'No, Dad, I will not eat them.'

'Why not?'

'Because I don't eat tinned carrots.'

'But you said that about the tinned mushrooms and the tinned new potatoes.'

'That's because I don't eat tinned mushrooms or tinned potatoes either.'

Dad peered into Adam's side of the trolley. 'And yet you'll eat tinned kidney beans? Where's the logic in that?'

Adam joined his father in peering at the tinned kidney beans in the trolley. Did he have a point? Was there really no difference between tinned kidney beans and tinned carrots? Adam was pretty sure that there was but he wasn't sure what. Other than the fact that in this day and age people like him didn't – with the exception of tinned pulses – eat any kind of tinned vegetables. Tinned vegetables were the territory of a different generation altogether,

'And what about tinned tomatoes?' added Dad as if reading his son's mind. 'They're in your trolley.'

'Everybody eats tinned tomatoes,' protested Adam. 'And anyway, tomatoes are a fruit not a vegetable.'

Dad shrugged and dropped the tin of carrots into the trolley while Adam wondered what he had done to deserve this: not only sharing his home with his dad but arguing with him about tinned vegetables. One way or another, he thought, as he trailed after his dad like a schoolboy, he was going to have to get his parents back together and he was going to have to make it happen now. He typed out a message to both Luke and Russell: 'Emergency pow-wow re: Mum and Dad. Tonight in the Beech, 7.30 p.m. NO EXCUSES!!!'

'I've just got stuff on my mind that's all.'

It was twenty minutes past seven as Adam walked into the front bar of the Beech and spotted Luke. He waved in Luke's direction to see if he was all right for a drink but he seemed to be lost in a world of his own so he ordered himself a solitary pint and made his way over to Luke's table.

'All right?' asked Adam, taking a seat opposite his brother.

'Yeah, fine,' replied Luke, who patently wasn't. 'You?'

Adam laughed. 'As good as I can be with a sixty-eight-year-old man as a housemate. Do you know what he said before I went out tonight? He asked me to spare a couple of hours next week to offer some input on a cooking rota and two-week meal planner that he had drawn up. I tell you Luke, I feel like he's made up his mind that he might as well put his roots down with me!' Adam expected a laugh or at the very least a grin but there was nothing. It was as if Luke hadn't heard a single thing that Adam had said.

In a bid to reserve all parent-related conversation until Russell decided to turn up, Adam tried to make conversation but Luke was so unresponsive that in the end Adam concluded he'd better ask the one question he was pretty sure Luke didn't want him to ask.

'How's Cassie?'

'She's fine.'

Now that he had got his brother speaking in whole (if brief) sentences Adam kept up the momentum. 'How's she getting on at work? I remember she had a big presentation coming up. How did it go?'

'OK, I think,' said Luke. 'To be truthful I don't really remember.'

Adam opened his mouth, about to ask further follow-up questions concerning Cassie's sister and family, but he was tired of being the only person at the table making an effort. Luke and Cassie, he concluded, must have had some sort of tiff, that much was obvious. He wished he had the guts to tell his brother to grow up. Luke had it all: a great job, a nice home and above all a proper, fully functioning relationship with an amazing girl. What could he possibly have to be down about?

'Look,' said Adam, aware that they were entering uncharted conversational waters, 'by all means tell me to mind my own business if I'm overstepping the mark here but is everything OK with you and Cassie? It's just that—'

'She's moved out,' said Luke. His eyes briefly flitted up to Adam's for a response and then back down to the table. 'It's only temporary. A few weeks. It'll all be sorted soon. We both need a little time, a little space to sort ourselves out. It's just . . . I don't know, we're in a tricky position. She wants to have kids.'

'And you don't?'

Luke nodded.

'Because of what happened with you and Jayne or is there something else?'

'It's Megan,' confessed Luke. 'I know it's going to sound mad but it just feels wrong to even consider starting another family let alone going ahead and doing it.'

Adam nodded. He had never imagined that Luke's problem might be this serious. 'It doesn't sound mad at all, mate,' he said, recalling how messed up his brother had been after he had stopped seeing Megan. It had been awful. The worst thing he had ever seen happen to his brother. Even though the whole family had pulled together to support him there had been moments when Adam had felt as though Luke might never recover. 'Megan is your kid. She's your family. I can understand why the idea of moving on like that would make you feel like you were giving up on her.'

'You know, Ad,' he began, 'there are times when it's all I can do to get through the day, I miss her so much. But I just hold on to the thought that one day she'll be old enough to come and find me. And she will, I know she will. And I'll be able to tell her my side of the story and we can reset the clock and start from scratch and we'll never have to worry about the past again.'

There was a long silence. Adam wasn't quite sure what a moment like this called for. 'We all miss her you know,' said Adam, choosing not to refer to Megan by name. 'I've got a picture of her on my bedside table. You know the one, it was taken that summer when she must have been about two and she's sitting on the picnic bench at Mum and Dad's and she's got that huge Bachelor cheeky grin stuck right on her face. She looks gorgeous.'

'I know the one,' Luke said quietly. 'And you're right about the cheeky grin too. It's trademark Bachelor through and through.'

Luke was clearly glad to have got all his thoughts about Cassie and Megan out of his system because they now fell into the kind of light and easy conversation that was their norm.

Russell texted to say he was running late so Adam got a pair of fresh pints and fixed his brother with a firm stare.

'Why are you looking at me like that?' asked Luke.

'Because I'm about to tell you something that's going to make you think a lot less of me,' said Adam, shaking his head in mock shame. 'It's a big brother thing, you see. I know you look up to me . . . some might even say idolise me, and what I'm about to say might leave you feeling let down.'

Luke clapped his hands in glee. 'Come on then, mate. Show me those feet of clay.'

'Well,' began Adam, 'before this whole thing with Mum and Dad kicked off I went out on a date.'

'In what way is that supposed to be news? It would be more likely to be a front-page splash if you went out and *didn't* go on a date.'

'Very funny,' chided Adam. 'But what I'm about to

tell you is quite a big thing for me, OK? So just shut up and listen: a little while ago some of the boys made a comment about me always going out with the wrong kind of girls and so basically I instituted a new policy on women.'

'This is brilliant,' spluttered Luke into his pint glass. 'The perfect antidote to all my woes! My brother has a new policy on women! What, pray tell, does this new policy state?'

'That I'm only allowed to go out with the right kind of girl.'

'Which means what exactly? You've stopped dating girls like that Scouser Paris Hilton lookalike who paraded around the launch party in little more than her underwear and a pair of kitten heels and are only dating librarians?'

'Sort of,' sighed Adam.

'So what happened? I take it you failed in your mission and are now back in the land of fake tans and long legs?'

Adam leaned in towards his brother in a conspiratorial fashion. 'What I'm about to tell you goes no further, agreed?'

Barely able to contain his mirth Luke nodded frantically.

'OK, so I went out on a couple of dates with a number of, you know, ordinary girls and they were lovely and all that but there was no spark.'

'No spark?' chuckled Luke. 'Oh, mate, this is pure comedy gold! My lady-killer brother on spark-free dates with a long line of librarians! What I would have given to have been a fly on the wall!'

'Look, you can mock me all you like, but this is my love life we're talking about which some of my followers would consider sacrosanct. So be more respectful before I slap you!'

'Fine,' said Luke. 'No more jokes.'

'So as I was saying I had these dates and there was no spark and I was on the edge of giving up when I met this girl . . . well actually you might even remember her as she was in my year at school, Stephanie Holmes?'

Luke shrugged. 'Name rings a bell.'

'Anyway, she was lovely in a cute kind of way but definitely not my usual type and so I decided to give her a chance and took her out for a coffee and well . . . she pretty much blew me away. She was smart, funny, intelligent and really good to talk to.'

'And what happened?'

Adam shrugged. 'I called her up for a date and she turned me down because – get this – apparently I wasn't her type! Now that's weird, right? How could she not like me?'

'Are you joking?'

'What? Are you going to give me some line about women all being different and how they're not all into good looks and charm?'

'Can you even hear yourself? You're like an ego on legs!'

'That would be the case if it wasn't true but I'm afraid

it is. I'm like a bloke version of Kate Moss and what bloke would turn down Kate Moss?'

'Me for starters,' laughed Luke. 'She's definitely not my type. Way too skinny.'

'You're telling me that if you weren't with Cassie, and you were single and you hadn't had a date with a girl in like . . . six months and then one day you open the front door and Kate Moss is standing there with that face, and those eyes of hers, and she says: "Luke, how about it?" you'd turn her down on the grounds that she's "not your type"?'

'Well put like that . . .'

'Exactly,' replied Adam. 'I am putting it like that because it's an undisputed fact that Kate Moss is every bloke's type. Now given that in the original scenario we were discussing I was a bloke version of Kate Moss why would any woman in her right mind turn me down?'

'But women *are* different,' sighed Luke. 'It's not always about looks with them. Some of them are a bit deeper. Some of them go for the stuff that you can't see and might actually be put off by the stuff that you can.'

'So what can I do about it?'

'Nothing. She's blown you out, mate. That ship has sailed.'

'You think I ought to forget about her?'

'Mate, all this is weirding me out so much it's untrue. But if you really want my advice – and why you'd want it I have no idea – I'd say forget all this right kind of women stuff and go back to doing what you do best.'

'What's that?'

'Being a bachelor. Believe me, bruv, nobody does it better than you.'

'It's about you and mum.'

'So where is it we're going again?'

It was the following day, just after eleven on a Sunday morning, and Adam was sitting in his car about to respond to his father's question.

'We're going to the Trafford Centre.'

'And why is it we're going?'

'Because I'm buying a cabinet from Habitat and I'll need some help getting it back to the car.'

Dad shook his head in disbelief. 'Once upon a time if you were buying something like that you didn't have to struggle getting it in and out of the back of a car. You just had it delivered.'

'I know, Dad, but times change, don't they?'

Dad didn't say anything but Adam could tell that he was still ranting internally about 'modern ways'.

In truth Adam wasn't actually taking his dad to Habitat but rather using it as an excuse to get his father into the car and take him back home.

When Russell had finally turned up at the pub the night before, Adam made it as clear as he could manage without the aid of diagrams that he had had more than enough of his dad as a house guest and it was time that one of his brothers took over the reins. Visibly baulking at the idea the moment it was aired both Luke and Russell countered that the answer to their problem lay in getting their parents to talk to each other. 'It's like this,' Russell had said. 'Dad hasn't got any real mates to speak of, has he? And neither has Mum. All they've got is each other so why could they possibly want to live apart? Which is why we've got to get them in the same room to talk things out. I'm sure if we can do that we'll be able to make this whole thing go away.' And that's how the plan (hailed by Adam as 'bloody genius') was born. Adam would convince Dad that he was taking him on a shopping trip but would in fact take him back home. Meanwhile Russ and Luke would tell Mum that they would be dropping round for an afternoon visit. Once at the house Adam (with the help of Russ and Luke) would persuade Dad to go inside and talk to Mum, and when that was all sorted the boys would leave their parents to it and head over to BlueBar for a celebratory pint.

Adam was relieved that there was a fair bit of traffic on the High Street because he was afraid that the five-minute journey to his mum and dad's house would be over all too soon. He hadn't given any consideration to what he was going to say to his dad, which made Adam panic slightly and the more he panicked the more he saw flaws in the genius plan. What if they made matters worse? What if their mum lost the plot and started talking about divorce? What if their actions forced

Dad to reveal why Mum had kicked him out thereby resulting in Adam never being able to look at his father in the same way again? For a few jaw-clenching moments Adam seriously considered turning the car round, taking his dad to Habitat and actually buying a cabinet. The thought of spending good money on furniture he didn't want seemed a lot more appealing than being the catalyst for this potential disaster.

In the end the only thing that kept him heading towards his parents' house was the prospect of his dad living in his spare room indefinitely and them ending up like some kind of modern Steptoe and Son. The thought of being permanently cast in the role of Harold Steptoe, and his dad in the role of the curmudgeonly Albert, made Adam shudder. No, much as he loved his father, the two of them had undertaken enough rebonding in the past month and a bit to last a lifetime.

'Listen Dad,' said Adam as they came to a halt at a set of traffic lights. 'It's like this: we're not going to Habitat and I'm not after a cabinet.'

'What do you mean? Have you changed your mind?'

'No Dad, I never was going to buy a cabinet.'

'Why would you tell me you needed me to help you buy a cabinet if you didn't want to buy one? It makes no sense but then what do I know.'

'Dad, this isn't about furniture. It's about you and Mum. I only said all that stuff about Habitat to get you in the car. You need to talk to Mum and sort out everything, OK?'

There was a silence. Adam didn't have a clue what was going through his mind but he was pretty sure it wasn't good.

'Look Dad, this really is for the best,' said Adam as they pulled off the High Street.

Dad said nothing.

'I know you're annoyed but in half an hour or so this could all be over.'

Still his dad didn't say a word.

'Just think about it, Dad, if you sort this out you could get back to your garden, you know how much you love your gardening.' He reversed into a parking spot right outside the house and switched off the engine. Adam pointed to Russ and Luke who were standing on the front doorstep. 'See, Dad? Russ and Luke came over to make sure that Mum was in and my job was to make sure you got here, so go on, just go in and talk to her and get this sorted.'

Finally his dad, clearly trying to control his anger, spoke. 'Son,' he said. 'I understand that you and your brothers think you're doing the right thing, and I understand that this must be quite upsetting for you but I swear to you that if you don't start this car up this very second and take me back to your place I will never have anything to do with you or your brothers ever again.'

Adam had never heard his dad talk with such vehemence and he obviously meant every word he said. As far as his dad was concerned Adam and his brothers had overstepped the mark by some way. For the first time in years Adam felt afraid, not of his dad, but of the situation. This wasn't just some overblown tiff. This really was the beginning of the end.

Starting up the car Adam watched a look of bewilderment spread across his brothers' faces as they made their way down the front path towards them.

'Dad, I'm sorry,' said Adam as he released the handbrake, desperately hoping for some kind of response. 'I'm really sorry. Say something will you? Just say something.'

But his dad said nothing.

'Sorry'

It was the following morning and Adam had been lying in bed for a good half-hour before he gave up and accepted that despite his extreme tiredness he was unlikely to get back to sleep any time soon. As he listened to the clanging sound of Dad searching around in the pan cupboard, no doubt looking for a frying pan for his regulation fried breakfast, Adam glanced over at the luminous red display of his digital alarm clock.

He decided to head into town and treat himself to something new and expensive that he didn't need. He picked up yesterday's clothes that were lying on the floor at the foot of the bed and put them on, shoved his feet into his trainers and went downstairs. Pausing to glance in the direction of the kitchen where his father continued his banging and clanking, he made his way out of the front door and closed it quietly behind him.

Adam and his father had not said a single word to each other since the previous afternoon. Passing each other in the hallway, in the kitchen or outside the bathroom their preferred method of communication appeared to be what was known within the family circle as 'the Bachelor glower' (brow furrowed, eyes narrowed, mouth set in a permanent scowl) which could variously be interpreted as 'Just stay away from me,' 'You have let me down badly' or 'I am so annoyed that I can barely look at you,' depending upon who was doing the scowling and the degree of facial manipulation that was occurring. This being the case Adam had opted simply to stay out of his father's way and as his dad had commandeered the front room with the widescreen TV Adam had remained upstairs watching the tiny portable in his bedroom.

Adam headed to the Arndale and spent a good hour or so wandering in and out of shops picking up anything that took his fancy from new jeans and trainers to a miniature laptop and designer watch.

From there, he made his way to Selfridges but as he passed the St Mary's Gate branch of Paperchase he found himself going inside. Adam couldn't remember the last time he had bought so much as a birthday card so what he was doing in the shop was a mystery but eventually as he browsed the aisles he was drawn to the blank greetings card section. There were cards of every description from arty-looking black and white pictures through to ones adorned with the faces of celebrities but the only type that interested Adam were reproductions of various artistic pieces. He selected a Rothko print entitled 'White over Red', picked up a pack of biros and took them to the till to pay for his purchases.

Adam changed his mind about Selfridges and doubled back on himself until he reached the Arndale branch of Caffè Nero where he bought an ordinary filter coffee (together with an impulse purchase of a blueberry muffin) and then sat down at a table towards the rear of the store. He took out the card from its paper bag, ripped open the cellophane, opened his new pack of pens and contemplated the open page in front of him. He took a bite of blueberry muffin, chewed, then finally committed pen to paper:

'Sorry'

He tried to imagine what Steph might feel when she read it. Would she like the card? Would she like the fact that it contained only a single word? Would she even know what he was sorry about? He wasn't sure but he needed to do it. Not because he was going to try and win her back (he was pretty sure that Luke was right that it was unlikely she was going to change her mind) but because he felt, for reasons he couldn't quite pinpoint, that it was the right thing to do.

Ten minutes later, having drunk his coffee, consumed his muffin and sealed his card in an envelope he checked his phone for Steph's address, scribbled it on the card and headed in the direction of the nearest post box.

Adam and his father continued to ignore each other for the next few days but over time his father's scowls became less scowly until by the following Friday morning Dad practically managed a smile as he entered the kitchen to make breakfast. By lunchtime he was even making tentative suggestions about a joint visit to Somerfield.

Grateful that the war was over Adam agreed not only to his father's trip to Somerfield but also to the joint purchasing of six cans of tinned carrots, three of new potatoes, several portions of boil-in-the-bag cod and half a pound of sliced ox tongue that his dad alleged was good for sandwiches.

Back at home Adam helped his father unpack the shopping, narrowly avoided an assignation with a white bread ox-tongue sandwich by pleading the need to work. Instead he escaped to a nearby café and started planning the mother of all big nights out because if there was anyone in need of letting his hair down Adam was pretty sure it would be him.

He met up with the boys at a bar on Thomas Street just after nine and made them trawl through the northern quarter until midnight when much to his disappointment three-quarters of the group went home citing various family commitments, moaning partners and sheer general fatigue as their excuse. Determined not to let the others rain on his parade Adam then led the remainder across the city to a host of bars and clubs that most of his friends wouldn't have stood a chance of getting into on a Friday night had it not been for Adam's influence with the door staff.

At just after two in the morning, in a bar called the Clover Lounge with two of the remaining nucleus of his friends talking about heading home, Adam noticed a girl who had clearly stepped straight out of the number one slot of an *FHM* magazine's 'High Street Honeys' feature. She was quite unmistakably, in fact unashamedly, making eye contact with him.

With all that had happened in recent weeks. Adam hadn't given the opposite sex a great deal of thought. Now, however, that a young, pretty and scantily-clad girl was making it clear that she was interested, he decided now was the time to give it a great deal of thought. The main question on Adam's mind was testing whether Luke had been right in his suggestion that he should stick to what he was good at: being a bachelor. Adam was indeed good at being a bachelor. Of all the bachelors he knew he was the best. No one (at least no one who wasn't playing premier league football) could out-bachelor him. He was the James Bond of bachelordom and there were guys in the bar who would have lopped off a limb to be him for a single night. But was that enough? Enough to make a life that wasn't completely devoid of all meaning? Adam decided to find out.

Making his way across the bar Adam engaged the girl, who turned out to be Danish (or possibly Swedish, he wasn't quite sure because he had been too busy looking at her legs to pay much attention to what she was saying) in conversation. Refocusing his mind from her legs to her lips Adam learned she had come to Manchester to see some university friends and this was her last night in town before heading back home, so she was desperate for the night to be as memorable as possible.

Clicking straight into 'Adam-on-the-pull-autopilot' within fifteen effortless minutes Adam had his arm round her slender waist, a beer in his hand and a big grin on his face that might as well have been a flashing neon sign announcing: 'Here I am, a thirty-eight-year-old single man with my arm round the kind of girl most mortals could only dream of.' If there was a heaven for bachelors this was it. This was cool of the shaken but not stirred variety. This really was the best a man could get.

'That sounds like a great plan.'

'You do realise that this is still blowing my mind, don't you?' Russell was looking across at Angie with real adoration in his eyes as they sat in an upmarket pizza restaurant on Wilbraham Road celebrating their two month anniversary. 'Look at us! After all this time and all that wasted mental energy you and I are a walking, talking, properly functioning couple! I even described you to Debbie, the receptionist, as my girlfriend! She asked me what I was doing tonight and I said I'm treating my *girlfriend* Angie to a posh meal.' He stopped and grinned. 'That is right, isn't it? You are my girlfriend. We are doing the girlfriend/boyfriend thing?'

'What are you like?' laughed Angie. 'Of course I'm your bloody girlfriend. And just so that you know, I've been referring to you as my boyfriend on Facebook for weeks now. I know it's the equivalent of when I was a teenager at school and used to spend whole biology lessons practising my "Mrs Robbie Williams" signature in my exercise book but I'm too happy to care. You make me happy, Russell Bachelor. You make me the happiest girl in the world.'

From the moment that Angie had kissed him, told him she loved him and (later that evening at her flat) tearfully confessed that it had been her feelings for him that had made her end her relationship with Aaron, Russell had felt as though he could switch off his inner worrier and get on with the business of life. Suddenly hating work, being broke and even being depressed about his parents' break-up and the Bachelor brothers' failed attempt to get their parents back together didn't affect him in the same way. Now that he knew he was loved and adored for the very first time he had a way at hand of keeping all of the bad stuff in perspective. And Angie did adore him. She hadn't bothered with any of the usual game-playing. She had simply laid it all out in the open: this is who I am and this is how I feel. And in return her openness and honesty had reaped massive dividends from Russell because after all this time in the wilderness he realised that this, rather than what he had experienced focusing all his thoughts and efforts on Cassie, was what love was meant to feel like: warm, tangible and secure.

'I love the fact that we're not playing games with each other,' said Angie. 'And I know this is going to sound cheesy but this is the best thing that's ever happened to me. Not only am I with my best mate but I'm also with the guy I want to be with most in the world.' She paused, blushed, and looked down at the empty plates on the table. 'I know I said I quite fancied a dessert but I'm suddenly not feeling quite as hungry as I was. What would you say to us getting the bill and heading back to mine?'

'That,' grinned Russell, assuming a Leslie Phillips-style leer, 'sounds like an excellent idea, my dear.'

Waking up at Angie's flat in Whalley Range the following morning Russell was surprised to find himself alone in the bed with Angie nowhere to be seen. He quickly dressed and made his way along the hallway checking first the bathroom, then the kitchen and finally the living room, where he found her sitting on the sofa in tears, a letter in her hand.

'Hey you,' he said, sitting down next to her. 'What's up? What are all these tears about?'

'This,' she said, waving the letter. 'I'm broke, Russ. I've reached the limit of my overdraft and now they're saying I've got to go and see them so that I can come up with some sort of plan to pay back the money I owe. But I can't! I've barely got anything to live on once I've paid the rent as it is.'

Russell took the letter and winced when he read the punchline. Angie was apparently five thousand pounds overdrawn.

'How did this happen? I thought you were really good with money?'

'I am usually but covering Aaron's share of the rent has nearly killed me.'

'So have you thought about moving?'

'Of course I have,' she tutted. 'What am I, stupid?'

'So why haven't you done it?'

'Because I know it'll make me miserable.'

Russell sighed. 'Well look, if you're desperate I could

probably loan you a couple of hundred for a while if that would be any help.'

Angie stood up and walked over to the window. 'I don't want your stupid money, Russ, OK?'

'Fine.' Russell wondered why this all suddenly appeared to be his fault. 'So what do you want then?'

Angie turned round. 'I want you to move in with me.'

'Move in?'

'Look, it's not like I'm asking you to hand over your testicles on a plate so there's no need to pull that kind of face. All I'm saying is that I'd like it if you'd at least think about it.'

'Don't you think it's a bit too soon? We've been together eight weeks! Even you'd have to admit that's not exactly long.'

'I've known you for years, Russ, it's not like we're some kind of overnight sensation, is it?'

'Yeah, but for the majority of those "years" we were just mates, weren't we? This is different. A new stage if you like and I'm not sure that we ought to be rushing things, that's all. I mean, what's to be gained?'

'Other than being able to spend more time together?'

'Look,' replied Russell, picking up on her sarcasm, 'there's no need to be like that. I'm not saying I never want to move in with you, just that there's no rush and no need to try and fix things that aren't broken.'

There was a long silence. Angie was far from happy. 'What if they were broken?'

'Are you saying that if we don't move in together

that we should split up? Because that sounds like an ultimatum.'

'Of course it's not!' Angie was unable to contain her exasperation. 'What kind of nutter do you take me for? I was just floating it as an idea, that's all, but now I've done it and seen your reaction you'll be pleased to know that I feel completely and utterly stupid. You're right, it is way too early. Just forget I even said anything, OK?' She picked up the letter from the sofa, headed towards the door and then stopped. 'Look, I'm going to get dressed and then why don't you let me take you to BlueBar for breakfast, my treat?'

Russell determined that the cohabitation issue wasn't going to spoil their weekend so he kissed her on the forehead, told her it was a great idea and tried his best not to panic.

'It's time to talk.'

Luke was in the kitchen heating up various bits of Marks and Spencer fare in preparation for Cassie's first official visit home in over three weeks. During this period Luke had spoken to her on the phone half a dozen times and while most of the calls had been related to the practicalities of everyday life the last few conversations had all been building up to her return home and above all the conversation about their future. Aware that once a date was set there would be no going back they had taken care to bat possible times and locations for their meeting backwards and forwards without any real determination. To have done so would have been too scary, too real. Finally the call had come. Cassie had sounded small and distant as the arrangements were made; the date, time and location were fixed for the following Thursday but there was no mention of the agenda, although Luke guessed it was probably a given.

Searching for a clean tea towel with which to wipe his thumb that had accidentally become covered in sauce Luke was about to wipe his hands on the back of his jeans when the phone rang.

'You sound breathless,' said Mum. 'Is everything all right?'

'Yes, everything's fine. I was just sorting out some stuff in the kitchen.'

Luke looked over at the new potatoes boiling away on the hob and reached across to turn the gas down.

'Are you sure everything's fine?'

'Yeah, Mum.'

'And what time is Cassie coming home?'

'About eight I think.'

'So not too long then?'

'No, not too long.'

'I'm thinking about you, you know.'

'I know you are, Mum. It means a lot to me.'

'I'm sure everything will be all right.'

'I'm sure it will too.'

'So you'll call me and let me know how things went? Not straight away . . . but maybe in the morning?'

'I'll see, OK?'

'Yes, of course. you'll take care though, won't you?'

'Will do, Mum. Speak to you later.'

Returning the phone to its charger Luke headed back over to the cooker, grabbed a knife and stabbed one of the potatoes to see if it was done. Then he reached for the open bottle of Merlot sitting on the counter next to the microwave, poured himself his third glass of the evening and took a moment to think about his mum.

Since hearing the news about Cassie his mum had gone from not calling him at all to her current rate of at least one phone call every two days. The last time that she'd been this persistent had been when he and Jayne were splitting up and that had continued for the best part of a year afterwards. Despite his reticence, Luke didn't mind the calls because they reminded him that being a parent was a job for life. No matter how grown-up your kids were supposed to be a part of you would always see them as your babies. The downside was the fact that his mum had problems of her own to contend with and Luke couldn't help but feel it should have been him looking after her rather than the other way round.

Luke pulled a bag of salad leaves out of the fridge and was about to arrange them artfully in a bowl when the doorbell rang. He wiped his hands on his jeans once again and made his way to the front door. Cassie was wearing her light grey mac and jeans and looked prettier than ever. Desperate not to overwhelm her as she came inside out of the rain Luke tried to resist the temptation to hug her but he couldn't help himself. Within a few moments he had wrapped her in his arms and was kissing her face and the fact that she was kissing him back strengthened his hope that the worst was over.

'I've made dinner,' explained Luke as Cassie hung her mac on the banister. 'Nothing flash, just a bunch of stuff from Marks and—' He stopped abruptly as he saw the smile fall from Cassie's face. 'I know,' he said before she could respond verbally. 'I know you didn't come round to eat. And yeah, I know we need to talk. But come on Cass, there's plenty of time for all that.

For now I just need you to sit down, have a glass of wine and enjoy yourself, OK?'

Nodding reluctantly she followed him into the kitchen extension where he poured her a glass of wine. As she admired the table setting and appreciated his efforts with candlelight he plated up the contents of the various trays and they sat and talked about work, and about friends and family and for a short while Luke felt it was just like old times.

'I could easily eat the whole thing again,' said Cassie, carefully placing her knife and fork in the centre of her empty plate. 'You didn't have to go to all this effort though. I would've been just as happy with a bacon and egg sarnie.'

Luke smiled. 'Do you remember those bacon and egg sarnies we had at that greasy spoon one time when we went for that walking weekend with your old university friends? It was like a half-baguette crammed with half a pig and half a dozen eggs. It was incredible.'

'Easily the best bacon sandwich ever. Although as I remember I couldn't finish mine and you wolfed down my leftovers in about a second!'

Luke was pleased they were sharing intimate old memories like this. 'Well sorry as I am to let you down in the bacon sandwich department I can promise you a cornucopia of delights when it comes to pudding. We've got a Belgian chocolate sponge thing, some of that posh ice cream with the big chunks of cookie dough and I even made your favourite: raspberry jelly.'

Cassie held her hands up in surrender. 'You made raspberry jelly? Oh, Luke, that really is sweet of you but I couldn't eat another thing, honestly.'

'No worries,' replied Luke. 'It'll keep. So what do you want now? Tea? Coffee? I bought some more of that herbal stuff during the week.'

'I'm fine on the tea and coffee front too.'

He nodded sagely. 'So I'm guessing this is your way of saying it's time to talk?'

Cassie nodded. 'Yes, it's time to talk.'

There was nowhere left to run so Luke pushed his plate to one side and made his case as best as he could. Although he hadn't exactly planned what he was going to say he knew the gist, along the lines that the last few weeks without her had been a living hell. 'Look,' he concluded, 'if there's one thing that your moving out has taught me it's that I honestly can't live without you. And I'm not even sure I want to wait until next year to get married.' He walked over to the kitchen counter, picked up an envelope that had been lying next to the mug tree and placed it on the table in front of Cassie.

'What's this?' she asked, looking down at the crisp white envelope.

'Two tickets to Barbados, leaving at the end of the month,' explained Luke sounding thoroughly pleased with himself. 'I've emailed the hotel and apparently as long as we give them enough notice they can sort out a wedding registrar from their end. So what do you say? How do you feel about the idea of becoming Mrs Cassie Bachelor in a few weeks?'

Cassie didn't say anything. She just stared blankly at the envelope in front of her. Luke began to get the terrible feeling that he had misjudged things completely. 'Is this about your family missing out on the wedding?' he asked. 'Because I was thinking we could have some kind of celebration here in Manchester when we get back.'

Cassie shook her head. 'You haven't mentioned it,' she said in a voice that barely registered above a whisper. 'You haven't mentioned it at all.'

Luke didn't understand. 'What do you mean, Cass? I haven't mentioned what?'

'Children,' said Cassie. 'You haven't mentioned children.' She shook her head in disbelief. 'You haven't changed your mind, have you? You haven't even considered changing your mind.'

'I thought you knew,' he said, shaking his head in horror. 'I thought you understood, Cass. There's nothing I can do about this situation, and that's just the way things have to be. But surely we're bigger than all that? Surely we're what's most important here. You and me. Surely everything else is just extra.'

'Extra!' spat Cassie. 'Is that what you think a child is to me? An extra? Is that what Megan is to you?'

'No, of course not.'

'Then why would you say that about the children I want us to have?' She rose to her feet as hot angry tears streamed down her face. 'I love you, Luke! I love you with my whole heart and to sit here and hear you dismiss the desire I have to start a family with the man I love as being a simple extra hurts me to my very core! It's almost as if I don't know you. This isn't about me choosing motherhood over you. If some medical reason meant that you'd never be able to have kids I wouldn't for a second regret staying with you – not for one second because I love you and you mean everything to me! But to know that you can have children but choose not to because of something over which I have no control . . . well, it feels like you're punishing me when I've done nothing wrong.'

'Of course you haven't done anything wrong. Of course not. But this is something I just can't do. I've never hidden this from you, have I? I've never lied to you about it.'

'So what do you want? A medal?' screamed Cassie, jabbing Luke in the chest with her fingers. 'No Luke, you never lied to me about this. It's true you were always honest and open about it. But do you know what else is true? It's the one thing in all the time I've known you that has never changed. Your looks, your way of seeing the world, the things you say and the way you say them: everything that makes you the person I love so much has grown and changed since I fell in love with you, thanks to time and experience, but this one thing from your past that you've held on to so tightly, that never has. Not time, not experience, not even my love has changed a single thing about that and that hurts me more than you'll ever know.' She pulled off her engagement ring and placed it flat on the table. 'When I said I'd marry you I imagined that in exchange for my giving myself completely to you, you would do the same to me in return. But you're not giving me everything, Luke, you're holding back and it's always going to be this way.'

'What is wrong with you?'

It was just after seven on the following Monday evening and Russell (who had arrived at his mum's sometime after six) was eating a hearty home-cooked meal of pork chops, potatoes, gravy and apple sauce while watching the tail end of *Channel Four News*.

'I was just wondering,' said Russell's mum in a deceptively casual manner that indicated the question she was about to ask had been on her mind since the moment he stepped through the door, 'have you heard anything from Luke recently?'

Russell shook his head. With the Bachelor Sunday lunch tradition out of the window he hadn't seen Luke for weeks, for which he was mostly grateful as – happy as he was with Angie – the last thing he wanted to do was tempt fate by spending time in Cassie's company.

'Why do you ask?'

Joan shrugged. 'Oh, no reason, I was just wondering, that's all.'

'I can give him a ring if you like?'

'Don't bother. I've left a few messages so I'm sure he'll get back to me when he's ready.'

Russell returned to his food even though it was clear

that something was going on. Whenever things were going on in the Bachelor family it was a given that he would be left out of the loop because his parents seemed unable to adjust to the idea that he was no longer a snot-covered schoolboy.

Finishing his meal Russell sat chatting about items on the news and about the rest of the family. His mum (who still wasn't looking or acting anything like her usual self) wasn't saying anything about the situation with his dad and although Russell tried several times to steer the conversation in that general direction she consistently refused to take the bait. Russell decided that the best thing would be to deliver the news he had come to give her.

'Listen, Mum,' he said somewhat reticently. 'I've got something to tell you.'

'Just a moment, Russell.' She reached for the remote control to turn down the volume, then settled back in her chair. 'Right, my sweet, you have my full and undivided attention.'

'You know my friend Angie? Well, she and I aren't just friends any more . . . we haven't been for a while now and we've sort of decided that we're going to move in together.'

Russell had made the decision that morning. Angie had been getting more and more down at the prospect of moving out of the flat and as they had been eating breakfast the solution had finally dawned on him. Having spent so long committed to a woman who had never loved him and never would the least he could do was have a go at commitment with a girl who genuinely thought he was the best thing since sliced bread. Angie had been so delighted that she had demanded they both pull a sickie and spend the whole day in bed. Russell had agreed but in the end had had to go to work anyway because the second he left a message with Debbie on reception telling her he wouldn't be in, Jeanette had called him back stating that if he didn't have a doctor's note on his return she would take immediate disciplinary action.

Russell looked at his mum to see if the message within the message had sunk in. Prior to this moment he had never mentioned that he had ever had a girlfriend let alone one with whom he might want to cohabit.

'Where will you live?'

'I'll move into her place in Whalley Range.'

'Have you told your father?'

'No.'

'What does Adam say?'

'I haven't told him yet either.'

There was a silence. Russell regretted telling Mum his plans. She had mistaken his offer of information for a request for permission and because she obviously thought it had the words 'bad idea' stamped through it like a stick of rock she was reluctant to grant it.

'I know it's a bit sudden,' said Russell in a fruitless bid to allay her fears, 'but it's what I want.'

Her face softened. 'Well, if it's what you want, son, then I suppose it's what I want too. And if you need anything like bedding or furniture you only have to ask.'

Deciding that this was as good a time as any to make his escape Russell helped his mum tidy away the remains of the tea before saying his goodbyes. At the end of the front path Russell turned left and reached into the pocket of his jacket for his phone: he had forgotten to switch over from its silent setting. He had two missed calls and four text messages and even without checking them he knew that they were all from Angie.

Message 1: Are you at your mum's? Hope all is cool. Ring me as soon as you can. Ange xxx
Message 2: Have just tried to call you. Call me if you need ANYTHING at all!!!!!
Message 3: Don't forget since you've decided to blow me out that I am going out with the girls tonight. Promise me that I will see you later at mine! xxx
Message 4: Am out with girls and missing you like crazy!!! Don't think I can make it through the evening without you! Come straight out when you're ready! Please call me as soon as you can!!! A xxx

Walking along the road reading the texts Russell enjoyed exactly how good being with Angie made him feel. This thing with his mum and dad was having an effect on him yet here he was with a spring in his step and a smile on his face. And it was all down to Angie. Still grinning Russell began typing out the following reply: 'Have left Mum's and am walking up to High Street. Will see you soon xxx.' He pressed send and was about to return his phone to his pocket when it rang. Assuming it was Angie, he answered the call straight away.

'Ange!' said Russell.

'Have another go,' said a gruff male voice that he immediately recognised as Adam's.

'All right, Ad?' Russell wondered if this was going to be an update about their father.

'As it happens, no,' replied his brother. 'My reason for being, my one motivation, the very thing that makes your brother the person he is has gone. But I'll have to share that with you another time, kid, because that's not why I'm calling.'

'So why are you calling then?'

'Because less than five minutes ago I had Mum on the phone saying that you're moving in with your mate Angie. I told her she must have got the wrong end of the stick and that you meant you're moving in with her in the sense that you'll be her flatmate or housemate or whatever. I'm just checking that is the case.'

Russell groaned. Enlisting Adam as her own personal enforcer was typical Mum behaviour when she had things to say but didn't want to be the one who actually said them. Now he would have no choice but to allow his elder brother to talk sense into him. It was the same when he had briefly toyed with the idea of getting a job instead of doing A levels, and again when he had considered dropping out of university and when he had thought about going to live in Holland. Each and every time he had shared these notions with his mum she had taken them to Adam who had proceeded to talk Russell out of doing whatever he'd wanted to do. Well it wasn't going to happen. Not this time.

'Actually it's not the case,' said Russell firmly. 'So just to make it clear: yes, I am moving in with Angie in the sense that Angie and I are now together and . . . well, we've decided to take things to the next level.'

'What is wrong with you?' said Adam incredulously. 'It's bad enough that you're shacking up with some bird two minutes after getting together. Don't make matters worse by using phrases like "taking things to the next level". You're meant to be a Bachelor, Russ, but the way you're talking makes me think that you should have been born a spinster!' Russell had heard the 'Bachelor/Spinster' thing many times before and didn't bother rising to the bait. Instead he held the phone away from his ear and let his brother continue. 'Anyway,' said Adam, whose voice Russell thought sounded a lot less annoying now that it was no longer being funnelled directly into his ear canal. 'I thought you and Angie were just mates. I remember you giving me and Luke a huge long lecture about how much we were missing out by not having birds as friends and now look at you – copping off with your supposed best mate. Not quite the higher love that you were preaching back then, is it?'

Russell put the phone back to his ear. 'Things change, that's all. We didn't mean for it to happen, it just sort of appeared from nowhere.'

'And how long exactly has it been? Mum was a little shaky about the timing.'

Russell sighed inwardly. Adam was heading towards victory. 'A little while,' he acknowledged.

'As in what exactly? Five months? Six?'

'A couple of months.'

'A couple of months? That's no time at all. What's the big rush?'

'There is no rush. It's just something I want to do.'

'Look, Russ, I know you think I'm pulling rank by doing the big brother thing but I do actually give a crap about what happens to you, OK? And all I'm saying is . . . well, put it like this: there have been times in the past when I've done things in the hope that they'll somehow sort out a problem I've been having, you know, in a "if-I-do-this-and-cross-my-fingers-it'll-stop-me-from-doing-the-thing-that-I-don't-want-to-do" kind of way.'

For a moment or two Russell thought Adam was talking about Cassie but he realised that the idea of his Jack-the-lad elder brother noticing anything to do with real live emotions was highly unlikely.

'I have no idea what you are on about,' said Russell finally. 'But thanks for the advice all the same.'

'Fine,' sighed Adam. 'Just don't say that I didn't warn you.'

'We are.'

It was just after four in the afternoon and Luke (who should have been at a meeting in Exeter) was sitting on the sofa in his T-shirt and boxers thinking about his old primary-school friend, Ben Cohen. Back when they were friends Luke and Ben used to be in and out of each other's house all the time and they got to know each other's families really well, so it was a real shock for Luke when one morning the teacher announced that Ben wouldn't be at school because his cab-driver father Harry had died of a heart attack. What made this even worse for Luke was that he and Ben had had a kick-around in the garden with Mr Cohen the night before. Luke felt weird that his friend didn't have a dad any more but even weirder when his friend told him on the telephone that evening that the funeral had already happened. 'That's rubbish,' he said. 'People don't get buried that quickly,' but then Ben passed the phone to his older sister Rebecca, who had no reason to lie, and she confirmed it was true, adding that they were now doing something called sitting shiva.

Over the years that passed Luke thought about his friend Ben Cohen and the story of his dad's funeral several times, usually inspired by other cases of excruciatingly embarrassing insensitivity which he had been party to, but today was the first time Luke had ever thought about that story in terms of the thing itself: the speed of the funeral. It really shocked him how one day you could be alive and kicking and less than twenty-four hours later you could be six feet under. The swiftness seemed almost indecent. How could you process what had happened in that short a space of time, let alone prepare yourself to say goodbye to a loved one? Surely these things took a week or so because that was what they needed logistically and emotionally? Surely everyone, no matter their religion or culture, was wired up with these same basic needs?

Evidently not.

Within twenty-four hours of Cassie handing back the engagement ring she had gone. Not just in the sense that she had packed more clothes and essential items for a few more days and headed back to her friend Holly's house but in the sense that by the time Luke returned home from work the following evening everything that she owned had disappeared. Her keys to the house (the mortgage was in Luke's name – putting her name on it was one of those things they had never actually got round to) were left on the kitchen table.

Luke hadn't been able to believe his eyes as he looked around the house and saw all her clothes missing from the wardrobe and various pictures and photographs gone from walls and surfaces. Items to which she had equal rights, like sofas and armchairs and the dining-room table and chairs, she had left behind as though so desperate to break all ties with Luke that she was forgoing her entitlements in a bid to speed her passage away from him.

Luke knew that the swiftness of her exit had nothing to do with threats, punishment or indeed retribution for his actions and everything to do with Cassie's own attempts at self-preservation. The longer a separation took the more drawn-out and arduous it would be for both of them in the long run. Cassie's version of ending things was swift and to the point. Get the practical stuff out of the way while you still feel numb. Do your mourning later, in private and in your own time. If Cassie had left the timing of this separation in Luke's hands it would have dragged on for months, featured frequent last-ditch attempts at reconciliation and ultimately ended badly enough to put them both off relationships for life. No, Cassie had done the right thing, the noble thing that in the end would be best for both of them. Even so, Luke wished that she had stayed because every second without her was empty.

Luke had called her mobile and it was all he could do not to throw the phone across the room when it went straight through to voicemail. Barely able to breathe for rising panic he dialled her office number in the hope that she might be working late and pick up without knowing that it was him but again every call was passed straight through to her anonymous electronic voicemail. Realising that he was running out of options Luke dialled her mobile number once more and plucked up the courage to leave a message: 'Cassie, it's me. We need to talk. I need to see you. We can't let this happen to us. We're better than that. I promise you we are. Please, please, call me back as soon as you get this message.'

Luke had ended the call and dropped the phone into his jacket pocket. His every fibre was primed for action but without a point on which to focus all this energy, it surged around his body pointlessly agitating his limbs as it looked for a way to escape into the world. He thought about jumping in the car and driving over to Cassie's friend Holly's house to see if she was there, but even in his heightened emotional state he could see the flaws in this strategy. No, the time for action had long since passed. If he had been here when she had been packing then maybe, just maybe he could have talked her round. Now all he could do was sit and wait and hope that she would call him.

He slumped down on to the sofa and switched on the TV. Determined not to be defeated by the fact that there seemed to be nothing on he flicked up and down the channels from news programmes, to repeats of British comedy classics. Luke tried his best to concentrate on the screen, wishing desperately that he could lose himself in the excitement and the explosions, but to no avail. The huge knot in his stomach refused to stay in place, shifting from side to side before finally breaking free and moving upwards and outwards into his lungs. All at once he was sobbing like a baby and the more he tried to stop the harder and quicker it came out. He felt like something had broken inside. It seemed the pain would never stop, so he called work and told them he was taking some time off in lieu, then switched off his mobile and unplugged his phone and proceeded to cut himself off from the world.

'There's honestly no need for symbolic bread-based gestures.'

It was quarter to one on a cold, wet Saturday afternoon and Adam (having spent the best part of five and a half hours sitting in his car staking out his local newsagent's like a TV detective) had just concluded that there was no option but to abandon his plan, return home and give serious consideration to his future now he had solid proof that Steph had ruined him for ever.

The reason Adam believed this was simple: his night with the gorgeous Danish/Swedish girl less than a week earlier had been an unmitigated disaster. Arriving in the early hours at the apartment she was staying in off Deansgate, he had allowed her to lead him to her room utterly convinced that this amazing girl with her fantastic looks and outstanding body would blot out everything from his doomed pursuit of the Right Kind of Women through to the problems with his parents' marriage. But half an hour later, as the Swedish/Danish girl dozed quietly at his side, he knew two things for sure: he no longer had the will or the inclination to lead this type of life and he missed Steph more than ever.

He started to hatch a plan: on the following Saturday morning he would get up as early as humanly possible, stake out the newsagent's where he had first met Steph and attempt to engineer an accidental meeting and then . . . he didn't know what exactly would happen after that. But Steph made him want to be a better person and that meant more to him than anything else in the world.

He glanced into his rear-view mirror to check the traffic before pulling away and was shocked to see a lone female figure walking up the road. While not daring to believe that it might be Steph, Adam nevertheless refrained from pulling away until he could be sure. Barely breathing until the figure had come close enough for full identification Adam was relieved as first the coat, the hair and then finally the face that he had thought of kissing so many times came into sharp focus.

Waiting until she had walked past and into Sanjay's, Adam leaped out of the car, narrowly avoiding being run over by a cyclist, crossed the road, walked straight into the newsagent's, picked up a copy of the *Mirror* and made his way to the till at which there was a six-person-long queue. Steph was number five and a balding guy with a long grey hippy-ish ponytail was number six. Adam tried to work out what his next move should be: the most straightforward thing would be to say hello to her on the spot but that would have given the lie to the casual nature of everything he was trying to engineer. No, she would have to discover him herself . . . or even better they would discover each other at the same time . . . and everything else would follow naturally. He took a deep breath. The queue was getting shorter. Steph was second from the front. The woman in front of her paid for her shopping. Steph was next. From behind the ponytail guy Adam could just about see her handing over the money for the paper. Adam prepared his face for their encounter: a casual smile and raised eyebrows of surprise (but not too raised).

Steph turned away from the counter, her eyes fixed on the headlines of her newspaper. Adam wanted to yell: 'Look up! Look up and see me!' but remained in mute despair as she walked past him and out of the shop. He couldn't believe it. All those hours spent in a cramped car and his mission was about to be thwarted by an absorbing headline! This was wrong, so wrong that it hurt. Adam looked at the headline, something to do with the number of people estimated to have died in a war on the other side of the world. He shook his head in disbelief. Why give a toss about people dying in a war halfway across the globe when none of it was affecting her? It wasn't as if there was anything she could do about it. Why couldn't she just be like normal people who wanted to read stuff about celebrities and only paid lip service to the idea of caring about the world? Adam watched her walk down the road. His heart could not have felt any heavier. He handed Sanjay a two-pound coin for the paper, dropped the change into the Save The Children charity tin and turned to walk away. Only he couldn't. Steph was blocking his exit holding her newspaper and brandishing a loaf of wholemeal bread that she had clearly forgotten the first time. She glanced up and saw him. She looked both shocked and surprised.

'Adam! How are you? Were you here all the time? I didn't even see you standing there!'

'I was . . . er . . . just getting a paper.' He waved the newspaper in the air. 'So how have you been? Are you well?'

'I'm good actually,' she replied. 'Work has been a bit busy but that's fine. How about yourself? Everything OK with the bar?'

Adam nodded. 'It virtually runs itself. I just turn up there sometimes so that it looks like I actually work for a living.'

There was a long pause and Adam wondered whether this was going to be the end of the conversation. Then, 'I got your card,' she said quietly. 'It was really nice of you to send it. I'm actually quite fond of Rothko.'

'It was nothing,' said Adam. He thought about saying something more in reference to the card's message but then thought better of it and made a joke instead. 'Truth is you came pretty close to getting a card with a cartoon of Garfield.'

Steph laughed. 'Now that would have been really strange because the only thing I like more than Rothko is a nice Garfield cartoon!'

Once again the conversation seemed to be drawing

to a close. Adam looked at the bread in Steph's hands. An idea popped into his head and he decided to let it run free. 'Can I pay for that?'

Steph looked confused. 'What? The bread? Why would you do that?'

'Think of it as a small act of penance on my part. Think of this loaf of . . .' he paused to read the label, 'Warburton's Wholemeal Farmhouse as our bread of peace. My way of apologising for several years of teasing at school and for any other misdemeanours that might have taken place since.'

'Really,' smiled Steph, 'there's no need for symbolic bread-based gestures. You can consider yourself absolved.'

'Really?'

Adam decided it was time to seize the moment. 'Well in that case I was sort of wondering if you'd like to go out some time.'

The look on Steph's face (acute embarrassment set off with a heavy frown) said it all but just to drive the point home she added, 'I appreciate the thought, I really do, Adam, but if I'm being truthful I don't think that would be a great idea.'

'I mean as friends,' said Adam quickly as he recalled the fact that he remained officially 'not her type'. 'You know, mates who hang out together and that sort of thing.'

'Still not a great idea.' Steph shook her head in a regretful manner that made Adam feel thoroughly dejected. He wanted to be somewhere else as quickly as possible and yet couldn't leave until a decent amount of time had passed in case she jumped to the conclusion that he had taken offence at being rebuffed. He counted to ten as quickly as he could and said: 'So, I suppose I'll see you around then?'

'And more likely than not it'll be in here.' With a half nod and an awkward smile in Adam's direction she walked past him to the till to make her purchase.

'Just gin gin will do for me.'

It was ten to eight on the Thursday of the following week and Adam was standing in the Slug and Lettuce in Didsbury looking around for a woman in a red coat with auburn hair.

The name of the auburn-haired red-coated object of his investigations was Lorraine Maconie, a thirty-four-year-old primary school teacher and part-time netball coach who was originally from Southend-on-Sea but now apparently lived in Didsbury. Adam (who since his rejection by Steph had let his friends know that he was now very much back on his pursuit of the Right Kind of Girls) had been put in touch with Lorraine via his friends Martin and Kay earlier in the week and after much toing and froing via their intermediaries they had agreed upon a date.

At five minutes past eight, just as Adam was beginning to wonder whether Martin and Kay had been playing some kind of elaborate joke on him, the door to the bar opened and he looked up to see a woman in a red jacket enter the room, scan the bar with one quick look and rest her gaze on him. Adam let out an audible sigh. Even from a distance he could see that this woman with her bobbed auburn hair and bootcut jeans was in no way, shape or form going to make it as a replacement Steph but he would have to give her a go.

'You must be Adam,' she said quickly. 'You look just like the photo Kay emailed. Sorry I'm late. I know Kay said eight o'clock and I always hate it when other people are late but I was just leaving my flat when the phone rang and I knew it would be my mum phoning to wish me good luck for my date with you tonight and if I didn't take it she would spend the whole night calling to make sure things were going OK.'

'It's fine,' said Adam, slightly taken a back by this sudden gush of nervous chat. 'It's really fine. Can I get you a drink?'

'A gin and tonic would be great.'

'Boodles? Bombay? Beefeater? Plymouth? Tanqueray?'

Lorraine looked confused.

'They're gins,' explained Adam.

Lorraine looked embarrassed as though Adam had caught her out, which hadn't been his intention at all. 'Oh, I forgot, you own a bar don't you? Just gin gin will do for me. Is that OK?'

'Of course.' Adam smiled. 'One just gin gin and tonic coming up.'

Returning to the table with their drinks Adam proceeded to ask lots of leading questions in a bid to show Lorraine that he was both interested in her and her responses and in between he tried his best to be as charming and as entertaining as he could manage. But no matter how hard he tried Adam found it impossible to get into the right frame of mind. For all his efforts, once again there was just no spark. No magic. Not a single indicator to alter his initial response the moment he clapped eyes on her that she was 'a nice girl but *so* not for me'.

As he headed up to the bar to get Lorraine another gin gin and tonic and wondered how he was going to make it to the end of the night, given that it was only nine o'clock and they had already scraped the bottom of the barrel to such an extent that the current topic of conversation was rumours of the city council being in discussions about reducing the weekly refuse collection to once a fortnight, his phone rang. Adam didn't recognise the number. Normally he didn't answer his phone to numbers he didn't recognise because of the dual hazards of irate ex-girlfriends and cold callers, but such was the failure of this evening that he would gladly have welcomed the distractions of either.

'Adam Bachelor speaking.'

'Hi, Adam, it's me, Steph.' Adam almost dropped the phone but quickly regained his composure. 'How are you?'

'I'm good, thanks.' A bunch of lads in the bar cheered in the background. 'Where are you? It's very noisy.'

'Nowhere exciting,' he said, wishing that she'd called him a few hours earlier when he had been in a location that made it sound less like he was having the time of his life. 'Just out for a drink with a mate.'

'Well I've been thinking about our meeting the other day and I feel really bad and I was wondering if you mean what you said about us being friends?'

'Absolutely,' he assured her even though this hadn't been strictly true at the time. 'I definitely want us to be friends.'

'And you're not just saying that as a ploy in the hope that something will happen between us later?'

Adam was about to respond but stopped himself at the last minute. Maybe this was a trick question to see if he really had changed. The old Adam would have strenuously denied any ulterior motive just to get what he wanted. The new Adam therefore had to tell the truth even if it hurt.

'Look,' he began, 'I can't deny that I still like you but if you want us to just be mates then I'm sure I can learn to live with that.'

'And it's not like there aren't literally thousands of better-looking girls to distract you in the meantime.'

'I thought you said you'd forgiven me?'

'I'm just teasing you, Adam! And as weird as it is to be the current object of your affections – let's not forget that at school you used to called me Four Eyes Holmes – I'm convinced the weirdness will wear off soon leaving behind what I hope will be a half-decent friendship.'

'So you want to be friends?'

'Yes, I do. And as our first act of friendship I think we should do something special.'

'Great! Well, a mate of mine is throwing a party to

celebrate the opening of his new bar in Tibb Street. We could go there if you like?'

'No,' said Steph firmly. 'No bars, no clubs and no fancy restaurants.'

'So what do you want to do then?'

'I was wondering if you were free on Saturday afternoon?'

'To do what?'

'Can't tell you. It's a secret.'

'What kind of secret?'

'If I told you that it wouldn't be a secret, would it?'

'Fine,' said Adam, who was so thrilled at the prospect of seeing her again that she could have revealed they were going seal-clubbing and he wouldn't have batted an eyelid. 'You name the time and the place and I'll be there.'

'Great,' said Steph. 'Why don't I pick you outside Boots on the High Street at half two on Saturday?'

'Sounds good to me.'

'Good . . . oh, and Adam? You should dress as though you were going to be undertaking some kind of exercise.'

'Exercise?'

'Yes,' she laughed. 'Exercise.'

When he finally got back to the table with their drinks, Lorraine had gone.

'Aliens? Farm animals? Girls called Sue?'

'You're . . . thinking . . . that . . . you've . . . got . . . a . . . new . . . found . . . respect . . . for . . . me . . . aren't . . . you?'

It was just after three on the following Saturday afternoon and Adam was lying on the floor of the badminton court at Chorlton Leisure Centre struggling to breathe and feeling seconds away from passing out with exhaustion. Half an hour earlier Steph had picked Adam up from outside Boots and kept him in the dark about what they were going to be doing until they had pulled up at the Leisure Centre. Adam had pictured them possibly hill-walking or even mountaineering; he had been more than a little disappointed when Steph's secret assignation had only involved a couple of games of badminton. Adam hadn't played badminton since school and then only under duress because even at the age of fourteen he had been sure that badminton was strictly for the ladies.

'What do you mean, new-found respect?' Steph picked up the shuttlecock lying next to Adam's head. 'I won every single game and now look at you! I wouldn't have thought you'd break sweat playing a game that you considered to be "strictly for the ladies"!'

'But . . . that . . . was . . . before . . . anyway . . . there . . . were . . . a . . . couple . . . of . . . moments . . . back . . . there . . . when . . . it . . . could . . . have . . . so . . . easily . . . gone . . . my . . . way.'

'In your dreams, Bachelor Boy! That was just me going easy on you so you didn't get dispirited. Even though I say so myself I am ace at badminton.' She held out her right hand to help him to his feet and he gratefully reached out and grabbed it. It felt soft and slender in his grip and even once he was on his feet he didn't want to let go.

'Right then,' said Steph, subtly extricating her hand. 'I'm heading off for a shower. I'll see you at the front when I'm done and then I'll give you a lift back to your place if you like. Given the way you look right now you don't stand much chance of making it home on foot.'

It was just after four when they pulled up in front of Adam's house.

'So this is you,' she said pulling on the handbrake. She turned to look at Adam. 'It was really nice of you to agree to playing with me today. Even though you were beyond hopeless I had a lot of fun.'

'So does that mean that I'll be seeing you again?'

'I dare say if you're at a loose end and fancy another thrashing at badminton you will.'

'And what about non-badminton-related events?'

'How do you mean exactly?'

'Let me take you out tonight. And before you say no, hand on heart I promise on pain of death that I won't try it on or anything. What I'm suggesting will be something along the lines of two old school mates who occasionally play the noble game of badminton having a meal together during which nothing other than eating and good conversation will occur. Come on Steph, what do you say?'

'Well, because you sent me that Rothko card, were a good sport about losing today and asked so nicely I will agree to meet you this once for dinner tonight. But that's all, OK?'

'Great,' said Adam. 'I'll have a ring round and see where has got a table free and let you know where to meet.'

It was just after eight and Adam was sipping a glass of bottled water and about to help himself to a bread roll when he looked up to see Steph standing right in front of him. She was wearing a black polka-dot top with a black cardigan and a black knee-length skirt, black tights and flat black pumps. She looked pretty but Adam couldn't help but smile at the thought that had Steph been given a brief to select an outfit that none of his previous conquests would have been seen dead in this was pretty much it.

Standing up to greet her Adam kissed her on both cheeks and Steph, seemingly unused to Continental-style cheek-kissing by men like Adam in the middle of south Manchester, had let confusion show briefly on her face.

Initially they talked about badminton again (Adam had had to lie down for most of the afternoon because of a shooting pain in his thigh) but after a while the conversation moved on to work. Steph had spent the previous week helping the shelter she worked at put together a bid for a funding application to local government that, if successful, would enable them to double the number of full-time staff they had on site and increase the number of women they helped by a third. Adam, who had spent most of his week doing very little apart from trying to sort out a new batch of dates with the Right Kind of Girls, felt obliged to embellish his account with tales of high-level meetings, various bits of 'paperwork-chasing' and a staff day out. He had impressed himself with his action-filled working week.

'So come on then,' said Steph later as Adam used up his final current affairs fact that he had cribbed from the *Guardian* specifically to impress her and the waiter cleared away their plates and handed out dessert menus. 'What is this really all about?'

'What is what all about?'

'This,' said Steph. 'You and me sitting here in this nice little restaurant like we're on some kind of a date: is this a joke or a bet?'

'No, of course not.'

'So explain to me why twenty-odd years down the line the best-looking boy at school – and before you flatter yourself let's not forget that there wasn't a great deal of competition – has been making overtures towards a girl whom he regularly referred to as Hopeless Holmes?'

Adam considered her question and decided that now was the time to reveal all. 'It's like this,' he confessed.

'A little while ago it was pointed out to me by my close friends that it might be time for me to stop dating . . .' He paused, wondering how a politically correct paper like the *Guardian* might describe the kinds of girls that he normally went out with. After a few moments of struggling he found the right phrase. 'Inappropriate women.'

'"Inappropriate?"' Steph seemed a little shocked. 'In what way?'

Adam tutted under his breath. This was the problem with political correctness: no one knew what anyone meant. 'What I'm trying to say is that I used to go out with . . . how shall I put it . . . the wrong kind of girl.'

'As in . . .'

'Well, you know,' shrugged Adam. 'The wrong kind like . . .'

'Like what? Aliens? Farm animals? Girls called Sue? Be more specific.'

'OK,' said Adam, 'I mean . . . lap dancers . . . and page three models . . . and page seven models . . . glamour models . . . various former members of the cast of *Hollyoaks* . . . numerous ex-girlfriends of premier-league football players . . . former TV reality show contestants . . . and pretty much any kind of girl who considers underwear as suitable outerwear in which to go clubbing.' Adam winced as he took in Steph's horrified face.

'Did you leave anyone out?'

'No, that is pretty much everything.'

Steph took a long sip from her wine glass. 'So are you saying that you used to date quite a few girls like that?'

'No,' replied Adam. 'What I'm saying is that I only ever dated girls like that.'

'Am I right in thinking that you're interested in me because it might be time to stop dating girls like that?'

'Look,' he began. 'It's complicated. All I know is that I'm done with that world.'

'How do you know?'

'Because I just know.' An image of the Swedish/ Danish girl flashed in his head.

'Am I supposed to be impressed by this news?' she said, fluttering her eyes lashes in a comically coquettish fashion. 'Oh, the gorgeous and mighty Adam Bachelor is no longer interested in girls who wear underwear as outerwear so now brainy girls with glasses stand a chance!'

'No,' said Adam curtly. 'I'm just saying that I am done dating the wrong kind of girls. I'm only interested in the right kind.'

'And they would be what exactly?'

'Girls you can have conversations with and who will laugh at your jokes; girls who can walk past a mirror without looking into it and aren't always worrying about their nails; girls who your mates like and your mum will think make you a better person; in short the right kind of girl would be a lot like you . . . but obviously not you because as you've been at pains to point out ever since we met, I'm not your type.'

'Three years.'

Once Steph had finished mocking Adam and his attempts to find the right kind of girl the rest of the evening went by in a blur. Deliberately steering clear of the topic of relationships, they chatted about pretty much everything else and at just after midnight with coffees consumed and second bottles of wine finished off their evening together had come to an end. Adam refused Steph's offer to go halves, paid the bill and said he'd walk her home.

'Tell me something about you that would surprise me,' she said, taking Adam by the arm. 'And when I say surprise me I mean really surprise me. I'm not interested in any revelations of the third-nipple variety or anything that involves you once having been a woman.'

Adam thought for a moment. 'OK,' he said, 'I've got something which you'll find surprising but it's not so much about me as about my kid brother Russell.'

'What about him?'

'You know I told you that my middle brother Luke has got a girlfriend called Cassie? Russell is in love with her.'

'Really? Did he tell you this?'

'Of course not,' said Adam. 'Me and Russ haven't got that kind of relationship. We talk about general stuff . . . fun stuff, not anything serious like love. If Russ wanted to unburden his soul he'd probably be more likely to go to Luke than me and given the circumstances that is never going to happen.'

'So how do you know then?'

'It's weird, but I've just picked up on it over time. Changes in Russ's face whenever Cassie speaks to him, the way he hangs on to her every word, snatched glances whenever he thinks no one is looking.'

'And no one else in your family knows?'

'Not as far as I'm aware.'

'And you're pretty chuffed about that, aren't you?'

'Well, wouldn't you be if everyone in your family had you pegged as a jack-the-lad with all the sensitivity of a house brick? I like being able to spot an acute case of unrequited love when I see one. It makes me feel human.'

'And that's your surprising thing? That you spotted your brother's longing for someone he can't have?'

'You sound disappointed.'

'No,' replied Steph with a grin, 'that tone in my voice is actual one hundred per cent shock and awe. I stand corrected, Adam Bachelor: despite what I might have implied earlier today there is definitely more to you than meets the eye.'

At Steph's front door Adam accepted her invitation to come in for a drink. Her terraced house was pretty much everything he expected it to be: ordered, girlie and the absolute opposite of his own. There were a few touches that he liked: a big pop art poster above the fireplace and the fact that as far as he could discern she didn't have a cat. Opening up a bottle of wine in the kitchen they continued chatting as though there really was going to be no end to the evening and then began a conversation about a travel adventure holiday to southern Asia that Steph had been thinking of going on with a friend. This had led to a conversation about holidays and travelling in general, and places they would and wouldn't like to go to one day, and somehow (Adam wasn't quite sure how but no doubt all the wine they had consumed had helped make a connection, no matter how tenuous) they'd got round to talking about relationships: specifically Steph's last one eighteen months earlier with a barrister called Rav.

'Maybe I shouldn't be saying this,' said Adam as Steph concluded the tale of the demise of her relationship, 'but Rav the barrister sounds like a right idiot. How long were you with him again?'

Steph shook her head in disbelief. 'Three years.'

'It took you three years to work out what a jerk he was?'

Steph took a sip of her wine. 'It's very kind of you to gloss over the facts, Adam, but things ended not because he was a jerk but because he went off with someone else.'

'But you would have worked it out though, eh?'

Steph shrugged. 'Who knows? At the time I thought he was the most wonderful man that I'd ever met but now – excuse the image – I wouldn't spit on him if he was on fire.'

'Believe me it was his loss, not yours.'

Steph raised an eyebrow. 'Do you think?'

'Absolutely.'

'I'm not so sure,' she sighed. 'He's married now and I heard on the grapevine that his new wife is expecting twins.'

'But you wouldn't have wanted all that with the wrong man, would you?'

'Rather than never having it at all? Sometimes I'm not so sure.'

'Who said anything about never having it at all?'

Steph shrugged. 'Let's look at the facts: I'm thirty-eight and single. Even if I met someone I wanted to be with tomorrow I couldn't begin thinking kids for another year by which time I'd be thirty-nine, and then of course there's the fact that my fertility is waning the older I get. So let's say optimistically it will take me a year to get pregnant by which time I'll be forty and this is only if I find the right man tomorrow. Now if you factor in the information that it's been six months since I joined an internet dating agency – and no, Adam, I'm not going to tell you which one – and in all that time I've been on three dates, only one of which managed to get to a second date before he was whisked off to Chicago by the company he worked for, then I think you'll appreciate why I feel more than a little fed up about men.' She flopped her head into her hands in mock shame.

Adam instinctively put his arms round her and held her as tightly as he could. After a while because the holding and squeezing thing didn't seem to be doing the trick he started stroking her hair and whispering that she shouldn't worry and that everything was going to be all right. He pulled her closer not as a means to take things further as might have happened in the past but rather to protect her. How weird was that? Adam had somehow become the kind of guy who protected girls like Steph from the affections of guys like him. It made no sense and complete sense all at the same time. This was what it felt like putting someone else's needs before your own. Adam was wishing that this moment would last for ever when something weird happened: Steph reached up and gently guided Adam's lips towards her own and then they kissed for two, possibly three seconds before Adam pulled away.

'Look, Steph,' he said quickly. 'You really don't want to be doing this.'

'And why not?'

'Because you'll regret it in the morning. I know it seems like a great idea now but wasn't it you who said you wanted to be mates and nothing more?'

'Yes.'

'And haven't I got the worst reputation of any man you've known?'

'Possibly.'

'So this,' he gestured to the space between them, 'right here right now is not a good idea.'

She nodded thoughtfully. 'Adam?'

'Yeah?'

'If I say something will you promise not to take offence?'

'Of course, just fire away.'

'Good, because the last thing I want is to offend you. So would you please just shut up and kiss me before you permanently ruin this moment for both us!'

Was this really a meeting of equals as she was indicating or a situation where one party was exploiting an emotionally charged situation for their own gain? wondered Adam. After a few moments of looking into Steph's eyes he had his answer: there was no exploitation to speak of but this certainly wasn't a meeting of equals. The balance of power was all in the hands of the woman opposite him on the sofa and he was powerless to refuse her demands.

'Did he put up much resistance?'

It was the following Sunday morning and Luke was lying in bed imagining that instead of being at some undisclosed address in south Manchester Cassie was actually downstairs in the kitchen assembling the items for their usual weekend breakfast in bed. In his mind's eye cupboard doors were opening and closing; pots and pans were being put on the stove; and Cassie would be making scrambled eggs on toast while the kettle boiled in preparation for their morning mug of tea. Luke pictured Cassie wearing her usual weekend morning uniform: a worn grey-hooded top over an old T-shirt matched with the grey men's pyjama bottoms that she had bought him from Gap for Christmas last year. Her hair would be tied back from her face, her skin devoid of make-up, and she would look completely and utterly delightful. In a moment or two things would start coming together: tea bags with hot water, butter with toast, eggs on plates, cutlery on tray and then very carefully she would bring it through the hallway and up the stairs until she would be outside their room.

After five long minutes in this imaginary world Luke realised that if he was ever going to move on from the past then he had to make some changes to his present circumstances. He climbed out of bed, picked up the cordless phone from its cradle on top of the chest of drawers and dialled his brother's mobile.

'Hello?'

Luke was completely thrown. The voice on the other end of the phone was female and distinctly croaky as if its owner had just woken up.

'Hi,' began Luke. 'I'm trying to get hold of my brother Adam, is he around at all?'

'You're Adam's brother!' The voice at the other end of the phone was suddenly a lot clearer. 'Hi . . . yes . . . sorry . . . Adam's . . . I'll just go and get him.' The sound went muffled but Luke could still make out the sound of his brother's laughter.

'All right, bruv?' said Adam, coming on to the phone. 'What's going on?'

Luke's curiosity was piqued. Was this another one of his brother's conquests? Was he finally done with all of that Right Kind of Girl nonsense? 'Who was that then?'

'A long story,' replied Adam. 'So what's up? No one's seen anything of you in weeks. Is everything OK?

Luke decided he wasn't that interested in his brother after all. 'I've been thinking about how since this whole thing with Mum and Dad kicked off you've had to bear the brunt of it and, well, it's time I did my bit, so while this might be the worst idea I've ever had I think I ought to take my turn in having Dad as a house guest. You've had him for way too long now so basically put the idea to him and if he's OK with it bring him and his stuff round here, say . . . next weekend and I'll take him off your hands.'

'Are you sure? With you going AWOL like that I guessed that you had your hands full.'

'I'm fine.'

'So she's back then?'

'No,' Luke swallowed. 'She's gone for good.'

'And you want Dad to come and live with you?'

'It'll be fine.'

'Fine? Luke, you've barely spoken a civil word to Dad since he left Mum and now you're coping with this thing with Cassie, how is it possibly going to be fine?'

'I don't know, do I?' snapped Luke. 'I haven't got a crystal ball and I can't mind-read either but we'll work something out. So do you want me to take him off your hands or shall I just get Mum to forward his mail round to yours until Christmas?'

There was a long silence that Luke took to be his brother imagining living with Dad until Christmas.

'OK, OK,' said Adam. 'Take him, he's yours. But go easy on him, all right? He's been through a lot and I've got a horrible feeling that it's still a long way from being over.'

On the Saturday of the following weekend at just after nine in the morning Luke looked out of the window of his front room to see Adam pulling up in his Audi with their father in the passenger seat. For the first time in what seemed like years he felt compelled to smile. Was there anything more incongruous than the sight of his sixty-eight-year-old father in a flash German sports car? Luke was sure there wasn't.

As Adam climbed out of the car and popped the boot open Luke wondered how it would be having his dad to come and live with him. It wasn't as though Luke harboured any animosity towards his dad. Though he hated how much his father's actions had hurt his mum he still loved him as much as he ever did. The problem was the sense of disappointment. By choosing to leave Mum he had let not just the family down, but himself too. Now he wasn't just his father who liked sport, gardening and TV game shows, but also some bloke who had secrets, thoughts, feelings and who knew what else going on inside his head, Luke didn't know how to talk to him any more. The normal stuff didn't seem normal and the new stuff was too odd to comprehend.

'Welcome to the Hotel Middle Bachelor,' said Luke, trying to be jovial as he went to help Adam and Dad with the bags. 'How are you, Dad?'

'As good as can be expected.' He winked in Luke's direction just like he used to do when Luke was young. 'So are you going to give us a hand with these bags or what?'

'Yeah, of course,' said Luke, somewhat relieved to discover that this was as awkward for his father as it was for him. 'You leave all that there and I'll sort it out.'

Later, Luke watched as Adam set their dad up in the living room with the TV on louder than strictly necessary before dragging Luke in the direction of the kitchen and closing the door behind him.

'Are you sure about this? Because it's not too late for me to take him back.'

'Of course I'm sure.'

'It'll be a baptism of fire all right,' warned Adam, 'I feel like I ought to leave you with some kind of manual. You know, things that you should and shouldn't do if you want to live successfully with Dad.'

'Like what?'

'Whatever you do make it clear at the start that in the twenty-first century it's OK to eat a main meal that doesn't feature lamb, beef, pork or chicken. You know I like a good steak as much as the next man but Dad nearly freaked out the one time I made him a vegetable chilli because there wasn't any road-kill in it. And the other key piece of advice is to make sure that he remembers to lock the loo door when he goes to the bathroom. I forgot to do that once and well . . . let's put it this way, I didn't ever forget again. Other than that he's OK as long as you let him watch whatever he wants on TV, make him regular cups of tea and drop plenty of hints about broken things that need fixing. Honestly Luke, that man loves mending things more than anything in the world. A while ago I mentioned a broken kettle that I was thinking about throwing away and last week he was up day and night trying to fix it.'

'And did he succeed?'

'Sort of. He spent about twenty quid on spare parts from some shop that he knows on the Manchester

Road. I didn't have the heart to tell him I could have got a brand new one in Tesco five quid cheaper . . . he just seemed so happy I had to let him have his day.'

Luke took out two cans of Coke from the fridge, opened them and handed one to his brother.

'So did he put up much resistance when you suggested that he came to mine?' asked Luke.

Adam shook his head and took a sip from the can. 'I think he could see that he was on the verge of outstaying his welcome.'

'And what did you tell him about Cassie?'

'Not a lot. It's not like you've actually told me a great deal. I just said that I thought you guys might have hit some kind of rough patch and that Cass was living with a mate for a while. Was that OK?'

'It'll do for Dad, won't it. He's not going to interrogate me like Mum would.'

There was a short silence and then Adam said: 'So it is really over then?'

Luke nodded. 'I thought we'd somehow miraculously work out a position where she'd forget about wanting to be a mother some day but it never happened.' Luke looked down at the floor and scratched his arm nervously. 'I can't believe this, you know. I just can't.'

'And there's nothing that you can do?'

'Like what?'

'Like changing your mind for starters.'

'Is that what you'd do?'

Adam shrugged. 'I don't know. It's a messy situation. I can see both points of view.'

'A nice piece of fence sitting there, mate, but no, I don't think I can change my mind.'

'That's a real shame. Mum'll be devastated when she finds out. First Dad, now this . . . she'll feel like the whole family is falling apart.'

'Maybe it is,' said Luke, looking out through the kitchen doorway in the direction of the living room.

'Families can be difficult.'

Monday lunchtime. Russell (along with ninety per cent of the population of Manchester's various office blocks) was in the Market Street branch of Tesco Metro getting together everything he needed to make dinner for Angie and himself that evening. In his shopping basket were the ingredients for baked potatoes and vegetable chilli: two large baking potatoes, a tin of chopped tomatoes, one small tub of chilli powder, a can of kidney beans, a tub of sour cream and a box of mushrooms. He was now trying to locate the chill cabinet that housed Tesco's cheese selection while simultaneously wondering if he was going to be able to fit all his shopping into the fridge they had at work.

Russell couldn't believe how much he was enjoying his life of domesticity. He liked waking up in the morning and feeling Angie's arms still wrapped round him; bringing her a morning cup of tea before he dived into the shower; automatically slipping bread into the toaster the moment he heard her flick on her hairdryer; the text messages and emails that they exchanged throughout the day; the fact that by three o'clock in the afternoon all he could think about was getting home so that he could see her. Even if all they did was eat pasta, share a bottle of cheap wine and watch *Waking the Dead*, it never felt as though the evening had been wasted.

Having located the cheese cabinet Russell selected a packet of on-offer Cheddar, dropped it into the basket and was about to head towards the checkout when he saw a familiar figure staring into the very next chill cabinet. It was Cassie. Without recourse to his conscious mind, his brain conspired with his lips and vocal cords to call out her name.

'Cassie!'

She turned, momentarily bewildered. 'Russ?'

How long had it been since he had seen or heard from her? Weeks? Months? He set down his basket of shopping, stepped over and embraced her just as he always used to do. Though he knew it was wrong it felt good to hold her and as his conscious mind caught up with his subconscious and issued a severe reprimand, Russell noticed that something wasn't quite right. Cassie's embrace wasn't as strong as it used to be; it felt as though he had been holding her while she had merely allowed herself to be held. He looked down and saw that her face was turned slightly in towards him and the palm of her left hand was open and flat against his coat. It was only then that Cassie's tears became audible.

'Are you all right?' he asked, craning his neck to look at her directly. She shook her head. 'What's wrong, Cass? Whatever it is you can tell me, can't you? I'm your kid brother.'

It was a reference to an old in-joke they came up with when Luke and she first got together. Cassie had commented to Russell that she had always wondered what it might be like to have brothers and Russell had joked that if she could put up with Luke for long enough she would find out as he and Adam would officially adopt her into the family and teach her the ways of the Bachelors.

'Come on, you can tell me, Cass.'

She sniffed, repeatedly wiping her eyes with the backs of her hands. 'You don't know, do you?'

'Know what?'

Cassie shook her head. Even though it was difficult to believe, Russell knew that the one thing in the world he had never thought would happen had become a reality.

'Oh, Cass,' he said, squeezing her tightly. 'Mate, listen, don't worry about a thing, OK? Let's get out of here and get you a stiff drink.' And without a second thought about the shopping that he had abandoned on the floor Russell led her towards the exit.

Just like Tesco Metro, the All Bar One on Kings Street was packed with the lunchtime office crowd but thankfully most of them seemed content to stand in large groups talking rather than sitting down at tables so after not too long a wait Russell and Cassie were served and found themselves a spare table at the rear of the bar.

Russell wasn't sure how to play this situation. The idea of Cassie and his brother having split up was just too bizarre. They were the perfect couple. What could have brought them to this point? Neither was the type to cheat, they got on like a house on fire and were engaged to be married. How could they of all people have gone wrong? The answer when it finally emerged took Russell completely by surprise.

'I can't believe it,' he said. 'You guys have really split up?'

'I can't believe Luke hasn't told you.'

'He wouldn't,' said Russell matter of factly. 'It doesn't work like that in our family. I was the last to know when his marriage broke down too. It's a younger child thing. The way it goes in our family is that Adam gets told pretty much everything, Luke knows what Adam chooses to tell him, Mum and Dad get informed on a need-to-know basis and I only find out when there's no way left of keeping it a secret. I don't think anyone in my family accepts that I'm not a snot-nosed schoolboy any more.'

'Families can be difficult.'

There was a long silence. Russell took several sips of his pint while Cassie absent-mindedly stirred the ice in what was left of her vodka and tonic. Russell had a million and one questions but wasn't convinced that this was the time or the place and yet there was one he couldn't prevent himself asking.

'I'm still finding this too hard to believe,' he said. 'There's definitely no way that you and Luke will get back together?'

Cassie shook her head. 'No way at all. It's horrible, Russell. Really horrible because I love him . . .' she corrected herself, 'I *loved* him so much but we couldn't make things work the way they were. It took all the strength I had to leave him. But looking into the future all I could see was the two of us growing more and more resentful of the things that we felt we didn't have.'

They talked some more, focusing mainly on the break-up. Cassie told him about their final conversation. Russell considered his own feelings about Jayne and the niece that he loved but never got to see. Russell had liked Jayne to begin with and had thought that she and Luke had been good together but though he was aware of Luke's faults and understood that there were two sides to every story the evidence spoke for itself: what kind of person would deny the child her right to see her father? Luke might have not been the best husband in the world but he had always been a good father and the Bachelors as a whole had done everything to support both Luke and Jayne. To have taken Megan away like that for spite seemed one of the most cruel acts one human being could perpetrate against another. It was no wonder Luke was so screwed up about starting another family but that didn't make his reasoning right. When you really love someone, thought Russell, you can't let the past dictate the future. When you love someone you have to put his or her needs above your own.

'Listen,' he said, as they jointly realised that they were fast running out of lunch hour. 'I meant it about being your kid brother. Whether you're with Luke or not, you're still family, so if you want anything make sure you ring me. Ring me for a chat, for a drink, or even if you just want someone to be with you while you sit in silence. I'm there for you Cass, OK? All you've got to do is ask.'

'Didn't mean to disturb you.'

Luke was pleased with himself. With a week of living with his father under his belt without a single argument between them he was now officially a saint. The key to his achievement was simple: shutting up in the face of provocation and making every effort to accommodate his father. When on their first Sunday as housemates Dad had woken him from a deep sleep by bringing in a tray containing a full English breakfast Luke thanked him profusely and ate it without question. When the following Monday evening he had returned home from work to discover that his father had pruned back the plum tree in the garden to such an extent that it looked like a very tall twig stuck in the mud Luke thanked him for his efforts and listened keenly to his somewhat radical theories on plum-tree maintenance. And when a few days after that Luke had decided to work from home in order to make some kind of headway through the backlog of admin only to have his father knock on his study door every hour on the hour asking him if he wanted tea/coffee/breakfast/lunch/dinner Luke didn't lose his temper. Instead he resigned himself to the fact that he was never going to get anything done for the rest of the day, called it quits at two p.m. and spent the rest of the afternoon with Dad tackling the nightmare of disorganisation and junk that was his garage.

During this time, although they discussed in a general fashion everything from the latest evolution of Russell's love life through to City's prospects in the premiership, they had yet to a say a single word about Dad's relationship with Mum or his own relationship with Cassie. Of course part of Luke was happy that this was the case. Thanks to his divorce he knew how uncomfortable such conversations could be when undertaken by two people as bad at communicating as he and his father. But at the same time, the longer these subjects went undiscussed the more prominent they became in his own mind and if he didn't do something about it soon, the subject would leap involuntarily from his lips as though he were suffering from a hitherto-undiscovered form of Tourette's Syndrome. With this in mind, pulling back his bedroom curtains and peering at the sun outside Luke made up his mind that today was going to be the day. He would make himself a coffee and then tackle the task at hand.

He was about to make his way downstairs when there was a knock on the door and Dad entered holding a plate with sausages, bacon, eggs and tinned tomatoes on it in one hand and a mug of tea in the other.

'Didn't mean to disturb you. Just thought you might fancy a spot of breakfast. I'll leave it down here, shall I?' He gestured to the floor at the side of the bed.

'Cheers, Dad.'

'Did you sleep well?'

'Fine, Dad. You?'

'Not so bad. That spare bed of yours is a lot more comfortable than you might think to look at it. Did it cost much?'

'I dunno, Dad. I can't remember. I've had it ages.'

Dad nodded but Luke could see that he didn't quite understand how his son could not know what price he might have paid for a major piece of furniture.

'Your mum and I paid six hundred pounds knocked down from twelve hundred for our current bed in the House of Fraser post-Christmas sale eleven years ago. Best bed I've ever slept in.'

Luke was unsure if his dad was genuinely enthused by beds or had simply run out of things to say that wouldn't result in a further widening of the space between them. Whether he had had his morning coffee or not, this was the ideal moment for him to talk to Dad.

'Dad?'

'Yes, son?'

There was a silence. Luke tried to frame the words.

'Son? Did you want to ask something?'

Luke shook his head. He decided to go with a bit of subterfuge to cover his tracks. 'I'm going to go out in a bit, do you want anything?'

'No, son.'

'Right then, I'll scarf this lot down and see you later, OK?'

Dad nodded. He was about to close the door behind him when he stopped.

'Luke? Don't you think it's time we talked about what's happening with you and Cassie?'

Luke let out a huge sigh of relief. 'Do you know what, Dad? I think you're absolutely right.'

Deciding that a change of venue was in order Luke suggested they go to a nearby pub but his father being his father offered a counter-suggestion: 'Why don't we go to Adam's bar? At least that way we'd be keeping the money in the family.'

Luke agreed and so half an hour later they entered BlueBar, found themselves a seat amongst the small scattering of weekend couples reading the papers and tucking into BlueBar's famous all-day English breakfast and got themselves a drink.

'Don't you think it's funny that Adam owns all this?' asked Dad as he took a sip of his half-pint of Guinness.

'I suppose so,' replied Luke. 'When was the last time you were here?'

'I think it was for Russell's twenty-fifth which has got to be a good couple of years ago. How old is Russell now? I always forget!'

'I have no idea. Twenty-seven? Twenty-eight? It's easy to lose count after a while.'

The two men fell into what Luke assumed was a comfortable silence until he looked over at his father's face to see that he seemed to be struggling with something.

'Are you OK, Dad?'

'I was just thinking about your . . . you know . . .

situation and well . . . you do know that you can't just let Cassie walk away like this, don't you?'

'There's nothing I can do, Dad. She wants kids and I don't: there just isn't any room for compromise.'

'But that's not quite true, is it?'

'How do you mean?'

'I mean it's not quite true that you don't want any more children. I know you, Luke, there's nothing more in the world that you'd like than to start a family with Cassie.'

'You don't seem to be getting what I'm trying to say, Dad. I can't move on without Megan in my life. I can't do it.'

'Then you've got to get Megan back in your life.'

'Don't you think I've thought of that?'

'I don't know, have you?'

'Of course I have but . . . but . . . it's just too complicated . . . too much time has gone by.'

Dad shook his head. 'Luke, just listen to me. I know you're scared. I know that deciding not to see Megan was the hardest decision you ever made. And I know that you're terrified of what she might think of you after such a long time. After all you've been through this is the last thing you want to do. But take it from someone who knows: sooner or later the past always catches up with you so you might as well deal with the consequences of your actions now rather than later, because you know what? If you do leave it until later with a girl as lovely as your Cassie there's a strong chance she won't be about for too long.'

'I wouldn't have called it a "ban" exactly so much as a veto . . .'

Russell was reaching for Angie's hand as they crossed the main road on their way back from a night out with Angie's friends. The evening had been a lot more successful than Russell had expected and he had been surprised to have so much in common with Angie's friends' boyfriends considering that at least two of them were accountants.

As Angie's fingers intertwined with his own Russell wondered if this might be the right time to tell her about bumping into Cassie the other day. It didn't feel right not telling her, especially as it had been a completely innocent conversation. Yet he was fearful about her response given the feelings that he'd once had for Cassie.

'So what do you fancy doing at the weekend?' asked Angie, oblivious of Russell's inner turmoil. 'Kate is apparently throwing some kind of surprise party to celebrate Jim's new job and has asked if we can go but we don't have to if you don't want to.'

Russell didn't reply.

'Look, Russ,' continued Angie. 'There's no need to

get all funny about it. We don't have to go if you don't want to.'

He came to his senses. 'What do you mean, funny? I'm sorry, babe, I was a million miles away. I've no idea what you're on about.'

She stopped and looked up at him. 'What's wrong with you? I feel like you've been somewhere else all night.'

'It's nothing really,' began Russell. 'It's just that . . . well, it's sort of weird but I heard today that Luke and Cassie have split up.'

'They've split up? How? Why? I don't understand. Didn't they only just get engaged?'

Russell nodded. 'It's all to do with kids apparently. You know how I haven't seen my niece in years all because of Luke's bitch of an ex-wife? Well it turns out that because of all that Luke told Cassie he never wants to have kids.'

'And Cassie does?'

He nodded. 'Apparently it all came to a head when they got engaged and he wouldn't budge and she wouldn't budge and so it's over.'

'That's so horrible,' she said, putting her arms around him. 'How's Luke taking it?'

'It wasn't Luke who told me. It was Cassie.'

The expression on Angie's face changed in an instant. Gone was the look of sympathy and concern and in its place was one of hurt and outrage.

'You saw Cassie?'

Russell nodded.

'So this isn't about you being upset because of your brother, it's you feeling guilty about seeing Cassie?'

'Look, it's not what you think,' said Russell. 'I was in town and I bumped into her, OK? I didn't know that anything was wrong between her and Luke and we were chatting and then she just came out with it and started to get upset so I took her for a drink.'

'You took her for a drink?'

'Yeah, honestly it was nothing flash. Just a quick drink and a chat. She was upset, that's all, and I was just trying to—'

'Don't you dare finish that sentence. Don't you dare tell me that you were only trying to comfort her!'

'Don't say it like that, Ange. Don't say it like I've done a bad thing here. I've not tried to keep it a secret so why are you having a go at me?'

'Could that be because you were in love with her for about a billion years and spent all day every day fantasising about her?' Angie jammed her hands deep into her coat pockets. 'I bet you loved it, didn't you? Sitting listening to her pouring out all her woes like you were the closest thing that she has in the world to a friend. I bet you lapped it up.'

'Look, it wasn't like that,' pleaded Russell. 'I was just being a mate, that's all.'

'And I'm supposed to feel better because you've said that?' snorted Angie. 'We used to be just mates, Russ, and look where we are now.' Pushing him away from her with her fists Angie walked off leaving Russell standing motionless in the same spot. When she was about twenty or so yards distant she called out: 'You must think I'm really stupid if you thought that I wouldn't be bothered by this, Russ. And I'm not. I'm not stupid and I'm not going to stand for it, OK? I'm not!'

The following morning Russell awoke from a cold and uncomfortable night on the sofa to find Angie kneeling next to him with her laptop underneath her arm. She was still in her dressing gown and her morning breath smelled distinctly of fresh cigarettes, which was an old habit that she only ever relapsed into during times of extreme stress.

Setting down the laptop Angie kissed him gently on the forehead. 'How did you sleep?'

'Badly.'

'If it's any consolation I had a terrible night too.'

'At least you were comfortable. I'd have been better off sleeping on razor blades than this stupid bloody sofa.'

'Look, Russ, I'm sorry. I know I overreacted. It was my fault. I know you were just trying to do what's right and I'm sorry if you feel I've let you down with my whole insanely jealous thing.' She opened her laptop and showed him the screen. It was open on her Facebook page and after a few moments of puzzlement Russell noted that her most current update status read: 'Angie is very sorry for being horrible to her boyfriend last night.' 'See? That's how sorry I am. Now all the world knows how horrible I've been to you.'

He laughed. 'I think that is the sweetest thing anyone has ever done for me.'

'Good,' smiled Angie. 'Because I mean it.'

Later, after breakfast, Russell and Angie left the flat and made their way to the bus stop. As they walked past the crowds of mums taking their kids to school Russell noted that Angie, who was not a morning person at the best of times, was being unusually chirpy, full of humorous stories and anecdotes as though taking it upon herself to be court jester for the day. Relieved that she was so determined to get into his good books he felt they had put the whole incident behind them.

'So that was our first row,' said Russell as they stood waiting for the 187 bus to take them into town, 'it's always good to get these milestones out the way as quickly as possible.'

Angie grinned. 'It would have been a lot better if it had been you who had gone off on one rather than me. I hadn't intended to reveal my bonkers streak for at least another six weeks.'

'Still, it's all sorted now, isn't it?'

She nodded. 'Yeah, we're all good. And anyway, it's not like you're going to see her again, is it. Just stay clear of Tesco and I'm sure we'll be fine.'

'What do you mean, not see her again? Are you banning me from talking to Cassie?'

'I wouldn't call it a "ban" exactly so much as a veto . . . but if you want to call it a ban then by all means feel free to knock yourself out.'

Russell couldn't believe it. 'So you're trying to tell me that I'm not allowed to talk to Cassie?'

'Are you trying to tell me you're planning to see her again?'

'Of course I'm not planning it! I'm not stupid. But I did say that if she needed to talk to anyone then she could talk to me. She's coming out of the end of a long relationship, Ange! All I'm doing is trying to be a mate to her.'

'Well I don't want you to be and anyway this is all academic. She won't want you hanging about reminding her of Luke, will she? Plus, she'll have her girl mates to do all of the crying and wailing stuff with. But if she does call just tell her you're busy.'

Angie reached up and kissed Russell as if to underscore two contradictory messages: a) that she was being light-hearted and b) that she wasn't being light-hearted at all and meant every single word. Either way it was clear from the kiss that as far as Angie was concerned that really was the end of the discussion. The fact that she was waiting for him to kiss her back was her way of asking if he was in agreement with everything that she had said. He of course wasn't in agreement with anything, let alone everything, but as her lips hovered millimetres away from his own he didn't have the strength to carry on the debate and so he kissed her back, convinced that as long as he did his best to stay out of trouble everything would work out fine.

'You are amazing.'

It was early evening on the following Monday, roughly a month into Adam's new relationship with Steph, and Adam was lying on his sofa like a lovelorn teenager rereading the last hour's worth of text messages from his beloved who was away until the following Sunday evening on a training course in Oxford.

Text message to Adam: What are you doing? S xxx

Text message to Steph: Am trying to read that book I picked up from your bookshelf last week: *Love in the Time of Cholera*. Not exactly fast paced is it? How's the course going? Ad xxx

Text message to Adam: Course is OK. People nice. Am missing you though. What manner of madness has possessed you to read *Love in the Time of Cholera*? You'll hate it. S xxx

Text message to Steph: Because it reminds me of you in that it's boring, long-winded and is yellow at the edges!

Text message to Adam: Ha! That is so mean!

Text message to Steph: I know! But seriously I am reading book because of you. Now that we are officially dating I feel I ought to put some effort into making myself appear as clever as you are. The last thing you need is for all your mates to think you've got so desperate that you've started dating down! Really wish you were here! A x

Text message to Adam: Ahhh! How sweet! I wish I were here too! And what do you mean exactly by 'dating down'? There's only one of us dating down here mate and that's you! Seriously, though, could not be prouder of you. Can't wait to show you off to my friends!

As Adam finished rereading Steph's final text a huge grin somehow bolted itself to his face and was refusing to budge. In a deliberate attempt to get rid of it he thought about the piles of invoices at work, but still it remained; then he thought about the fact that the night before last some yob had smashed not just one but both of his wing mirrors and how astronomical the quote had been to get the work done at his local dealership and still it remained; finally he pulled out all the stops and thought about the fact that he hadn't been to the gym because of all the time he'd been spending with Steph and how his midriff was feeling a little bit 'looser' than normal undoubtedly because of all the food he'd been eating with Steph and still the grin remained. There was no doubt about it. This grin was staying put.

Nothing had been the same since their kiss on the night of their first date. Waking up fully clothed in her arms underneath a duvet on her sofa the following morning Adam knew he had just experienced the single best night of his life; and the contrast between his night with Steph and the million one-night stands that he had shared with the Wrong Kind of Girls could not have been more marked. They had talked. They had laughed. But above all they had connected on a more fundamental level than he had ever experienced.

Feeling as though he needed to mark his arrival into the world of fully functioning adult relationships, Adam had carefully extracted himself from Steph's limbs, borrowed her front-door key and sneaked out to the North Star Deli on Wilbraham Road where he picked up two hot chocolates and a huge box of freshly baked pastries. Just as she was stirring from her sleep he presented his purchases to her and had been more than a little startled when she gave him the oddest of looks. Adam's imagination had gone into overdrive as he reasoned that perhaps a surprise breakfast of hot chocolate and freshly baked pastries might have been ex-boyfriend Rav's signature move and now she was thinking about him. Apologising profusely for stirring up memories from the past Adam had been about to get rid of the offending items when Steph had explained that she was looking at him oddly because Adam was being so nice to her. Perplexed at this complexity of thought processes Adam let out a sigh of relief and told her it was no big deal. He sat down on the sofa next to her, turned the TV over to one of the music channels and encouraged Steph to start eating and as they slurped hot chocolate, scoffed down pastries and took it in turns to perform a variety of comical reconstructions of R&B music videos, Adam felt sure that he was on to a good thing.

Back at his own place some time in the mid-afternoon Adam had been about to go to bed when he had received a text from Steph that read: 'Hey you! Am off to bed just wanted to say good night and a huge thank you for the most fun that I've had in a long while. You are amazing. Sleep tight. S xxx.' He had replied straight away (something along the lines that he too had enjoyed himself) and for the rest of the week that followed a constant stream of warm, funny and intimate messages bounced between her phone and his without a single call taking place until, on the following Saturday morning when desperate to see her again, he had called her up directly and asked her out on a second date.

Adam had suggested all manner of restaurants and bars that they could go to but Steph had politely rejected each of his suggestions and instead offered up one of her own: the cinema. Adam had driven them both into town where they then visited the Cornerhouse and watched a French film with subtitles. Indifferent to the film (which to his mind was needlessly complicated) Adam had instead contented himself with simply holding Steph's hand in the darkness while making plans about where they would go to eat afterwards. And later still, full to the brim as they left the small Portuguese restaurant off Deansgate that he had selected, he had driven them back to Steph's house where they had sat up until the early hours talking about nothing.

Now after weeks of dates covering everything from art exhibitions to folk artists in Levenshulme (plus a week-long separation) Adam was now well beyond 'like' with Steph and though he insisted on baulking at the word 'love' whenever his subconscious threw up the concept late at night, at the same time there were moments when he couldn't help but conclude that if what he was feeling looked, smelled and tasted like 'love' then chances were that it probably was.

And now that she was away the clarity of thought that separation sometimes brings persuaded him that there was one last hurdle left before he could relax fully into this new era of his life. Picking up his phone Adam typed out the following message: 'I think it's time you met my family,' and pressed send.

'Are you ready?'

'I think we ought to cancel.'

It was just after ten on the following Sunday morning and Adam was standing at the cooker in Steph's sun-filled kitchen making breakfast for the two of them while Steph sat at the table in the middle of the kitchen and in preference to reading the open newspaper instead chewed pensively on a fingernail.

'Cancel?' Adam turned down the gas underneath the eggs he was currently frying. 'Why would you want to do that?'

'Because I'm not ready!' she said, only half joking. 'I need more time. You know you only get one opportunity to make a first impression.'

'I don't believe you! You've travelled all over the world, stood up to address meetings crammed full of ludicrously rich and powerful business people and run divisions that made a lot of money for your company and you're scared of meeting a little sixty-seven-year-old woman who wouldn't say boo to a goose and her two reprobate sons – who to be frank should be more concerned with impressing you than the other way round. What is wrong with you?'

'I'm nervous, that's all.'

'You'll be fine. All you need to know is that Mum likes fussing during dinner so there's no point in asking her to take a seat, Luke is bound to be a bit off with you because his life is falling apart and Russell . . . well Russell will more than likely fall in love with you the second you say hello.'

'You say all this like it's some kind of a joke! Meeting your family is actually kind of a big deal, you know. I mean, what if they don't like me?'

'Then they won't invite you back.'

'I'm serious, Adam. This is a really big deal.'

'To be fair it's not a really big deal – it's actually *a lot* bigger than that. I didn't want to freak you out but since you're already halfway there anyway I suppose it's time I told you the truth: I have never, ever, ever in all my thirty-eight years brought a girlfriend –' He stopped and raised a solitary ironic eyebrow. 'I take it you are officially my girlfriend now, aren't you?' Steph rolled her eyes in a weary fashion. 'Good,' said Adam, and then continued – 'back to my parents' house for Sunday lunch.'

'Never?'

'Not ever.'

'And you're telling me this now because?'

'Because basically you could walk in that house, slap my mum in the face with a wet fish, put your feet on the table and fart the National Anthem and my family would still think you're the best thing since sliced bread.' Adam paused and turned up the heat under the frying pan until the oil began to froth and spit. 'So are you ready?'

'Yes.'

'For breakfast or to meet my family?'

Steph took a deep breath and exhaled. 'Both.'

From the moment that she first received Adam's text about meeting his family Steph had gone into panic mode even though Adam tried his best to point out that the Bachelors 'weren't the kind of family you have to worry about impressing'. No matter what Adam said to reassure her Steph refused to be reassured and instead demanded that with the little time they had left Adam should make sure she was up to date with every single last bit of Bachelor family trivia.

As they ate breakfast together Steph began to calm down enough to read out various snippets of news she thought worthy of discussion. Although Adam had little or no interest in the article about the investigation of a corrupt MP or the one about the playwright who had written a play that had a bunch of people he had never heard of up in arms, Adam liked the fact that Steph *was* interested in these things. As he sat watching her half chewing on a fried egg sandwich while simultaneously getting irate over a comment in the letters pages he finally accepted something that had only partially occurred to him before this moment: Adam Bachelor (bar owner, man about town and current holder of the title 'second best-looking bloke in Chorlton') had fallen completely and incontrovertibly in love with Steph Holmes.

'Mum this is Steph,' said Adam as he stood in his mother's hallway. 'And Steph this is Mum.'

'I'm so pleased to meet you,' said Joan, in what Adam noted as her 'this is the voice I would use to meet the queen' manner. She was wearing her 'these are the clothes I would use to meet the queen' clothes too, a pale lilac outfit that Adam had only seen her wear once before at his eldest cousin's wedding. She shook Steph's hand, invited her into the front room and asked if she would like a cup of tea.

'I'd love one,' said Steph. 'Is there anything I can do to help?'

'Oh, no,' said Joan. 'I think I've pretty much got everything under control. How do you like your tea? I'm guessing you don't take sugar.'

'You've guessed right,' said Steph. 'No sugar for me but apart from that I'll take it as it comes, thanks.'

Nodding to herself appreciatively as if Steph's no-sugar-in-tea stance was indicative of some great moral worth of which she approved, Joan left the room and returned five minutes later with two cups of tea on a tray, served in the china which only ever got used at Christmas or for visitors of international importance.

'Adam tells me Sunday lunch at your house is a bit of a tradition, Mrs Bachelor,' said Steph as Joan handed her and Adam (even though he hadn't asked for one) the cups of tea. 'I think it's great that you've managed to get your boys to sign up to it.'

'I've always felt that it's important to have family time,' said Joan, taking a seat. 'The boys know I don't care about lavish birthday presents or Mother's Day gifts but if there's one thing guaranteed to make me happy then it's making the effort to come here on a Sunday.'

'She makes it sound like we've got a choice in the matter when it's actually a rule of membership!' joked Adam. 'There was a time a few years ago when I missed a month of Sundays in a row and I swear mum was on the verge of making me hand over my keys to the house!'

'That's not true!' said Joan. 'I don't want Stephanie thinking I'm some kind of tyrant.'

'I'd never dream of thinking anything of the sort, Mrs Bachelor,' said Steph. 'No, I'm just pleased you've invited me to join you. I can't remember the last time I had a proper Sunday dinner let alone the kind Adam's described to me. I hear your roast potatoes are legendary.'

If there had been any doubt in Adam's mind that Steph wouldn't be a hit with his mum it evaporated from this moment. One potato-related compliment was pretty much all it took to make Joan putty in Steph's hand. Seizing the opportunity to make a good first impression Steph chatted away to Mrs Bachelor about the art of the Sunday dinner before widening the conversation to include cake baking, bread making and the pros and cons of organic vegetables. By the time that the doorbell rang and Russell's face appeared at the bay window they were chatting away like long lost friends.

'Stephanie,' said Joan with Russell and Angie in tow, 'I'd like to introduce you to my youngest son Russell and his friend Angie.'

'Lovely to meet you both,' said Steph, rising to her feet and shaking both their hands. 'I know it's a cliché but I've heard so much about you I feel like I already know you.'

'And here's another right back at you,' said Russell. 'Was all of it bad?'

'Adam was actually very complimentary,' said Steph.

'Now I know you're fibbing,' said Russell grinning. 'My big brother never has a good word to say about me.'

'It's true,' said Adam 'Steph was just being polite.' He grabbed Russell around the neck and put him into a headlock.

Steph looked worriedly at Angie as the two brothers wrestled. 'Are they always like this?'

'Pretty much,' replied Angie. 'But you'll get used to it.'

Just before one, Luke turned up and the last introduction of the day was made.

'Steph,' said Adam, 'this is my middle brother Luke: the brains of the family.'

Luke nodded sullenly. 'Hi.'

There was an awkward silence. Adam tutted under his breath and wished that for once in his life Luke could make the effort to be civil. Everybody was aware that his life was falling apart so there was no reason for him to keep making the point.

'Right,' said Joan, immediately coming to Adam's rescue. 'Now let's sit down and do what we're all here for: eat!'

As predicted Steph proved to be a big hit. Russell had started chatting to her about literature the second he spotted a novel by an author he liked poking out of her bag. Luke managed to pull himself out of his current slump long enough to reminisce for a good few minutes about their school days; and Mum seemed buoyed by Steph's presence and much more like her old self even though it was obvious how keenly she felt the absence of both Dad and Cassie. Determined to make the best of a bad job Mum had deliberately sandwiched Steph between herself and Angie, and much to the consternation of the men at the table the three had got on together like the proverbial house on fire. With the exception of when his auntie came to stay, Adam had never seen his mum this animated and he was sure that much of his disquiet came from the fact that their once male-dominated household now seemed to be going the other way.

Volunteering to help clear the table and do the washing up, Adam seized the opportunity to talk to Mum alone in the kitchen while she set out the various dishes of dessert.

'So what do you think, Mum? She's great, isn't she?'

'She's lovely, son. You've picked a right winner there, that's for sure. I don't want to make it seem as though you're hopeless, Adam, but you won't mess things up, will you?'

'No, Mum, of course not.'

'I think she'll be good for you. She's exactly what you need.'

'I'm sure she'll be pleased to hear that, Mum, but you're making it sound like she's on to a rough deal and I ought to get her down the aisle before she works out what's going on.'

'I wasn't saying that, Adam. You're a fine young man and I can't imagine that there's a girl in the world who wouldn't be thrilled to have you in her life.'

'Now that's more like it! And once you're out of earshot I'll make sure to let her know just how lucky she is.'

Helping his mum with the various offerings she had prepared for pudding, Adam followed her back to the dining room where pretty much all of it was demolished within the hour. Keen to prolong the afternoon, Angie suggested they all go for a walk in the park and even though Adam insisted that he didn't really 'do' walking in parks, Mum worried that she didn't have the right kind of shoes and Luke claimed that he just didn't fancy it, they all ended up putting on their coats and heading out for a turn around Chorlton Park before returning home for a cup of tea, a doze and a chat in front of the TV. If there was a top hundred moments in his family history Adam would cherish, this one was it, although he couldn't help but feel guilty about enjoying it so much given his father's absence.

Later, having already said their goodbyes, Adam made an excuse about having forgotten his mobile in order to have one last word with his mother.

'Have you forgotten something?' she asked as he walked through the front door.

'No, Mum,' he replied, determined to get straight to the point. 'I came back because I wanted to talk to you about Dad. Today was great, wasn't it? But it just didn't feel right without Dad being here. I know you don't like talking about it but no matter what happened between the two of you it's time that you made up. Whatever he's done, Mum – and believe me I don't doubt for a second that Dad's at fault here – even without knowing what it was, I can tell that he's sorry. I know it and you'd know it too if you just sat down and spoke to him.' Adam stopped. It was clear from the thin line of his mum's mouth that he had succeeded in ruining what had been one of the best days the Bachelor family had had in a long time.

'Because if you are, I for one think it's a bad idea.'

It was the Wednesday evening of the following week and Luke was sitting in the Beech draining the last dregs from his pint glass while Adam looked on bemused.

'Come on then,' said Adam. 'I know you've got something you want to tell me, you don't normally just call up out of the blue and invite me for a drink, so why don't you give us both a break and spit it out?'

Luke grinned. 'That would be too easy. I'll tell you what though, while I'm building up to my big news why don't you take a moment or two to tell me more about that young lady you brought along to Mum's on Sunday.'

'What's to say?' Adam was keen to play his cards close to his chest. 'You've met her. What did you think of her?'

'I thought she was lovely. In fact too lovely for a guy like you. Is it serious?'

'Do you think I would've introduced her to Mum if it wasn't?'

'Fair point. Introduce Mum to a girl and you know she'll be asking questions about her for years to come.

I still can't believe it though. My big brother going out with a proper three-dimensional girl with a full set of opinions and a fully hardwired brain!'

'Yeah well,' said Adam, tiring of the scrutiny, 'I suppose it had to happen some time.' He took a sip from his glass. 'While we're avoiding your main topic of discussion how's Dad?'

Luke shrugged. 'He's all right I suppose but even I can see that being without Mum is starting to take its toll. You know how busy he was doing things when he was living at yours and when he first moved into mine? Well, this past week all that seems to have ground to a halt. When I go out to work he's still in bed and when I come back he's slumped in front of the TV and the sink is full of washing-up.'

'You know why that is, don't you?'

Luke shook his head.

'It'll be the wedding anniversary that's doing it.'

'Of course! It's only a couple of weeks away. With all that's been going on lately I'd practically forgotten about it but you're right. I can't imagine that it's slipped Mum's mind or Dad's for that matter. For all their talk of being casual it was going to be a big deal for them. So what do we do?'

Adam shrugged. 'What can we do other than cross our fingers and hope for the best?' Adam drained his pint and looked over at his brother. 'So now that we're both in as cheery a place as we can possibly be are you going to tell me this news of yours or what?'

'Well, it's like this,' began Luke. 'I'm feeling a bit

odd and I need a second opinion on something I've just done.'

'What exactly?'

'I made a phone call.'

'Who to?'

'To Jayne,' replied Luke. 'As in Jayne my ex-wife.'

Searching out his ex-wife's telephone number after his conversation with his dad Luke had been disappointed but not surprised to discover that the last number he had for her was no longer working. Refusing to give up after his first setback he searched out the last communication he had received from Jayne's solicitor and then wrote requesting that they forward Luke's contact details along with a message that he wished to get in touch with her. Determined to keep up the momentum he then found the contact details for Jayne's parents and a number of her close friends and left messages with all. While there was no doubt that his scattergun approach had as much potential to drive her away as it did to make her contact him, he really didn't have a choice. As his father had pointed out, every moment that passed in which his situation remained unchanged was potentially another moment in which Cassie could be getting closer to someone else.

A week and a half after his initial burst of activity Luke returned home from work to discover a solitary answerphone message and heard the voice of his ex-wife for the first time in years. The message simply said that she would call back later and hope to find him in.

The effect on Luke was immediate and he found himself choking back tears at the thought that this call might represent a first step towards seeing his little girl again.

Two days later she called back just as Luke was thinking about going to bed. The conversation although short was warmer than Luke had imagined possible given their history and she suggested that they meet up at the nearest opportunity. Without offering her current whereabouts she asked if he still visited London; he assured her that he would meet her whenever and wherever she chose.

'You did what?' spluttered Adam. 'Why would you do that? You're not thinking about getting back together, are you? Because I for one think it's a bad idea.'

'Of course I'm not thinking about getting back with her. This isn't about her so much as Megan. Seeing her is the only way I'm ever going to be able to see Megan.'

'So when are you going to see her?'

'Next Wednesday in London. I've booked the whole day off. There's a bar in Covent Garden that we used to go to when we first moved to London that's still going so I said I'd meet her there and we'd decide exactly what to do after that.'

'And she sounded OK?'

'She seemed a bit . . . I don't know, edgy I suppose, but it was nowhere near the hard work I was expecting. I don't know if I'm reading too much into all this but it was almost as if she knew that one day I'd call and because I had she was at least going to make this bit easy for me.'

'And there was no mention of Megan?'

'Not a word.'

'And what do you make of that?'

'Nothing. Neither of us mentioned Megan but Jayne knew as well as I did that she was the reason I was calling.'

'And choosing London? Do you think they live down there?'

'Maybe, who knows? She could have got a new job or moved that way with a new partner. We could spend all day speculating but what would be the point? All that matters is that I see her. Because if I see her then I'll get to see Megan and then I'll be able to stop living in the past. After that if it's not too late Cassie and I will finally be able to get on with our lives.'

Arriving home from BlueBar some time after ten Luke really wanted to call Cassie and tell her about everything that was going on. He even got as far as scrolling through his phone book for her mobile number before turning it off and throwing it on to the sofa. He knew it wouldn't be fair to intrude in her life until everything that was broken inside him was fixed.

Luke started to tidy up the house but even as he began loading the dishwasher his heart wasn't in it and he wandered back into the living room, pulled down one of three photo albums sitting on the shelf and opened it up.

On the first page was a picture of Luke and Jayne taken on the first day of their honeymoon in the

Seychelles. They were standing by the edge of their resort's swimming pool with the blue-green Indian Ocean acting as the perfect backdrop. Luke looked into the eyes of this younger version of himself and marvelled at just how much he had been in love. They had both believed their love would last for ever. And after all these years apart older, wiser versions of their past selves would soon be coming together in the hope of making sense of the mess things had become.

'She's amazing.'

Today was D-Day. After barely a few hours' sleep he was up, showered and dressed at six a.m. and following a hurried breakfast had called a cab to take him to Piccadilly even though the train he was booked on wasn't leaving until five minutes past nine. Loitering on the concourse for the train to be announced, Luke had been amongst the first passengers but as his carriage filled and everyone around him pulled out laptops, books and newspapers for their journey he noted he was the only person doing nothing. He took off his jacket and stared out of the window, lost in his thoughts.

A few hours later Luke had made his way to Leicester Square by Tube and then walked along Long Acre to his destination. Descending the steps into the bar he ordered a coffee and took a seat at a table opposite the entrance so that he would be able to see Jayne the moment she walked in.

The bar hadn't changed a great deal from the days when it had acted as a second home to Luke and Jayne. The distressed-looking piano at the rear of the room, the basic and uncomfortable seating, the persistently wobbly tables, all were the same. Thinking how comforting this lack of change was in a world where everything else was in a state of flux, Luke waited patiently for his coffee to arrive and was in the middle of stirring two large lumps of brown sugar into it when he noticed the glass doors to the bar open and Jayne was standing in the doorway looking right back at him.

What surprised Luke wasn't the fact that his heart immediately started racing or that he automatically rose to his feet in anticipation of her arrival but rather that the anger and bitterness he had felt sure would flood his system the moment she arrived failed to make its expected appearance. The unsettled feeling in his stomach was evidence it was still there but what was missing was the trigger. Luke had thought that the very act of being in the presence of this woman who had ruined his life, who had taken away the person he had loved most in the world, would have been more than enough to cause him to vent the full force of his anger. After he had first stopped seeing Megan there had been times when all he had thought about was having his revenge on Jayne, making her experience a fraction of the suffering he had felt at her hands. Now all that hatred and bile, though present, was under control, waiting, lurking, for its moment of release.

Exchanging wary smiles in lieu of physical contact Luke asked Jayne what she wanted to drink, ordered it at the bar and then returned to his seat.

'I knew that you'd call one day,' said Jayne quietly. 'I knew that you'd want Megan back in your life.'

'I always wanted Megan in my life, Jayne. Always.'

'I know, of course you did. I didn't mean it like that, I meant that . . . I don't know . . . I meant that I knew you'd never forget her. Despite everything that happened I always knew that you weren't that kind of man.'

'How is she?'

'She's amazing.' Jayne reached into her bag and pulled out an envelope full of photographs. 'I had these printed up for you. You know the kind of thing . . . birthdays, Christmas, holidays.'

Luke grazed his fingers across the envelope but didn't open it. 'Thanks. I really appreciate the thought.'

One of the bar staff arrived with Jayne's coffee and set it down in front of her. She looked around. 'This place hasn't changed much, has it?'

'No, not really.'

'What made you choose it?'

Luke shrugged. 'I don't really know you any more and you don't really know me. So it seemed sensible to choose somewhere from back when we did know each other.'

'I'm glad you did,' said Jayne.

Over the next half-hour she proceeded to tell Luke the story of her life from the point at which he had ceased to be a part of it, although at times she seemed to be deliberately vague as though fearful that her words might at some point be used against her. From what Luke could gather Jayne and Megan had only lived in Brittany for a year before homesickness resulted in both her and her parents returning to Bath. Having been employed in a number of part-time jobs while Megan was young Jayne was now working in marketing for a computer software company and was apparently doing very well. Interspersed amongst all this were various tales of failed relationships and long and involved rows and complications with her parents that seemed to indicate she was no longer living with them. After listening patiently for a long time Luke sat up abruptly, looked her straight in the eye and said: 'I don't care about any of this, Jayne. I really don't. All I care about is Megan. I want to know how she is and I want to know where.'

'I'm sorry,' she said quickly. 'I know I should've come to the point but I couldn't help myself. I got scared when I heard that you were trying to get in contact with me. Before I say anything more I want you to promise that this isn't about trying to take her away from me.'

Luke couldn't believe what he was hearing. How dare she sit across from him and demand that he promise not to take their daughter away when that was exactly what she had done to him? How dare she make any demands of him? That seemingly innocent comment unlocked every last bit of anger that he felt towards her and he lost all sense of proportion and level-headedness. 'And what if it was, Jayne?' he said, slamming his open palms down on the table in a sudden burst of anger. 'What if it was about me wanting to take our daughter away from you? Would that be your worst nightmare? Because if so then maybe I should try it! At least then you'd know what my life's been like since you took her away from me!'

Everyone in the bar was looking at them so Luke tried to calm down but it felt like an almost impossible task. All he wanted to do was vent all the pain and the anger that he had stored up for so long. He wanted to yell and scream at Jayne until she was in tears.

'I can't do this,' he said, standing up abruptly. 'I thought I could but I can't. If you're any kind of human being at all you'll tell Megan that her dad loves her with his whole heart and will never ever forget her. But as for this . . . me talking to you here and now while you dare to ask me not to do the things you've done to me, well we're done. And we're done for good. I never want to see or hear from you ever again. Megan will come and find me one day, I know she will. And when she does I will tell her every last twisted and evil thing that you have done to keep us apart.'

'I think you did a better job of being a member of the Bachelor family than any of the rest of us ever did.'

It was the following Thursday evening and Russell was on his way out of work when his mobile rang.

'Hello?'

'Hi, Russ, it's me,' said Cassie needlessly. His breathing had speeded up simply at the sound of her voice.

'Hey you,' he replied. 'Is everything OK?'

'Everything's fine. I'm just calling because . . . well . . . when I last saw you . . . you mentioned that if I ever needed to talk to someone . . . you don't have to of course, it's just . . . I don't know, I feel like all my friends . . . they're great and everything and I'd be lost without them but none of them really know Luke . . . do you know what I mean? Not in the same sense that you and I know Luke and I'm still trying to make sense of it all and I'm finding it really difficult and it's our anniversary next week and anyway I was thinking about it all and . . . well, I don't know, I just sort of hoped that you wouldn't mind . . . you know, for old times' sake at least, meeting up with me.'

'Listen, it's fine, Cass. Really. I'd love to meet up with you. I said you could call me any time and I meant it. When were you thinking?'

'Well, I was actually thinking about tonight if that's convenient?'

Russell felt sick with tension. He couldn't possibly do tonight. Angie had been texting him all afternoon about the special meal she was making for him. There was no way he would be able to get out of that without causing his early demise. He could however do the weekend. Angie was heading up to Blackpool first thing on Saturday morning for her friend Rebecca's hen do and had already informed him that if the last hen do was anything to go by it was unlikely that she would make it back to Manchester before Sunday evening. 'I can't really do tonight, Cass. I've got something on which I can't cancel but how about Saturday? Maybe in the afternoon. I could do any time that you like then. We could go for a coffee or something?'

'Thank you,' said Cassie, genuinely pleased. 'Why don't I text you tomorrow and we'll work out the details?'

'That sounds great,' replied Russell. 'Hear from you tomorrow.'

For the first few moments after waking up on Saturday morning Russell felt as though this was just another ordinary day. Although Angie was nowhere to be seen he could hear her in the shower through the thin walls of the flat and feel the last traces of her body's warmth lingering on the sheets. Thinking about Angie made

Russell happy. Thinking about Angie going away for the weekend however made him feel nervous and thinking about Cassie in any way, shape or form made him feel as if he was the repository for all the guilt in the world.

The main reason for his guilt was because he had agreed very much against Angie's express wishes to see Cassie that afternoon but there were other more subtle reasons to feel guilty too. The first was that he had yet to tell Cassie he even had a girlfriend, let alone that he was living with one. Why for instance had he chosen to tell her that he had 'something on' rather than the more accurate 'my live-in girlfriend's cooking dinner for me'? Then there was the fact that, faced with the dilemma of when to see her, an alternative time had come to him so quickly – and why Saturday afternoon of all times? If he really didn't have any feelings for her then why hadn't he simply suggested that he saw her in the evening? Had he chosen an afternoon meeting because he thought it was safer? And if it was safer, what danger exactly was he trying to prevent? Russell had a bad feeling about the day. A very bad feeling indeed.

At five minutes to one Russell made his way up the steps to the Lead Station and poked his head through the doors looking for Cassie. Generally speaking Russell avoided places like this at the weekend because they tended to be packed to the rafters with people having better weekends than his own but when Cassie sent him a text suggesting this as a potential venue he had said yes immediately.

Ordering a coffee at the bar Russell wondered if he should have waited until she arrived but then just as he was in the process of calling the waitress back over to cancel his order Cassie walked in and with her entrance he seemed to lose the power of speech.

She made her way over and within a few moments was squeezing him tightly as she had done a million times before, except this time it felt different, more intense, as though they were sharing some kind of unspoken bond. Russell didn't want the embrace to end. He relished feeling needed by her. He loved being someone who had the power to comfort her instead of simply being her 'kid brother'.

'So have you heard from Luke at all?' asked Russell twenty minutes into their conversation.

Cassie nodded. 'We spoke last week about a few loose ends: bills that needed paying, mail that needed forwarding, that kind of thing.'

'And did you get any sense that he wanted to . . . I don't know . . . fix things?'

'He was in tears by the end of the call. We both were. It's just a horrible situation. It's like he's stuck in this continuous loop that doesn't make any sense. He says he loves me and he wants to be with me and would never want to deny me anything that would make me happy and then in the next breath he's telling me that I did the right thing and that I have to move on because he can't see any way round this mess. Does that make any sense to you?'

Russell shrugged. 'It's hard to say, Cass. It broke his heart when he stopped seeing Megan. He wasn't himself for a long time afterwards. So I can sort of understand his reluctance . . . not that you might do what Jayne did . . . but he probably sees the idea of having more kids as some sort of betrayal of Megan.'

Cassie just sat shaking her head for a while, clearly trying her best not to cry. 'Have you seen him lately?' she asked eventually. 'Is he doing OK?'

'I haven't seen him in a while,' replied Russell. 'I only know Dad's living with him now because Mum mentioned it in passing. I think that's what's wrong with all us Bachelor men . . . we're completely crap at communicating with each other.'

Cassie attempted a smile and just about succeeded. 'Oh come on, Russ, that might be true of your brothers but it's hardly true of you, is it?'

'I think it might be, you know. I talk to Mum because I was her last kid and so she and I are a bit closer than the rest of the family but since all this stuff with Dad kicked off, I've barely seen him. Adam always seems really busy and Luke's pretty much kept himself to himself. I don't think you really understood this but you . . . well, you were really good for us all. You brought us all out of ourselves and made us more relaxed. I mean take that whole fortieth anniversary thing you were planning. Obviously it doesn't look like that's going to happen now but if it hadn't been for you none of us would have given it a thought. I think you did a better job of being a member of the Bachelor family than any of the rest of us ever did.'

'I've done the male-dominated household and let me tell you, it's hard work.'

Russell and Cassie talked for hours. In fact they talked for so long that only when Cassie excused herself from the table to make a trip to the loo did Russell emerge from the trance-like state into which he had fallen during the time he had spent in her company. Looking around the café it became apparent how much time had elapsed. The faces of the patrons at surrounding tables had changed without him even registering their passing and the influx of newcomers (women with babies, couples reading newspapers, groups of friends all laughing and joking with each other) who had appeared as if by stealth was startling.

Double-checking that Cassie was nowhere to be seen Russell pulled out his phone and finally read the text messages that he had deliberately chosen to ignore. They were all from Angie.

> **Message 1:** Hey you, just to let you know that we arrived safely, have had a long boozy lunch and are now heading for the rollercoasters! Miss you loads. A xxx

Message 2: Have just been showing the girls all the pictures of you that are on my phone. They are all in agreement that you are by far the best-looking boyfriend I have ever had! Don't let your head swell!!!! Love you loads. A.
Message 3: It's cocktail time! Love you xxx
Message 4: It's still cocktail time!!!! xxx
Message 5: Cocktail time has claimed first casualty. Bride to be's sister is throwing up in loos as I type!!! Miss you crazy legs! A xxx

Russell was about to compose a reply that would go some way to making recompense for his earlier non-replies when another message arrived.

Message 6: Am v. drunk!!!! Have I told you how much I love you? RUSSELL BACHELOR YOU ROCK MY WORLD!!!!!!! XXXX

Nervously biting his lip as he kept look out for Cassie Russell typed the following reply: 'I'll make sure that we're well stocked with Nurofen for your return home!!! Love you, you mentalist! R xxx' and then pressed send just as Cassie returned to the table.

'What's up with you? You look a little bit shifty.'

Russell looked up. 'It was nothing,' he said, quickly shoving his phone into his trousers pocket. 'Just a mate sharing a bit of an in joke that we've got going on. So what now?'

'Haven't you got anywhere you need to be?' asked

Cassie. 'Come on Russ, there's no need to be polite. You've gone way beyond the call of duty now, OK? You don't really have to waste any more of your weekend looking after me.'

'I have no plans,' said Russell with a grin. 'Because like you I have no mates and no life so why don't we carry on hanging out together until one or other of us gets bored?'

'That's what you really want to do?'

'No, Cass, that's what I *really, really* want to do.'

'You do realise that you're making both of your brothers look like poor choices in comparison, don't you?'

'Yeah, I've been thinking it's about time someone put them in their place.'

Allowing Cassie to take his arm Russell made his way out on to the pavement where Beech Road was now practically swimming in smug-looking couples who were doing the weekend strolling thing. Russell couldn't help a small glow of pride at the thought that every one would jump to the conclusion that he and Cassie were together. It was like being in a dream and yet fully awake. If he didn't keep his mouth shut he would be sure to involuntarily communicate the pleasure he was feeling in a fashion that would leave both of them severely embarrassed.

With no plan in mind they strolled aimlessly, content to simply walk and talk in what remained of the day's sun, and eventually found themselves heading into Chorlton Park where they sat down on a bench overlooking the children's play area.

'How could anyone not want one of those?' asked Cassie,

pointing out a little girl wearing a pink T-shirt and yellow shorts chasing after a ball. 'Look at her, she's adorable.'

'You're right.'

'Do you want to have kids one day?'

The question took him by surprise. 'Me?' he spluttered. 'Do I want to have kids?'

She laughed. 'It's not that hard a question, is it?'

Russell thought for a moment. 'Yeah. I suppose I would like to have them some day.'

'Girls? Boys? Don't care?'

'Girls definitely,' said Russell. 'I've done the male-dominated household and let me tell you, it's hard work.'

'And a female-dominated one isn't? Even when I was a teenager I used to feel sorry for my dad having to put up with me and my sister and all of our ballet lessons, pony obsessions and constant demands for new clothes when all he really wanted was someone to take to the park for a quick kick around with a football. And I don't know how he must have felt when we first started going out with boys. He must have worked out a way of blanking it all from his mind!'

'None of that bothers me. I've always liked girls. They're more straightforward and loads easier to talk to about stuff.'

'You'd make a great dad. You'd be really understanding and patient.'

Russell looked back over at the playground where two little girls, clearly sisters, were sitting on the see-saw taking it in turns to scream at the top of their voices. 'How about you?' asked Russell. 'Judging by what you've just said my guess is that you'd like boys.'

'And you'd be wrong. I wouldn't care one way or the other. Boys, girls, I wouldn't mind. I'd like at least three though. Three's a good number for a family, don't you think?'

Russell shrugged. While he was sure that he hadn't missed out on anything being the youngest child of three he suspected that Luke harboured a few issues about being the middle child.

'Kids are important, aren't they? They bind you together with the love of your life and ground you completely.' She began to get upset. 'I just don't get it. Why didn't Luke want to start a family with me? Why did I have to make a choice between the man I love and having children that let's face it I might never have? It's just not fair. Luke got to experience being a dad, why shouldn't I get the chance to be a mum?'

As Cassie started to cry Russell put his arms round her and concentrated on the sensation of her body pressing against his own. Part of him wanted to say something that would comfort her but most of him wanted to kiss her and so he reached out, gently lifted her chin until her lips were perfectly positioned with his own and then did so. For a moment or two he was convinced that she was kissing him back but as quickly as the moment had begun it was over.

Cassie regained her composure, stood up and moved away from him. 'I'd better go,' she said, avoiding his gaze. 'I'd really better go.' Without another word she turned and walked away.

'Let's not keep madam waiting.'

Saturday morning found Adam loading up the boot and back seat of his car with weekend suitcases. For the first time he and Steph were going away overnight to attend the wedding of one of Steph's university friends in Stratford-upon-Avon.

'Do we really have to do this?' moaned Adam, who would much have preferred to follow their usual relaxed routine of eating nice food and taking in cultural events that he wasn't interested in. 'If there's one thing I loathe it's going to the wedding of a complete stranger.'

'She's not a complete stranger,' said Steph patiently. 'She was one of my best friends back in my uni days.'

'But she's not any more, is she?'

'You're more than welcome to stay here if you like but I'd just like to point out that you would be missing out.'

'On wedding cake and pointless small talk with strangers?'

Steph shook her head and raised an enigmatic eyebrow. Eventually he got the message. 'Are you saying what I think you're saying?'

'I might be.'

'Really?'

'Well, put it this way: I've spent a small fortune on underwear and I really don't want it to go to waste.'

'Right then,' said Adam, starting up the car. 'Let's not keep madam waiting.'

For the most part the drive down to the Midlands along the M6 was uneventful. Adam steadily worked his way through the playlist that he had made for the journey on his iPod while Steph dozed in the passenger seat in a bid to make sure that she didn't fall asleep at the reception, but just outside Stoke the traffic came to a complete standstill and Adam began to wonder whether they would make it to their destination at all.

'Worried about us making it on time?' asked Steph.

'Amongst other things.'

'I can't help you on traffic jams but I might be able to help you with the other stuff if you want to share.'

Adam squeezed Steph's hand briefly. 'I'll be fine.'

'That's the thing about you,' said Steph, sitting up upright. 'You like to cope. Coping is what you do. But have you thought that there might be a more straightforward solution?'

'Like telling people what's on my mind?'

'It's a novel approach but I've heard it actually works for some people.'

'OK, it's like this: basically I was thinking how if I'd met you back at the beginning of the summer and you'd asked me to go to this wedding I would've had to say no.'

'Because you don't like weddings?'

'No, because Monday is supposed to be my parents' fortieth wedding anniversary and we'd have thrown the party that we were planning for them today.'

'Oh, Adam, why didn't you say? The last place you'll want to be this weekend will be at a wedding. Look, let's forget it and turn back home or better still go off on an adventure for the weekend.'

'You really would do that, wouldn't you,' said Adam, surprised by the rush of love that he felt for her. 'You really wouldn't care if we didn't go.'

'Not if it's going to upset you, of course not. So where should we go instead?'

'Nowhere. I'm fine with us going to the wedding. There's nothing I can do about my parents, is there? I didn't tell them to split up so I'm guessing it's up to them to get themselves back together if it's what they want.' The traffic had started to move. 'Anyway,' he pulled off the handbrake and they started crawling forwards, 'maybe this whole wedding anniversary thing will make them take a long hard look at everything they're putting at stake. Maybe it'll make them see just how important the family really is.'

For the next hour all Adam and Steph did was talk about family. Steph spoke about her mum's illness and her subsequent passing away but also about all the good times that they had shared as a family of two. As she spoke about her past Adam found himself gaining a deeper understanding of why Steph was the way she was and of the things that she really wanted to get from life. Suddenly the conversation they had

had about her ex-boyfriend and the tears she had cried on the night they first got together made much more sense. Steph hadn't been lamenting the end of her relationship but rather the passing of what must have felt like her last opportunity to make a family of her own to replace the one that she had lost.

Arriving at their destination just before midday Adam and Steph made their way down the long and winding driveway of what was clearly a former stately home.

'This must have cost a bomb, if they've hired the whole place,' said Adam, looking out at the expanse of greenery towards the huge house mounted in the middle of the landscape. 'What did you say your friends do again?'

'She works in the City and I think he's some kind of top guy in the Civil Service. Sarah's always telling me about how he's just had a meeting with this or that minister so he must be quite important.'

Adam lifted up his sunglasses and looked at Steph. 'You do realise that I'm not going to have a single thing in common with these people, don't you?'

She leaned across and kissed him. 'Doesn't matter, my friend,' she replied. 'All I care about is that you have everything in common with me.'

Pulling into the car park at the rear of the hotel Adam and Steph unloaded their bags, checked into their room, got changed and were back downstairs in the reception waiting area within the hour.

'You look great,' said Adam, taking in Steph's simple but elegant dark green dress.

'And you don't look so bad yourself. A touch like an East End gangster but in this context that's no bad thing.'

The afternoon went a lot better than Adam had expected. Determined not to embarrass Steph he gave his best efforts to the making of small talk even when the small talk got so tiny that it was invisible to the naked eye. He refrained from overindulging at the free bar despite waiters thrusting champagne into his hand at every opportunity. Some time after eight when the cake had long since been cut, speeches made and first dances taken, Steph turned to Adam and smiled.

'What?' he asked, eyeing her suspiciously.

'I want to go.'

'Where?'

Steph rolled her eyes. 'Where do you think? Back to our room. I keep thinking about our lovely room and the fact that we're not in it. They'll kick us out by midday! Let's sneak out now before we're missed!'

Laughing as Steph grabbed his hand Adam followed her out of the ballroom and they ran full pelt along the corridor, through the main reception and up the stairs to their room. After frantically searching around in her clutch bag for the keys Steph opened the door, pulled Adam in and once the door was fully closed threw herself on to him showering him with kisses as they both began to undress. As Adam struggled to take off his jacket without removing his lips from Steph's his phone rang. He reached inside his pocket in order to switch it off for good and inadvertently noticed that the call was from his mum.

'Talk about timing!'

'What is it?'

'It's my mum. I'd better take it just to make sure that she's all right. Is that OK?'

'Of course. Anyway, I could do with a minute to get this dress off without ruining it.'

'Hi, Mum, everything OK?'

'No,' she replied. 'It's not. It's not at all. I've decided I'm going to divorce your father.'

'But why? I don't get it, Mum. Whatever it is it can't be all that bad, surely?'

'Well it is to me.'

'What has he done? You can't expect to take things this far and not tell us.'

'He had an affair.'

'Dad? An affair? Are you sure? When exactly?'

'Forty years ago.'

Part 3

'I don't understand.'

It was one in the morning as Adam pulled up in front of Steph's house and switched off the car engine after the 117-mile journey from Stratford-upon-Avon to Manchester.

'Are you sure you won't stay over at mine?' said Steph. 'You wouldn't have to talk if you don't want to. I just want to be with you, that's all.'

Adam shook his head. 'I'm fine, honest,' he replied, half wondering if she was aware that this was the beginning of the end for them. 'I just want to get some sleep.'

He climbed out of the car and took Steph's luggage out ready to take it up to the house but she made him put it down so that she could put her arms round him.

'If you won't stay with me then at least promise that you'll call me first thing in the morning. I won't pry or anything. I just want to know that you're OK.'

'Of course,' nodded Adam. 'First thing in the morning.'

They kissed, a long, slow kiss, and then picking up her bags Steph made her way to her front door. Adam watched as she opened her door and then closed it behind her. Taking one last look at her house as she switched on her bedroom light he drove away into the night.

The past few hours had been some of the toughest in his entire life. With his mum in tears at the end of the phone he had listened to the story of his father's affair that had shocked him to his very foundations.

According to his mum, before she and Dad got married they had been friends with another young courting couple from the area called Janet and Charlie. At some point in the proceedings his dad's friend Charlie had broken his engagement with Janet and run off to a new job and a new life in Aberdeen, leaving Mum and Dad back in Manchester to sweep up the pieces. His mum and dad had ended up spending a lot of their spare time comforting Janet which ultimately led to the inevitable back at Dad's lodgings off Cheetham Hill Road. It was six months before Adam's parents' wedding and as the affair continued Janet eventually confessed to Adam's dad that she was in love with him and pleaded with him to leave his fiancée. After various threats to tell Adam's mum (and even at one point to take her own life) Janet finally said she was leaving Manchester for good and that she would never see Dad again, which was exactly what happened.

'I don't understand,' Adam had said. 'If this all happened forty years ago why has it come out now?'

'It was the day that Luke and Cassie announced their engagement,' his mum revealed. 'Do you remember while Luke was helping me make the tea for everyone, Cassie, I think it must have been, asked your dad to get the wedding album out and he ended up telling you all the story of how Janet hadn't turned up for the wedding and how your Aunt Rose had had to step in as maid-of-honour at the last minute?'

Adam struggled to recall Dad getting out the wedding album let alone his story about Mum's maid-of-honour but with some prompting it had come back to him. 'But I still don't understand, Mum, why would you make a connection all these years later about something that happened forty years ago?'

'Because of the expression on his face as Cassie retold the story when Luke and I walked in the room,' she had explained. 'Your dad just looked guilty, son; he looked as guilty as sin. But it was only when I finally plucked up the courage to ask him all those weeks later that I knew for sure. Before he'd even answered my question I could see from his look of relief that he just couldn't lie to me about this one thing any more.'

His mum tearfully explained how even though it would hurt her as much as it would hurt his father she had come to the conclusion that getting a divorce was the only option. No matter which way she looked at the situation and no matter how hard she tried to forgive him and move on, she just couldn't do it.

'Believe me, Adam, there's no one who wanted to save this marriage more than me but I can't get over the fact that he lied to me, and not just once or twice but every day for forty years. I love him dearly, and I always will, but this is something I can't bring myself to forgive.'

Adam ended up staying on the phone for a good half-hour listening to his mum say pretty much the same thing over and over again, but then she told him that she was going to stay with Aunt Rose for a few days and asked if he would tell his brothers about the divorce because she didn't have the strength to do it herself. All Adam wanted to do was head back into the hotel room where Steph was waiting for him and tell her everything. That was what his heart was telling him even though the thought of being this open and honest about something so painful was uncharted territory for him. But the moment he saw the look of concern on Steph's face, the moment he realised the real reason he had spent so long in pursuit of the wrong kind of women, was the moment that he couldn't follow through with his actions. In Steph, who had in their short time together proved herself the perfect confidante, he saw his worst nightmare writ large. If he told her how he was feeling, if he poured his heart out to her, if he pulled down his final barricade and let her inside the one place that he knew to be safe then he would never be able to hide anything from her ever again. Not a single thought, not a single feeling; effectively she would have the keys to his consciousness and would be free to come and go just as she pleased. The thought of this terrified Adam. It terrified him to his very core. Not because of what she might do with her access but rather with the newness of it all. This wasn't a game whose rules he understood and right now he didn't care to learn.

So instead of being open and honest Adam chose to disguise his upset as best he could. Refusing to go into the details he said only, 'Some more stuff with my parents has kicked off and I need to go.' He suggested that Steph shouldn't let him ruin her weekend and should stay and get a lift back to Manchester with one of her friends. But Steph refused on the grounds that 'a night on my own in a beautiful hotel room without you would be a nightmare,' so she too had packed her bags and they had made their way to the car.

For the two-hour journey back up to Manchester Adam barely said a word. And even though his actions were amongst the biggest clichés in the male behavioural lexicon this awareness didn't help him in the slightest. It didn't help to know that he was 'emotionally withdrawing' from Steph. All that mattered was that the more distance he put between himself and Steph the more secure he felt. And nothing, not Steph, not his conscience, not even love itself was going to get in the way of his mission to be alone.

Reaching home Adam kicked off his shoes, dumped his bags in the hallway and was about to go upstairs when his phone vibrated. A message from Steph: 'I love you.' He switched off his phone and without thought or reflection made his way up to his bedroom, closed the curtains, crawled under the duvet and finally allowed himself to be consumed by exhaustion.

'Because it wasn't just a small tiff.'

It was late morning. Adam had showered and dressed and was heading downstairs for breakfast when his phone rang. His heart immediately began to race. It would be Steph checking to see how he was. If he spoke to her she would know that something other than this thing with his parents was up. She would ask him what was the matter and he would have to stonewall her which would end in a row and then at the height of all the yelling and the accusations and counter-accusations he would finally tell her and it would be all over. Adam shuddered at the thought of it. Steph deserved better than that. Steeling himself not to answer the call he glanced at the screen and breathed a huge sigh of relief. It was Russell, just his stupid, impetuous, kid brother Russell.

Adam's mind suddenly flipped back to the events of the previous night and specifically his promise to tell his brothers everything that had happened. It was just after midday and he had yet to say a word to either of them about the events of the previous night. He was reluctant to make the calls for a whole host of reasons but the main one was that once he told his brothers the news they would be looking to him for leadership and he didn't have any to offer.

Adam answered the call. 'All right you? What's up?'

'Nothing much. I've just dropped in at Mum's and she's not in. Just wondered if you knew if she'd gone to church early or whatever.'

'She's not there. She's gone to Aunt Rose's for a couple of days.'

'Really? She didn't mention that when I last saw her and you know what she's like about making plans weeks in advance. Is everything OK with Aunt Rose?'

'Yeah,' replied Adam. 'It's just that . . .'

'What?'

'Look . . . I don't mean to be melodramatic but what are you doing now?'

'Nothing much.'

'Do you fancy meeting up? How about North Star in twenty minutes? I'll buy you breakfast.'

There was a long pause that Adam didn't quite understand. Normally Russell would bite his hand off at the prospect of free food. 'Just the two of us?'

'Yeah,' replied Adam, attempting to keep his tone casual as he wondered why Russell was so desperate to avoid the company of Luke. 'Just the two of us.'

Entering the café already bustling with breakfasting couples Adam spotted Russell at the window table reading a newspaper. He greeted him with a back-slappy hug and insisted that they order breakfast straight away. That done, and a fresh filter coffee in his hand, Adam returned to the table where Russell was now observing him with a curious eye.

'Where's Luke then?' asked Russell.

Adam shrugged. Perhaps he'd been making two and two make five by concluding that Russell's earlier question about Luke was related to his feelings about Cassie. 'I dunno, I haven't spoken to him in a while. Why?'

'Just wondering how he was. I know this Cassie thing must be getting him down and having Dad living with him can't be easy.'

Adam smiled. 'Maybe you should take your turn. I'm sure Luke could do with a break.'

Russell looked horrified. 'I can't. Really I can't,' he spluttered. 'Is that what this is all about? Me taking on Dad? You've got to be joking. I live in a flat!'

'What kind of idiot are you?' said Adam impatiently. 'Of course this isn't about Dad moving in with you.'

'So, what then?'

'Mum and Dad . . .' Adam decided there was no point in sugar-coating this. 'Are getting divorced.'

'Divorced? But why? Why are they getting divorced over a small tiff?'

'Because it wasn't just a small tiff.' Adam told him the whole story.

Russell took the news about their parents very badly. There was no doubt in Adam's mind about that. Russell's first response was to demand that Adam should come up with a plan. 'So what are we going to do?' he asked. 'Do we try and get them back talking again? I know it didn't work last time but maybe it can this time.' This was exactly what Adam had been dreading. He didn't know what to do or say and it was only after an extended period of silence that Russell realised there *was* no plan. 'We've just got to accept that this is the way it is,' said Adam eventually. 'Mum's made her decision.'

Adam stayed for another half an hour before suggesting that Russell should come with him to tell Luke. At the mention of Luke's name Russell's mood had changed and he was back on edge as he had been at the beginning of their conversation. Russell conjured a whole horde of reasons why he couldn't come over to Luke's but Adam didn't believe one of them. This was definitely about Cassie and more than likely Russell had done something – Adam didn't want to guess what exactly – really stupid. Resigned to telling Luke alone he hugged his kid brother goodbye and mentally prepared himself to take on the role of bearer of bad news.

'I knew something was up,' was Luke's immediate response. 'In fact I was going to call you last night myself as Dad was acting so weird but I kept telling myself that I was overreacting. Mum called here about nine and asked to speak to Dad, which threw me completely. When the call was over, Dad looked on the verge of tears and I couldn't get a word out of him. All he's done since is sit in his room. He's not even been down for something to eat. I've never seen him like it. He really loves her, you only have to look at him to see that.' Luke shook his head in disbelief.

'I know it makes no sense but I think her mind's made up. The way she sees it is that the only solution is to move on and put the past behind her.'

'How's Russell taken it? How come he isn't here?'

'I'm guessing he wanted to be by himself or something.'

'So he took it badly?'

Adam nodded. 'Still, he took it better than I thought.'

'I suppose he's not that snotty little kid who always wanted in on our games any more.'

'Yeah, I think at twenty-nine our baby brother has finally grown up.'

Venturing upstairs Adam knocked on his dad's door and let himself in. His dad, dressed for the day, was sitting on the edge of the bed staring out of the window and didn't even turn round as he entered the room.

'All right, Dad?'

His dad said nothing.

Adam decided it was best not to push things but even so couldn't leave without one last check that this time his parents' stories were matching.

'So is it true, Dad? What Mum said happened all that time ago?'

He turned and looked at Adam with tears in his eyes. 'It's true,' he said. 'Every last word.'

Adam stood frozen to the spot.

'I'm sorry, Dad,' he said eventually. 'I'm really sorry.'

'Me too,' he replied and then turned back to gaze out of the window. Adam noiselessly backed out of the room and closed the door behind him. His phone vibrated from inside the front pocket of his jeans. He pulled it out and saw that he had a text message from Steph. 'I still love you.' He gazed at it blankly for a few moments playing the words over in his mind and then he deleted it and headed back down the stairs.

'Then let's talk.'

Saturday. Mid-morning. And over seven days since Adam had last seen or spoken to Steph. He was upstairs in his office at BlueBar staring into the screen of his laptop trying to find the previous month's VAT figures when his mobile vibrated. He glanced at the screen and then seeing whose number it was he simply closed his eyes, shook his head and put the phone back on the desk. For a moment or two he tried his best to concentrate his mind on the figures on the open Excel spreadsheet in front of him, convinced that he had perfected the art of divorcing his emotional life from his day-to-day life, but within seconds his eyes were drawn back to the phone as he waited barely daring to breathe for the familiar electronic 'ding' that would signal the arrival of a voicemail message.

He listened to her message and was about to call her back when he stopped. He still wasn't ready. He needed more time, another point of view. He grabbed his car keys and left the bar. His head still buzzing with things that needed to be done and decisions that needed to be made, Adam reasoned the best thing he could do was to kick-start his day by ticking an item that had been bothering him for some time: his mum. He hadn't spoken to her since the night of the wedding and even though he was aware via his brothers that she had been back home from Leeds for a few days now he hadn't called. Partly because he felt he had enough on his plate but mostly because the longer he avoided her the less likely it would be that he would fall apart in her presence.

'Were you just passing?'

Joan had been sitting on the sofa watching TV when he arrived. He kissed her cheek and sat down.

'I've come to see you, Mum. See how you're doing.'

'Do you want a cup of tea?'

Adam shook his head. 'I'm fine.'

His mum stood up and headed for the kitchen. Realising that this was her way of saying she felt more comfortable talking about whatever it was they were going to talk about if she was doing something else, he followed.

'We need to talk, don't we?' she said, filling the electric kettle and setting it down on its base. 'I know it's hard. I know you think that I don't see how difficult it is for all of you boys, especially you, Adam, but I do.'

'Why especially me?'

'You're the eldest. You think you've got to sort everything out for both your brothers. You think the world of your dad. You think I'm letting you down . . . I can carry on if you like.'

'I don't think you're letting me down.'

'Yes you do. And I don't blame you but you need to understand how much finding out what your father had been up to really hurt me. I just couldn't believe that he would behave like that.'

Adam sat down at the kitchen table. 'I'm having a hard time believing it myself. Did you really have no idea all these years?'

Mum shook her head and opened a new packet of tea bags while the kettle boiled away in the background. 'When Charlie left Janet I really felt for her, because back in those days the four of us used to do everything together. I used to imagine the four of us getting older, settling down and having kids; I thought they would always be in our lives. So when Charlie left my first thought was to rally round Janet and make sure she was all right. I told your dad I was determined that Janet shouldn't feel left out and so whenever your father and I went out, whether it was to the pictures or even just for a walk on a Sunday afternoon, we took Janet along with us.'

The kettle clicked itself off and Adam watched in silence as his mum poured out some of the hot water to heat up the mug like she always did and swilled it around before emptying it into the sink, dropping in a tea bag and covering it with fresh hot water.

'Knowing what I know now of course,' continued Mum, 'I suppose the signs were all there, although they were more apparent in Janet than in your father. As our wedding drew nearer Janet seemed to get more and more offish with me as though I'd done something to upset her. I put it down to the fact that she was on her own and missing Charlie and tried my best to be understanding. But when she didn't turn up on my wedding day, well, I was so angry with her, Adam, I can't begin to tell you. You just don't do that kind of thing to someone who's been such a good friend to you – I felt like she had deliberately set out to ruin my day. Once my sister stepped in as matron-of-honour I decided that I wasn't going to give Janet a second thought. Of course after the wedding I picked up little bits of gossip about her from people who had heard from her. She had moved to London and one or two people suggested she had run off because of a secret love affair that had gone wrong but I never for a minute thought it might have anything to do with your father. Your dad just wasn't that kind of man.'

'I know you think I'm making a fuss about nothing. I know you think it happened forty years ago. Why is she making a big deal out of it after all this time? I know how you and your friends live these days. You think that things like that don't matter and though it may surprise you I do hear about the girls in your life from time to time.' She took a sip of tea and went on. 'It's no way to live a life with all these girls coming and going with never a mention of love or affection. Don't you ever get lonely? Don't you ever want something more substantial?'

Adam didn't know where to look. How had this happened? He could tell from her tone of voice that her questions were far from rhetorical and she was unlikely to give up without a response.

'I'm not like that any more.'

'Good. But when you were didn't you get lonely? Didn't you ever want something more substantial?'

'Of course.'

'So why did it take you until now to do anything about it?'

'Because I thought I'd got plenty of time. Things are different from in your day. People don't feel in such a rush to get things permanently nailed down. These days people just want a bit more time to themselves.'

'And that makes them happy?'

Adam shrugged. 'Do you want me to speak for all of them or just me?'

His mum smiled. 'Just you.'

'I dunno, Mum, I really don't. I used to be happy once upon a time but not any more.'

'Because now you've got Steph?'

Adam nodded. 'She's different.'

'She seems lovely. A proper kind of girl.'

Adam smiled. *A proper kind of girl.* 'That would be one way of putting it.' He suddenly felt himself brimming over with self-consciousness. 'You're not messing about here are you, Mum? Is this you channelling the spirit of Oprah?'

His mum laughed. 'I'm taking the opportunity to talk to you while it's here. We never really get to talk like this do we? And I suppose that's fine because you're you and I'm me and that's just the way things are but don't you think that while we've got this window open we ought to make the most of it?'

'Of course,' said Adam.

'OK,' said Mum. 'Then let's talk.'

The next hour or so was possibly the strangest of his life as his self–consciousness faded and he talked to his mum as he had never done before. Not only did he sketch out exactly how he used to live his life but when she asked for specific details (the kind which in any other context would have seen him go into cardiac arrest) he gave them to her. Although there were times when she seemed shocked and disappointed by his behaviour, Adam never doubted that the honesty was a good thing for the both of them. Concluding the story of his life so far with his recent pursuit of the right kind of girls and his relationship with Steph, he asked her with an almost child-like innocence: 'What shall I do, Mum? What shall I do to get my life the way I want it to be?'

'I don't know, son,' she replied, 'but I always find the best thing is to trust your instincts.'

'Just because they're not concrete, just because they're not tangible, just because they often fly in the face of what you assume is logic and reason doesn't mean you can ignore them.'

Steph looked as lovely as he remembered. She was wearing the same black dress and cardigan as on their very first date. Just thinking about that made Adam wish he had the power to rewind time, to go back to the beginning and replay their courtship from its humble beginnings only this time paying attention to the details. He would never meet anyone like Steph again and even if he met someone similar there would be no way that they would want to be with him. Meeting Steph was one of those once-in-a-lifetime occurrences like Halley's comet or an eclipse of the sun. Adam waved to get her attention and after a few moments she spotted him, made her way over to the table and greeted him with a huge kiss.

'I know it's not cool,' said Steph, still holding on tightly. 'I know I should be acting a bit more pissed off than I actually am because you haven't returned one of my calls this past week but I don't care about games when it comes to you. I've really bloody missed you, Adam, and I don't care if you know it.'

'For what's it's worth,' said Adam as he wondered whether given what he intended to do tonight he was about to cross some moral line, 'I've really missed you too.'

Steph sat down and they ordered a bottle of wine and began looking through the menu. The restaurant specialised in modern Portuguese food and gave them plenty to talk about as they tried to work out what to order. By the time they had decided any initial awkwardness had evaporated leaving behind only what had existed before things had gone so awry: the warmth, fondness and intimacy that comes from being in the presence of someone who has seen the very inside of your soul.

As Steph took a long sip from her glass she fixed her eyes on Adam as though she was wondering if this was the right moment to ask a difficult question. He nodded as if to give her permission to ask whatever she wanted.

'So how are things with your parents?'

'Not good.'

Steph looked at him intently, clearly waiting for him to bring her up to speed. He tried to gauge how he felt about the idea of talking about his parents to her and realised that he was fine. A week had gone by; though still sore the wound was healing nicely enough. He could relay what Steph wanted to know without triggering something deeper. And so he set about telling the story of his father's forty-year-old affair.

Steph listened carefully and without comment until Adam had finished. 'As a woman I completely understand how horrible it must be for her.'

'Why as a woman?' asked Adam. 'Don't men understand betrayal?'

'I'm not saying that, Adam. It's just that . . . well, men are a lot more practical, aren't they? I don't think that's too harsh.'

Adam shook his head. 'No, not really.'

'And because of that practical nature you, your dad and your brothers are all thinking: "Instead of focusing on the one bad thing that happened the best part of forty years ago why doesn't she just focus on the forty-odd good years that came after it?" '

'OK, we may have had a conversation along those lines.'

'And the rest! But that's fine because that's how men work: they think practically. But your mum won't be thinking like you. She'll understand your arguments and she might even acknowledge the plausibility behind them but she won't *feel* them. And most men never really understand that feelings matter. Just because they're not concrete, just because they're not tangible, just because they often fly in the face of what you assume is logic and reason doesn't mean you can ignore them. We can't. We're not made like that. Feelings are the foundations of everything and if something shakes those foundations it affects everything else. Nice as it would be if we could just accept that and move on, what for you is a matter of reasoning for us is a matter of basic structural engineering law. You just can't argue with bricks and mortar, Adam.'

The rest of the meal passed by without event as Adam and Steph fell into their usual comfortable groove chatting about everything and nothing as though they had all the time in the world. Every once in a while Adam felt a twinge of guilt that he had yet to talk about his reasons for not having seen her all week let alone the conclusion he had come to. He hoped that when crunch time arrived he would have changed his mind but in any case he didn't want to spoil the evening.

'I'm glad all this is behind us now,' said Steph later that night as they stood in her kitchen while she poured out two glasses of wine. 'I don't mind admitting that there were a few moments this week when I thought you were going to do a runner on me. But we've had such a nice night together that . . .' She paused, set down her wine glass on the kitchen counter and hugged him. He felt more and more like a fraud the harder she embraced him. As she turned her head up to kiss him he realised that the moment he had been dreading had finally arrived and he couldn't prevent it from happening.

'I can't do this, Steph,' he said quietly. 'I thought I could but I can't.' She pulled away with a look of confusion on her face. 'I don't understand, what's going on?'

'This isn't working. It's not working for me and it's not working for you either. I'm not right for you. I wanted to be but I'm not.'

'Is this because of your parents?'

Adam shrugged. 'It's complicated.'

'Oh, don't give me that! Of course it's complicated. People are complicated. If you have any respect for me at all at least tell me the truth. Help me understand what's going on in your head.'

Adam didn't want to explain. He didn't want to talk. He just wanted to get as far away as he could before she persuaded him to change his mind. 'Talking about it isn't going to change a thing. Why can't you accept that I'm just not the right guy for you?'

'Because it's not true! And I know it's not true because I have never met anyone who has been more right for me. So if you think that I'm going to make it easy for you to walk away just because things in the rest of your world are a little bit shaky then you've got another thing coming. I have too much respect for both of us to let something so good end like this. You need time to sort out everything in your head and time to work out for yourself that I am the best thing that has ever happened to you. So this is what I propose: go away right now and start thinking and then a week from now you call and tell me what you've decided. If you still want out then by all means walk away and I won't say a word to stop you. I'm not scared of being on my own. I was used to it and I'll get used to it again. But if you want me and I mean really, really want me, then this time next week you will call me, we will meet and we will take this relationship all the way. And I'm not just talking about us seeing each other a couple of times a week and taking the occasional holiday together. I'm talking about us both jumping feet first into the deep end because this is it, Adam Bachelor: you and I are each other's last chance at happiness.'

Adam looked at her aghast. This was the last thing he had expected. 'If that's what you want then fine,' he said. 'But I wouldn't be any kind of friend if I didn't tell you that it won't make the slightest bit of difference whether we do this now or in a couple of weeks. My mind's made up.'

'Well,' said Steph firmly, 'that might well be the case. But my mind is made up too and I'm not changing it.'

'I knew you'd do this.'

'So what's this all about?' said Cassie briskly.

It was just after five on the following Saturday afternoon and Luke and Cassie were sitting at a table in the Horse and Jockey.

'That's how it is now?' said Luke. 'We don't do pleasantries any more? We just get straight to the point?'

'You know as well as I do that meeting up like this is only going to make things harder. You've made your decision and I've made mine so what's the point in dragging this out? I don't mean to be harsh, Luke, but that's the way I feel.'

Luke nodded. Cassie was right. He was making things more difficult than they needed to be but at the same time he had to put up a fight for her. What he couldn't understand was why Cassie wasn't doing the same. Had she moved on? Was she seeing someone else? Luke pushed the unbearable thought to the back of his mind.

'You're probably right. Maybe I should just come to the point. And I would if I knew what it was. All I know is that everything is falling apart.'

'Like what?'

'My parents for one. They're getting divorced.'

Cassie was shocked. 'Divorced? I thought it was just an argument that got out of hand?'

'It was a bit more than that,' said Luke. 'I don't want to go into all the details but it turns out that Dad had an affair just before they got married which Mum only found out about recently and now she knows . . . well . . . she just can't seem to get it out of her head.'

'Your poor mum. She must be heartbroken.' Cassie reached across the table and placed her hand on top of Luke's. Luke felt a brief glimmer of hope.

'The thing is, Cass, even though we've split up I feel like you're the only thing keeping me afloat right now.'

'I am really sorry about what's happening with your parents. They're both lovely people. But I don't know what you want from me. I don't know what you want me to say.' She drew back her hand. 'I'm sorry, Luke, but that's just how it is.'

Sensing that in a few moments Cassie would stand up and walk out Luke was filled with desperation. He had taken a gamble and used up his last chance to get her to come back with him and all for what? A few words of sympathy? He couldn't let her go without telling her how much she meant to him. 'I met up with Jayne,' he said quickly. 'That's how much I want for us to get back together. That was the real reason I called you today. I wanted you to know that I'm still trying to make things right.'

Luke could see from the hopeful look on Cassie's face that his news had done the trick and not only did she want to know more but even now she carried a small hope that their break-up wasn't permanent. 'So what happened? Have you seen Megan? Will she let you have access?'

Luke's mind flicked back to that day in London. He had wandered through Covent Garden in a daze in an attempt to put as much distance as possible between himself and Jayne. He had ended up sitting alone in a crowded pub in Bloomsbury desperately trying to keep it all together as Jayne repeatedly called his number. When eventually she'd left a message he had deleted it without listening to a word.

Returning to Manchester he had tried to lose himself in work but found it impossible to concentrate on anything other than feelings of self-loathing and intense hatred towards his ex-wife. And for the week that followed all he had done was work, drink and avoid phone calls from worried family and friends because he had run out of all options bar one: contacting Cassie and hoping that she was missing him enough to reconsider her stance on wanting to start a family.

Aware that his reasoning was utterly selfish Luke had resisted making the call but every day the arguments seemed more powerful and persuasive. Did it really matter if she never got to be a mother if she was happy in every other respect? Wasn't he too sacrificing his hope of a happy family life for the greater good? What was the point of them both being miserable apart? There was no guarantee that Cassie would meet anyone else, let alone anyone with whom she might want to start a family. It all made sense to Luke. He wasn't being selfish. He was being sensible, pragmatic even, and making the best of a bad situation. But what had finally tipped him over the edge into making the call was his father. The man was broken. Luke was in no doubt about that. He was about to lose the most important thing in his life all because he had waited too long to make it right. The short leap in imagination it took to compare his father's situation with his own was enough to make him call Cassie.

'It's complicated,' said Luke, cringing at the realisation that having built up Cassie's hopes he was about to let her down in a big way. 'The meeting,' he stammered, 'it didn't quite go the way I planned and . . . well . . . the truth is I let her get to me and ended up walking away.' He reached across the table and held her hand. 'But whether I see Jayne again or not this is evidence of just how much I love you. I'm trying to sort things out, Cass, and all I'm asking is that you come back home so we can try and sort them out together.' She was crying. 'Please Cass, I'm begging you: come back home.'

'I knew you'd do this,' hissed Cassie snatching away her hand. 'I knew you'd try and get me to come back without a single thing having changed. And it hasn't, has it? You still won't start a family with me but you won't let me get on with my life without you either. That's how selfish you've become. You don't care about me or about my feelings. You think it's OK to keep stringing me along? Well it's not! And if you think

I'm going to spend one second more thinking about you, Luke, you are sadly mistaken.' She picked up her bag, her face full of fury. 'I don't know what I was expecting when I agreed to meet you today but I'm really glad that I did because it's shown me first hand just how weak you think I am. And you were right, Luke, I was weak. Since I left you my only hope was to save what we had. But I can see that I've only been fooling myself so badly that it's laughable. Well, no more. No more waiting. No more hanging round. I'm going to put as much distance between you and me as humanly possible. I'm going to make sure that even in my weakest moments there will never be a way back for us. It's over between you and me, Luke. The last bit of love I had for you has gone away for ever.'

'I am different.'

It was minutes after eight in the evening and Russell was sitting on the sofa listening to Angie's amusing rant about how early episodes of *Friends* should be banned because seeing the characters all young and thin like that was needlessly cruel to people in their thirties.

'You think I'm joking but I'm not.' Angie pointed at the TV screen. 'It's horrible! I used to be as thin as Monica and now look at me!'

'Look at what?'

Angie lifted up her top and wobbled her belly. 'This!'

'That's just normal! You don't want to be one of those stick-thin girls who are always yakking on about this diet and that diet. I thought you were different.'

'I am different. I just want you to like me, that's all.'

'I do like you.' He leaned forward and kissed her. 'In fact I more than like you. I love you.'

'Ah, but would you love me more if there was less of me?'

'I couldn't love you more than I do right now.'

Angie narrowed her eyes and squinted at Russell. 'Is that a good thing or a bad thing?'

'Is what a good thing or a bad thing?'

'Being unable to love me more. I'm not sure I like the sound of that. Shouldn't there always be room for improvement?'

'Not if what you've got is perfect in the first place.'

Despite his assurances the last few weeks with Angie had been something of a rollercoaster ride. Following Russell's attempt to kiss Cassie things were strained to say the least. Unable to cope with the guilt, Russell's behaviour had been erratic in the extreme. He couldn't sit down for more than a minute at a time, was always checking his phone for missed calls and unnoticed text messages and wasn't able to hold a conversation without making it obvious that his mind was elsewhere. And then the thing with his parents had happened and all the talk of affairs and divorce had knocked his world sideways to the extent that he didn't know what to feel or think any more. So he had decided to do neither and to concentrate his efforts on the things where he could make a difference: improving his relationship with Angie and avoiding Luke and Cassie at all costs.

The avoiding Luke and Cassie part was easy enough. Since the day of the kiss he hadn't seen or heard from Cassie and now all that was needed was for Cassie to continue keeping his indiscretion to herself and everything would be fine. On the keeping Angie sweet front things were going so successfully that earlier that day at his suggestion they had been out for a long lunch with a bunch of Angie's friends and assorted partners. The occasion had gone reasonably smoothly considering that Russell still didn't know Angie's friends all that well. The women had appeared suitably interested in the collection of anecdotes he offered them, the men managed not to spend the entire afternoon talking about sport and the food in the Japanese restaurant had been just the sort of thing that Russell liked. There had been talk of carrying on back at Angie's friend Suzie's flat but a number of key players opted out due to previous engagements so that plan fell apart pretty quickly. Russell was grateful for the early end to the festivities as on the whole he had managed to present himself to Angie's friends in a half-decent light and had not drunk enough to set him on a trajectory that usually resulted in him dancing/ confessing his love for Neil Diamond's early output/ falling asleep on a complete stranger's shoulder. So now they were at home and without the welcome distraction of other people, Russell felt distinctly on edge.

'I'm going to grab a beer,' said Russell, standing up. 'Do you want one?'

'I shouldn't really, should I?' yawned Angie. 'Well all right, I'll have another Bud if you insist.'

Russell headed down the hallway to the kitchen and was in the process of pulling two beers out of the fridge when his phone vibrated to let him know he had a text. Setting one of the bottles down he pulled out his phone, looked at the screen and was so shocked by the name he saw that he almost dropped the bottle in his other hand.

Returning to the living room Russell tried his best to act as if nothing happened but it was virtually impossible.

The text message had said: 'Hi, it's me. I know it's late but we need to talk. Am out with friends at the Pitcher and Piano in Didsbury. Please come over and meet me if you can. We'll be there until late. Cass xxx.' Russell half wondered whether she had sent the message to him rather than his brother by accident but there was something about the tone, wording and timing of the message that convinced him he was wrong. Whatever, Russell knew that he didn't have it in him to resist her call. There was too much he needed to say to her. Too many apologies he wanted to make in person. And he needed to make sure that she wasn't about to do something crazy like tell Luke what had happened.

'Listen,' he said. 'I know this is a pain but I've just had a text from Luke and Adam and they want me to meet them down at BlueBar later to talk about my Dad.'

'What about him?'

'Well I'm guessing that Luke probably wants me to take my turn at having him for a while.'

Angie covered her mouth in horror. 'You haven't told them your dad could move in here, have you? Not that there's anything wrong with your dad. He's lovely. But there's barely room to swing a cat in here let alone a pensioner.'

Russell managed to raise a smile. 'Me, you and my dad living in a flat this tiny! Are you insane? Of course I haven't agreed to it. But I do need to go and make my case, OK? You know what they're like. They think they can boss me about all they want.'

'OK, fine,' replied Angie reluctantly. 'But you don't have to go right now, do you?'

Russell looked at his watch and reasoned that he probably needn't leave until about eleven. 'I'll be fine for ages,' he agreed and turned up the volume of the TV so they could carry on watching *Friends*.

'Excuses don't come into it.'

Luke was still in shock. He had never seen Cassie that angry. He hadn't thought such bitterness was possible from someone as sweet natured as her. He played over their meeting time and time again to work out how something so straightforward had ended up going so wrong. The answer was always the same: he had displayed a level of misjudgement so catastrophic that it eclipsed every wrong thing he had ever done before.

He could see his mistake now. He had come to her thinking that his efforts with Jayne would be enough to show that he was trying. But the time for trying had been over long ago. All that mattered was a result and he hadn't one to offer.

Luke called Cassie's mobile to apologise but her phone was switched off and his call went straight to voicemail. He left a message that was short and to the point: 'I'm sorry, Cass. I'm really sorry. Call me when you get this and let's talk.' He was desperate enough to seriously consider driving up to Harrogate to see Cassie's parents in the hope that they might agree to act as intermediaries, when his dad emerged from the living room.

'I didn't hear you come in,' said Dad. 'Have you been back long?'

Luke shook his head. 'I only just stepped through the door.'

'Have you been anywhere nice?'

'Not really.'

'Are you hungry? I can make you something to eat if you like.'

'I'm fine, Dad, honest.'

'Tea? I was just going to make one anyway.'

Luke looked at the car keys in his hands. What was he doing even thinking about going to see Cassie's parents? He needed to stop and think about what his next move was going to be instead of lurching from one bad idea to the next. 'Thanks, Dad, tea would be great.'

Luke sat down on the sofa and looked around the room. Dad had been watching a documentary about World War II on the History Channel but by the looks of things (chiefly the many plates and mugs stacked up on the coffee table) he hadn't been anywhere other than this room all day.

Luke had been monitoring his father's gradual decline ever since he had heard about the divorce. He now spoke, went outside and ate less than he did before and all talk of his situation being temporary had evaporated. As much as Dad had brought his current situation on himself, Luke couldn't help but feel for his father and their situations were not dissimilar. All they wanted were the women in their lives back by their sides where they belonged but this was tantamount to asking for a miracle.

'I went to see Cassie,' said Luke as he and his father sat drinking their mugs of tea. 'That's where I was earlier.'

'Did it go well?'

'It went as badly as it could have done. I think I used up my one chance there, Dad.'

'One chance?'

'Since she left I felt confident that she would always give me one last chance, you know, to make things right and basically I think I used it up trying to sell her something that she was never going to buy.'

Later that evening having progressed from tea to Guinness Luke decided to ask his father about something that had been preying on his mind.

'Dad? I was wondering how you knew that Mum was the one. You know, the one you wanted to marry and spend the rest of your life with?'

Dad shrugged. 'I just knew, that's all. No one made me happy like your mother did. No one made me smile like she did. Just being around her . . . I don't know, it made me feel I was right where I was meant to be.'

'So what changed?'

'Changed?'

'You and this other woman.'

'It's hard to say without it sounding like a long list of excuses and you know I don't do that. I was in the wrong. That's all that matters. And what I did hurt your mother. Excuses don't come into it.'

'I think they do though, Dad. Knowing why we did things is how we learn not to do them again, isn't it?'

'I can tell you one thing, son, knowing what I know now even if the opportunity were there I would walk a million miles in the opposite direction just to get away from the mistake I made. But that doesn't help you, does it?'

'Not really, no.'

'To be honest I don't really know the exact reason why I did it. I could tell you that it was a matter of opportunity, that I got lost in the moment, that I lost my senses, that I was vain and flattered by the attention. I could tell you all this and more, but it wouldn't change a thing. I did it, got caught and why I did it just doesn't come into it. That's what's wrong with your generation. None of you want to put your hands up and admit you're guilty because you're all too busy looking for ways to prove why it was never your fault in the first place. What you forget is there's a reason why actions have always spoken louder than words: words are cheap but the actions can cost you everything.'

Luke took his father's words to heart. He settled his dad down in front of the History Channel and headed upstairs to make the call that would sort out his, Cassie's and Megan's lives once and for all. His dad was right, and not just about him needing Cassie. His parents needed their granddaughter back in their lives too because if there was one thing Luke had learned through all his recent traumas it was this: family, whether by blood, love or devotion, is everything.

'Jayne, it's me, Luke,' he said as she answered the call. 'Listen, I'm sorry about calling you so late and really sorry about what I said last time and the way I acted. It was all well out of order. I shouldn't have spoken to you that way. Not in a million years.'

There was a silence for a few moments.

'I know it was tough for you, Luke, coming to see me like that. And maybe I did deserve to hear some of the thing that you said but if we're ever going to move on then we need to come to terms with the past.'

'You're right,' said Luke, 'which is why I'm calling. I need to see you as soon as possible so that we can get this all sorted. I need to see Megan.' His voice cracked. 'I really do. And I'm ready to meet whenever you are.'

'How about Monday?'

'Monday? That'll be fine. Same time? Same place? I can be on an earlier train if you like.'

There was another silence. 'Luke, there's something I need to tell you. The thing is, I don't actually live in London.'

'But I thought that—'

'I know, and I did it deliberately. When you first got in contact I didn't know what you wanted and I thought it would be easier if you believed I lived miles away.'

'So where do you live?'

'Manchester,' she replied. 'We're living in Manchester.'

'It's all about Luke.'

Russell handed the driver a ten-pound note, collected his change and climbed out of the cab. With his destination only a few feet away but heavily guarded by two ferocious bouncers Russell felt compelled to look down at his white Converse and wish that he had made more effort but as he approached the entrance the doormen smiled and opened the door for him. He was taking a moment to get his bearings when Angie's friend Susie and her boyfriend Steve (both of whom had been at the Japanese restaurant that afternoon) suddenly appeared in his line of vision.

'Russell!' exclaimed Susie. 'What are you doing here? I thought you and Angie were heading home!'

'We did . . . we were . . .' He attempted to pull back from blind panic. 'What I'm trying to say is that yes, we did go home but then some mates of mine called and so I decided to come back out.'

'I never knew you were such a party animal! So did Angie not come?'

'No, she was a bit tired.'

'She works too hard, that girl!' said Susie, reaching for her boyfriend's hand. 'I'm only here because some mates of Steve were here for a while but they've all gone home so we're off now.' She leaned forward and kissed him on the cheek. 'Anyway, have a good time and hopefully I'll see you soon.'

Russell was convinced he was about to pass out from the sheer effort it had taken him to lie to Susie. And to make matter worse they hadn't even been good lies! Why hadn't he been consistent and said he was meeting his brothers rather than inventing random mates? What was he going to say to Angie if Susie ever mentioned bumping into him? How would he explain why he was in Didsbury when he had told her he was heading over to Chorlton? What if Susie was right now in the back of a cab sending Angie a text telling her that she had just spotted him? The potential for damage didn't bear thinking about and so Russell decided not to think about it.

He scouted around the bar for Cassie and eventually spotted her and her friends lounging on a pair of sofas next to the French doors at the back. By the time Russell was halfway across the room she was already on her feet, and as he arrived she threw her arms round him and kissed him, lips closed, but full on the mouth. Russell had no idea what was going on. Had he walked into some kind of alternate universe? The rising cackles of laughter from Cassie's friends informed him that the explanation was simple: Cassie and her friends were incredibly, undeniably drunk.

'I'm so glad you've come, Russ,' said Cassie a little too loudly. She turned to face her friends, swaying slightly. 'Everybody, this is Russell, the sweetest boy in all the world who was very nearly my brother-in-law.' Cassie's friends, five women of equal sobriety, waved at Russell. Cassie turned back to Russell to do the reverse introductions. 'Russell, this is Dina, Luce, Julia, Charmaine and Erin aka the best friends a girl could ever have.' Grinning inanely she put her arms round him and squeezed tightly. 'I bloody love you, you know. I bloody love you to bits!'

The next hour of Russell's life was bizarre. Somehow Cassie ended up perched on his knee while she and her friends continued to drink steadily, all the while getting louder. At one point there was singing and then later some dancing, and then later still some slow dancing. As the only man in the group Russell found himself passed around like a cut-price gigolo. Every time he managed to get away (usually insisting that he needed to head out to the loo) the girls would come and find him and even when he did manage to get Cassie on her own so that he could ask her what was going on she would always make some excuse (the need to buy a round, a text message that needed to be replied to or a song that needed to be danced to) and off she would go. Some time later a member of the bar staff came over and informed them quite forcefully in the middle of their group rendition of 'I've Had the Time of My Life' that if they didn't quieten down he would have no choice but to throw them out. The girls took this as their cue to call it a night and the next half-hour went by in a flurry of whispered phone calls to boyfriends and husbands (for those who had them) and (for those who didn't) shouty phone conversations with minicab operators all demanding lifts home. Soon after, having waved goodbye to each of her friends in turn, Russell found himself getting into the back of a Crimson Cars minicab with Cassie.

The driver glanced up into his rear-view mirror. 'Where are you looking to go, mate?'

Russell was about to open his mouth when Cassie piped up, 'Chorlton. We're going back to Chorlton,' and reeled off her address. 'That's all right, isn't it?' she said, slipping her fingers between Russell's. 'You're coming back to mine, aren't you?'

'Yeah, of course,' he said, barely able to get his words out properly. 'Yeah, of course I'm coming back to yours.'

It was nearly three as the minicab pulled up outside a nondescript block of purpose-built flats opposite a Tesco Metro. As Cassie searched around in her bag for her keys Russell paid the driver, took a quick look at his watch and wondered how he was ever going to come up with a plausible excuse for being out this late that wouldn't result in Angie causing him permanent harm. This night was too weird for Russell to take any real pleasure from it until he knew what the punchline was going to be. As it was he was simply too on edge to think that any good could come of it at all. He needed to find out what was going on and he needed to find out now.

'Found them!' said Cass, waving her keys victoriously in the air. She put her arm round his waist. 'Come on,' she said, shivering. 'Let's get inside.'

He didn't move.

'What are you doing?'

'I was going to ask you the same question. What's going on here, Cass? Why did you send me that text? And what am I doing standing here right now? This might sound a bit naive but I really don't know what's going on.'

For a moment he thought she was about to kiss him, properly kiss him, but then she shook her head. 'Why don't you come inside? I'll make us a cup of tea and some toast or something and then I'll explain why after tonight you'll probably never want to speak to me again.'

'I don't want to come in, OK?' He sat down on the edge of the pavement with his head in his hands. 'This was about you and Luke, wasn't it?' He looked up at her expectantly. 'It's all about Luke.'

Cassie sat down next to him. 'I'm sorry, Russ, honestly I am. You must think I'm the world's worst bitch. I don't even know myself why I called you tonight . . . I wasn't thinking it through. It's just that . . . well . . . I met Luke earlier today. We had a massive row and . . . and . . . I just got sick and tired of all the toing and froing he and I have been doing. I just wanted to draw a line underneath us once and for all—'

'And you thought you'd use me to do it? But I really cared about you, Cass!'

'I know,' she said quietly. 'What I've done is unforgivable.'

'You don't get it. That kiss . . . that day when I kissed you in the park. It wasn't a spur-of-the-moment thing. Cass, I have loved you for the longest time. Ever since that night when you first met Luke I've been mad about you. There have been times when all I could think about was you. So don't tell me what you did was unforgivable. I know it's unforgivable because I'm the one who won't be doing the forgiving.' He was about to walk away when something made him stop. He looked across the road and standing next to a car with Susie and Steve in it and looking for all the world as though her heart was breaking in two was Angie.

'That's different.'

The list of things on Adam's mind as he lay in bed that Sunday morning thinking about the day ahead was long – very long – from the stack of invoices on the desk in his office at BlueBar through to the thirty or so voicemail messages currently on his phone that he had yet to listen to let alone answer. But above all these problems hovered one he couldn't ignore: the fact that today was Steph's deadline.

Even though nothing during the last seven days had changed his mind, Adam was still keenly aware of the deadline. Was he making the mistake of his life? Didn't it make more sense to live alone than constantly in fear that he would mess things up? Yet Steph had seemed so sure, so convinced of her position that Adam couldn't dismiss it out of hand even though he wished he could.

Making his way downstairs and into the kitchen, Adam came face to face with the other thing on his mind which he had been hoping had been a figment of his imagination.

'I didn't dream it then,' said Adam, looking over at Russell who was sitting at the kitchen table with a plate of hot buttered toast and a steaming mug of coffee in front of him. 'You really did turn up at my house at four o'clock in the morning looking for a place to stay?'

Russell took a large bite of his toast. 'I'll be out of your way as soon as I can, OK?'

'There's no rush,' said Adam, making himself a coffee. 'It's not like I'm not used to having family members as house guests these days. Anyway, now that you've slept on it are you going to tell me what's happened or are you going to make me piece it together myself?'

'Me and Angie had a bit of a row.'

'I'd guessed that much. What about?'

Russell didn't reply. Adam decided he would help him out. 'Would it by any chance have been about Cassie?'

Russell looked up, confused, guilty. 'Why would you say that? Who's been talking to you? Did Angie ring you? What's she been saying? Whatever you've heard it's not true, OK?'

'So you're not and have never been in love with Cass?'

'Of course not!' Russell walked over to Adam as though the very act of positioning himself in closer proximity to his brother made his case more convincing. 'Is that what Angie has been saying? That I'm in love with Cassie? She's mad. She doesn't know what she's talking about. All that happened is we had a row and Angie . . . well Angie is a bit of a drama queen to say the least.'

'Have you finished?' asked Adam. Russell looked at him blankly. 'Look mate, Angie hasn't been in touch with me, and just for the record even if she had your little display of amateur dramatics there wouldn't have convinced me in the least.'

'I don't get it. How do you . . . ?'

'I've known for ages, mate. No one told me, no one had to tell me. It was obvious.'

'How obvious? Obvious enough for Luke to know?'

Adam put his hands on Russell's shoulders. 'Calm down, OK? Obvious to me but no one else has mentioned it so I'm guessing the only people who know are you, me and Angie.'

Russell sat down again. 'Nope, Cassie knows too. Ad, this is a mess. A real mess.'

Adam stared at Russell in disbelief. 'What have you done, Russ? How does Cassie know?'

'I met up with her a while ago. She wanted to talk about how things were with her and Luke and to cut a long and extremely embarrassing story short I tried to kiss her and she ran a mile.'

'And Angie found out about this?'

Russell shook his head sheepishly. 'No, she didn't know anything about it and I regretted it straight away. It was stupid, Ad, really stupid but then last night Cassie asked me to meet her at some bar over in Didsbury. So I lied to Angie and told her I was going out with you and Luke but I went to meet Cassie. I didn't know what she wanted. I just knew I had to go. She'd had some kind of row with Luke and was drunk enough to be considering using me as a way of getting back at him . . . and before you say anything nothing happened. And nothing would have happened. She was just angry, that's all.'

'So where does Angie come into it?'

'When I arrived at the bar I bumped into a couple of Angie's mates. I'm guessing texts were sent, conclusions were jumped to and soon enough Angie was fully up to date with the fact I had lied about where I was going. Her mates must have gone and picked her up and she must have followed me back to Cass's house just to make sure she hadn't got the wrong end of the stick.'

'But nothing happened with you and Cass?'

'Nothing at all. And that's what I tried to tell Angie. But when her mates drove off and she wouldn't answer her phone the only thing to do was head back to the flat and hope she would talk to me there.'

'And she wouldn't let you in which is why you came to mine?'

Russell nodded. 'Her phone was switched off and she wouldn't open the door. It was a choice between sleeping in the communal hallway or coming over to yours.'

'And how do you think she'll be now? If you explain will things be OK?'

Russell shook his head. 'Not a chance. I lied about meeting up with Cass. That's as much evidence as she needs. Her catching me in the middle of an embrace was just the icing on the cake. The thing is, Angie knows . . . everything about Cass and how I felt about her and she always has done. It's the price you pay for turning a friendship into something more: you end up being more exposed than you'd ever be otherwise. When we were just friends I never hid anything from her because there was never a reason to. And then I lied and worse still I got caught out. She won't have anything to do with me now, Ad, and the thing that really hurts is I haven't just lost a girlfriend I've lost my best mate too.'

'Once maybe, but not any more.'

Russell was at the flat. After knocking loudly enough to wake at least one of the neighbours he finally let himself in and after standing in the hallway calling Angie's name and listening for sounds of occupation he came to the conclusion that she was either not in or else was lurking with some kind of implement in her hand ready to brain him the moment that she saw the opportunity. Of the two options Russell preferred the latter, reasoning that perhaps if the blows she struck inflicted enough damage she might:

a) feel better about herself
b) feel enough remorse to make her forgive him.

Bracing himself as best he could he tentatively ventured into the flat checking first the living room, quickly followed by the kitchen (plates still in sink but nothing out of the ordinary), the bathroom (no sign of a shower), the bedroom (evidence that she had at least slept in there at some point) and finally the airing cupboard (just on the off chance). Russell was disappointed to discover no sign of Angie. Had she gone away? He narrowed it down to a couple of educated guesses: her friend Katie's house or her parents' place in Chester. As Russell stared at the empty beer bottles from the night before still sitting on the coffee table it occurred to him that a few months ago had Angie felt angry and hurt and in need of someone to talk to she would have turned to him. Right now she would have been cuddled up in his arms listening to him reassure her that everything would be all right.

Russell called her mobile again and although it rang out (so at least it was no longer switched off) she still didn't answer it (meaning either she couldn't hear it or was choosing to ignore it) and it went straight through to voicemail. Russell decided against leaving a message. Twenty seconds later he decided that perhaps he ought to leave a message after all and called her back. With his phone pressed up against his ear he began mentally preparing the message when he noticed something odd: he could hear (albeit faintly) Angie's phone ringing nearby. It had to be hers. Angie was the only person in the world who could entertain having the opening bars of the world's most annoying song ('La Macarena') set as her ring tone. Russell followed the sound of 'La Macarena' out of the living room and into the hallway. Hearing the sound of a key in the front door he realised that Angie was much closer to home than he had assumed.

Ignoring Russell as if he were a bin bag that she had forgotten to put out with the rest of the rubbish, Angie brushed past him, headed to the kitchen and slammed the door behind her. Slowly coming to the realisation that the longer he stood gawping at the wrong side of the door the worse it would be Russell plucked up the courage to follow her.

Angie was leaning against the kitchen windowsill. She no longer looked quite as angry, just disappointed that he was still there.

'I was hoping you'd gone,' she said flatly.

'Is that what you want?'

'Why would you care what I want? From the evidence of last night it's patently clear that what *you* want is far more important to you! You want Cassie? Then go ahead and have her because I don't want anything more to do with you.'

'It wasn't like that, Ange, you have to believe me. She sent me a text asking me to meet her. She sounded like she was upset and I knew you'd never agree to my seeing her and so I lied.'

'How many times?'

'What?'

'How many times have you lied to me?'

Was this the appropriate moment to tell the truth? Russell was pretty sure it wasn't. 'Last night was the only time. Really it was.'

'Are you trying to tell me that last night was the first time you've seen Cassie since I asked you to stop spending time with her?'

'Yes, yes of course.'

For a moment Russell thought he might be off the hook but then she held out her hand. 'Give me your phone.'

Russell played for time. Had he deleted all of his texts to and from Cassie? 'What for?'

'What do you think I want it for? If you're telling me the truth you won't have any problem handing it over, will you?'

'Fine.' Russell reasoned it was worth the risk. With his heart thumping at double time he reached into his jacket pocket and handed the phone to Angie. 'Here you go.' He shook his head in disbelief. 'I can't believe you don't trust me. I'm telling you the truth. Last night was the only time.'

'We'll see about that, won't we?' said Angie, apparently scrolling through for his text messages. When she pressed the call button and put the phone up to her ear Russell shifted uncomfortably.

'What are you doing?'

'Calling your girlfriend,' replied Angie. 'Cassie might be a lot of things but I'm pretty sure she's not a liar. So do you know what? If I ask her how many times she's seen you she, unlike you, will tell me the truth.'

'OK, stop!' said Russell, closing his eyes as he surrendered with both hands aloft. 'Put down the phone and I'll tell you everything.'

Angie shook her head. 'You think I'd trust a word that comes out of your mouth? Once maybe, but not any more. You're a liar, Russell Bachelor. A liar and a coward.' Angie pressed the end call button and tossed the phone on the table. 'I bet you never even told her about me, did you?'

'Ange, please . . . just let me explain.'

'Explain what exactly?' snapped Angie. 'How you met up with her behind my back? How you didn't think you were doing anything wrong because you were only trying to be a friend? How you thought it would be OK to lie to me because I would never understand how you felt? How you thought this was something you had to do? Come on Russ, which bit do you want to explain or have I covered all the salient points?'

Russell looked down at the floor. 'Ange, I know this is a mess. All I'm asking is that you understand that I never meant for any of this to happen. I never meant to hurt you.'

'And that makes it all right? Poor Russ never meant to lie to my face and make a fool out of me by carrying on behind my back! It was an accident! Surely not even you believe that? I told you not to see her, Russ. I told you! And do you know why? Not because I wanted to be cruel. Not because I was jealous. Not because I didn't sympathise with her predicament. It was because I knew this would happen. And I knew because I know you, Russell, like no one else does. And what breaks my heart is that you don't know me. Because if you did you wouldn't be standing here hoping I'll forgive you. That's never, ever, going to happen.'

'She calls him by his name.'

Standing in front of the Wilmslow Road branch of Café Rouge Luke paid the driver of the minicab he had had to call that morning when his car battery had been flat. Burying his change deep in his jeans pocket he took a moment to calm down. It didn't work of course. The shaking in his left hand was evidence enough of that.

Luke was overwhelmed by Jayne's news. That she and Megan had been living in Manchester all this time! It didn't bear thinking about.

Luke had wanted to know all the details – all the whens, whys and hows – but sensing Jayne's reluctance to talk and, more importantly, afraid of scaring her off he had no choice but to let it go. Determined not to ruin his chances of making things right he pushed all thoughts of injustice to the back of his mind to concentrate on what really mattered, and when she finally suggested that the two of them meet the following day in Wilmslow he said yes without a moment's thought.

'Luke.' Jayne stood up as he approached her table. She was wearing a white shirt and jeans and despite the immaculate layer of make-up he could tell she had spent much of the morning in tears. He wondered whether he felt sorry for her. He wondered whether she had spent the entire night imagining this moment. Finally he wondered whether any of the love he had once felt for her still lurked in some forgotten corner of his heart.

He sat down and she handed him a menu, which he declined politely. A waitress approached their table and Jayne ordered a cappuccino while Luke, fearing a scenario where he would be stuck looking at Jayne with nothing to say or do, opted for a straight filter coffee.

'Listen,' began Luke, 'I know I'm in danger of repeating myself but I do need you to know how sorry I am for walking out on you last time. I thought I'd be all right seeing you but obviously I was wrong. Still, that's no excuse, so, I'm sorry.'

'It's probably the least I deserved given the way things were in the past.' She stopped and looked at him steadily. 'I don't mean to make excuses, Luke, but I was a mess back then. I didn't deal with any of it – being a mum, the end of our marriage – very well.'

'I understand all that. We were both young. We made a lot of mistakes. But what I don't understand . . . the thing I've really never understood is why you made it so difficult for me to see Megan when you knew how much she meant to me. She was my life, Jayne. Even when we were at each other's throats you knew that. So why would you do it?' He had much more to say. But there was little point in saying it if it frightened her away for good.

'You're right,' said Jayne, avoiding eye contact. 'I should never have used Megan to get at you. No matter what went on between us you were always the best father in the world to her.'

'So why do it when you knew how much it would hurt me?'

'Because that's exactly what I wanted to do.'

'Because you thought it would be easier for me to move on than it would for you?'

Jayne shook her head. 'That might have been part of the reason but it wasn't the reason in itself.'

'So what was it?'

'Because I was still in love with you.'

'I don't get it,' he said eventually. 'You acted this way for love?'

'That's what I thought at the time.'

'And now?'

'I know I couldn't have been more wrong.'

The waitress arrived with their coffees and for a while neither of them spoke, lost in thought. Luke had a thousand and one questions and when he finally made eye contact with Jayne he could see, almost as if he were reading her mind, that now she had revealed the worst there was nothing to be afraid of asking.

'Where are you living now?'

'About ten minutes from here. I remarried a year and a half ago. We met in Bath. Megan thinks the world of him. John works for a big insurance company and when they asked him if he would head up a new office in Manchester he leaped at the chance.'

'And it never occurred to you to contact me? What if I'd bumped into you in town or something?'

'I thought about that all the time, Luke. But have you never had something that you knew you had to do but been unable to find the strength to do it?'

He knew she was right. He asked the question that was currently weighing on his mind. 'What does Megan call him?'

'She calls him John,' she replied. 'She always has done.'

Luke nodded. It was a relief but not much of one. 'And where does she think I've been all this time? Does she remember anything about me?'

'She remembers bits. And she's got photographs. She does ask about you from time to time but she understands that the situation was complicated.'

Luke put his palms up to his eyes as if to force back the tears that were forming. 'I want to see her,' he said quickly. 'I need to see her.'

'I know you do,' said Jayne. 'And I'm not going to stand in your way.'

'I hate the phone going in the middle of the night.'

Entering the gates of Chorlton Park Adam wondered what he was doing there. He was looking for somewhere to wait out the time that remained of Steph's deadline and decided that the best things he could do would be to:

a) Keep occupied
b) not wait indoors.

He had toyed with driving out along the A6 to the Peak District with only his iPod for company to spend ten minutes or so taking a look at nature before jumping back in the car and returning home but had neither the energy nor the inclination to follow through with it. Taking a walk up to the High Street before heading to the bar to do some work he had ended up in the park.

Adam sat down on a bench near the children's playground and automatically pulled out his phone as he always did whenever he found himself at a loose end. Soon he was trawling through all the text messages that Steph had sent him which in their own brief and funny way told the story of their relationship.

Even reviewing their relationship in his head Adam found it hard to believe. How of all people had he managed to find love and, even more alarmingly, with Steph Holmes? It was as if someone had flicked off a switch in his head from the moment he had bumped into her that fateful day in his local newsagent's. Now that it was back on he could see how he had been fooling himself thinking that he could maintain any kind of long-term relationship when his parents, who were practically built for it, couldn't even manage to do so.

He knew he ought to feel cheered that somebody as wonderful as Steph genuinely cared about what was going on in his life but he couldn't. It was as though the news of his parents' divorce and his father's infidelity had hardened him, changed him in some profound way. He felt closed off not just from Steph but also from the person Steph had made him want to be.

He looked at his phone and began typing out the following text message: 'I'm sorry but I just can't seem to change my mind.'

At home that night Adam switched on the TV and headed into the kitchen to make himself some toast. With the toast popped and buttered went back into the living room and began scanning his collection of DVDs for something that would keep his mind off his parents and Steph. Plucking from the shelf something suitably action-heavy and dialogue-light Adam slipped the disc into the DVD player and pressed play. The film had barely got past the impossible-to-fast-forward-through legal stuff at the beginning of the disc when Adam's phone rang. Reasoning that it was best to get all distractions out of the way he picked up the phone and was surprised to see Luke calling.

'All right, mate,' said Adam. 'You find me just about to start watching the *Blade* trilogy. I'm more than happy to press pause and hang on for a bit as long as you get your arse in gear. I might even have some of that microwave popcorn in—'

'Adam, just listen for a second will you?' interrupted Luke. 'I've got some bad news. It's about dad. Something's wrong with him. We don't know what yet. But the ambulance is here and I'm going with him. You go and get Mum and I'll see you at the hospital.'

Adam's mum was on the doorstep waiting with her coat on and a large handbag over her arm as he pulled up outside his parents' house to take her to the hospital. As she made her way down the front path Adam reached across the passenger seat and opened the door. She offered Adam a half-smile by way of a hello and then handed her bag to him as she climbed into the car and put on her seat belt.

'So what do you know?' asked Mum after a few minutes of silence.

'I'm guessing everything that you know, Mum. Luke called me after he called you. He hadn't a great deal of time to talk, as he was just about to get into the back of the ambulance. He told me he was in bed asleep, heard a loud crash from upstairs, went up and found Dad collapsed on the floor outside the bathroom. He called nine-nine-nine straight away and when they arrived they did some stuff with Dad to get him stable and now they've taken him to South Manchester.'

'That's all I know too. I was in bed when Luke called. I hate the phone going in the middle of the night. It's always bad news. When Grandma died that call came in the middle of the night too.' She looked at Adam. 'Has someone called Russell?'

'He said he'll see us at the hospital.'

'How did he take it?'

'He was shocked and upset but for Russ seemed pretty together.' Adam looked over at Mum. 'He'll be all right.'

'I hope so.' She turned to look out of the window.

'We *are* cursed.'

'We're here to see George Bachelor,' said Adam as they presented themselves at the main desk of the emergency department. They had waited for twenty minutes in the queue behind a young man whose shirt was caked in blood, an elderly woman and her carer and a worried looking middle-aged man and his teenage daughter. The temptation to eavesdrop had been overwhelming and grateful for the distraction Adam had listened in to conversations about injuries sustained during altercations outside nightclubs, unexpected side effects of new medication and enquiries about boys involved in motorbike accidents before he reached the front of the queue and was allowed to tell his own tale. 'I'm his son. He came in a while ago.'

The woman behind the desk nodded and looked at the screen. 'Bachelor, George, forty-four Woodford Road?' Adam nodded. 'He's in with a doctor in bay three but he should be going up to a room on the ward within the hour. His other son . . . a Mr Luke Bachelor is with him at the moment. I'm afraid we only allow two people at the bedside at a time.'

'That's fine,' said Adam. He looked at Mum. 'Just do a swap. You go in and see him and I'll wait here for Russ.'

After watching his mum disappear with a nurse Adam made his way to the waiting room and took a seat in the farthest corner he could find. He had been in enough hospital emergency waiting rooms over the years to know that the best thing was to keep himself to himself but as he was rummaging around for his iPod he looked up and saw Russell. Adam waved and within a few moments Russell was sitting by his side.

'Any news?'

Adam shook his head. 'Me and Mum only just arrived. She's in with Dad and Luke at the minute. I told her I'd wait here for you.'

'I couldn't believe it. What do you think it was? A heart attack? Dad always seems like he'd go on for ever.'

'And he will,' said Adam firmly. 'Whatever it is he'll be all right. He just might have to take things a bit slower, that's all.'

'How did Mum react?'

'As you'd expect. She hasn't said much but I'm wondering if she blames herself.'

'I was thinking she might go that way. But she shouldn't. Things happen. That's just the way it goes. What do you think it'll mean for the divorce?'

Adam shrugged. 'Since when has it ever been easy to guess what Mum will do about anything?'

Russell smiled. 'Do you remember that time you got sent home with a letter from school about punching Sean Ellis in the face and you were crapping yourself because you thought she was going to do her nut? When she asked you why you did it and you said because Ellis was picking on me, she said, "Don't do it again," and that was it!'

'That's Mum all over. Who knows how her mind works?'

The two brothers fell into an awkward silence. Adam folded away the headphones of his iPod and was about to ask Russell if he wanted a drink from the machine in the corner when Russell spoke.

'I've got news,' he said quietly. 'Me and Angie are definitely over. For good.'

'When did this happen?'

'This morning.'

'Well if it makes you feel any better,' said Adam. 'I've pretty much messed up things with Steph.'

'The girl you brought to Mum's that time?' Adam nodded. 'Why would you do that? She was really nice.'

'So was Angie.'

'What is wrong with us Bachelors? Do you think we're cursed?'

'I must admit I have been sort of thinking the same thing.'

'The evidence stacks up, right? Mum and Dad, you and Steph, Luke and Cass and now me and Angie. We *are* cursed.'

'It would be a lot easier to deal with if we were,' said Adam, 'but do you know what? I don't think it's true.'

'So what *do* you think the problem is?'

'The same one that afflicts blokes the world over but for some reason seems to affect our family more than most,' said Adam. 'We just don't know when we're on to a good thing and even when we do know we can't stop ourselves from screwing up.'

Adam went to get two coffees. He handed one to his brother and they sat talking about everything that was going on repeating themselves in a way that neither of them seemed to mind until Luke arrived.

'How is he? Any news?'

Luke nodded. 'He's going to be OK. He's asleep now but Mum and I have been chatting to his consultant and they think he must have accidentally doubled up on his blood pressure tablets. Although what happened was pretty severe, because the ambulance got there so quickly it was nowhere near as bad as it could have been. Anyway, they've given him a whole bunch of stuff to keep him stable and as long as there aren't any major changes over the next couple of hours they should be able to tell us in the morning when we can take him home.'

'That's fantastic,' declared Adam. 'Has Mum said anything about that? You know, Dad coming home?'

Luke shook his head. 'She's not said much at all. But you can tell it's really tearing her up seeing him like this. She'll take him back, surely? I mean, I can take a few days off work but I'll never be able to look after him properly.'

'Don't worry about it,' said Adam. 'He can come back to mine. It's not like I haven't got the time. The bar practically runs itself these days.'

'And you know I'll be there to help out too,' added Russell. 'We've got flexitime at work so I can do mornings or early evenings or whatever will make things easiest. Just let me know.'

Luke rubbed his eyes. 'I can't believe how late it is. I've told Mum she should go back home and we'll sit with Dad but she won't hear of it. Once you guys have been to see him I'm more than happy to sit with her until morning. Who's going up next?'

'Russell,' said Adam firmly.

'Fine,' said Russell even though he had been considering arguing the point. 'I'll see you both in a bit.'

'Good news?'

Adam and Luke watched Russell disappear and both looked around the waiting room as if searching for inspiration.

'I've got to get out of here even if it's just for a couple of minutes,' said Luke. 'Are you coming?'

The two of them made their way to the exit and out through the automatic doors that led to the car park where a small but valiant number of smokers were shivering over late-night cigarettes.

'It must have been a real shock finding him like that,' said Adam.

'For a moment or two I thought that . . . well, you know what I thought . . . anyway once I realised he was still breathing I was so relieved all I could concentrate on was calling an ambulance as quickly as possible. Everything that happened after that is just a blur.'

'Well, it sounds like you saved Dad's life.'

Luke shrugged and looked down at his shoes. 'It was good having him living with me, you know, seeing him every day like I used to when we were kids. It's not the same when you leave home; you haven't got that same day-to-day interaction. And I don't think I'd realised that until Dad came to stay. I didn't understand how much distance there was between us. Of course I used to pop in, say hello, talk about the weather, eat some food and then go but I never really talked to him, not properly. Not like I do with Mum. Why is that? Why is it so difficult?'

'It's just not what we do, is it? Me, you, Russ and Dad, we talk but we don't really say anything. Not anything meaningful anyway. It's the women who bring us out of ourselves. When we were at home it was Mum and now it's your Cass or Russ's Angie or even my Steph . . . It's them who show us what life is really all about. Without them . . . I don't know . . . I think we're all just a bit . . .'

'Disconnected? Lost? Hopeless?'

Adam smiled. 'All of the above.' He looked over at his brother. 'Me and Russ have been having a heart-to-heart and apparently he's split up with Angie.'

'Already? How come?'

'It's complicated.'

'But things with you and Steph are all right?'

Adam shook his head.

'If it's any consolation,' said Luke. 'I've got some good news that you might like to hear.'

Adam laughed. 'That's hard to come by in this family. Of course I want to hear it. Fire away.'

'It's a long story but this morning I met up with Jayne again. You'll never believe it but she and Megan are living right here in Manchester. Anyway, we've cleared the air and this afternoon I finally got to see Megan again.'

'That's the best news ever!' said Adam, throwing his arms round his brother. 'How is she? What's she like?'

'She's amazing.' Luke had tears in his eyes. 'Absolutely amazing. The sweetest little angel you could ever wish to meet. And it wasn't weird and it wasn't strange, it was the best feeling ever. Honestly mate, she looks like a miniature version of Mum, I'm not kidding you. The eyes, the face, the smile. I can't believe I never noticed it before. It's pure Mum.'

'Do her and Dad know yet?'

Luke shook his head. 'I was planning to tell Dad tonight and then with all that's gone on I thought it would be best to wait until Dad's properly awake and tell them together.'

'That's great news, Luke,' said Adam, embracing his brother once again. 'You must be walking on air.'

'I am. I really am.'

'And what about Cassie? Have you told her yet?'

Luke's face suddenly became serious. 'It's complicated on that front. The last time we saw each other it basically ended in a huge row with her storming off. She feels like all I've done is mess her around and now I've finally got my act sorted it might be too late.'

As the wind picked up the boys headed back inside the waiting room and warmed themselves with a coffee while taking it in turns to recall favourite memories from their childhood. In the middle of Adam's version of the time that Luke broke his arm while falling out of a neighbour's apple tree, Russell appeared and gave

Adam the nod so he made his way upstairs to see his father face to face.

The room was quiet. Mum was sitting by Dad's side but it was impossible to make out her features in the half-light. Dad's eyes were closed and his breathing deep and regular as though he were fast asleep. Adam pulled up a chair and sat down next to his mum.

'He'll be all right, you know,' he said quietly. 'He'll be fine. We're Bachelors, aren't we? We're virtually indestructible.' She took his father's hand and looked straight ahead.

'I blame myself.'

'That's nonsense, Mum. Of course it's not your fault.'

She reached for his dad's hand. 'I knew your father was ill. He'd been having problems with his health before he left. It seemed like every day he was up at the doctor's for one thing or another and don't get me started on the cocktail of tablets he had to take. I had to stand over him to make sure he remembered. Did he remember to take them when he lived with you?'

'I didn't even know he was taking any tablets.'

'He wouldn't have wanted you to know. That's your dad all over, isn't it? He doesn't like people making a fuss. It was all I could do to get him to let me help him so he certainly wouldn't have wanted you to get involved. That's just his way.'

Adam had no idea what was going on with his parents any more, whether the divorce was still on or if once Dad was better he would be going home with Mum but in that one small action, that movement of one hand towards another he had seen something that he hadn't seen in his family for a while: hope. Whether or not his parents got back together there was still an awful lot of love left between them, the kind of love that even the worst foolishness couldn't erode and even a hardened cynic like Adam had to stand back and admire.

Part 4

'I am what I am.'

At the sound of his alarm clock Adam cracked open first one eye and then the other and hit the snooze button. He didn't go back to sleep though. Who could possibly sleep with this much on their mind?

Things continued to pile up at work but he had promised Mum he would nip down to Toys Я Us to buy a present or two for Megan on behalf of the family for when they were all supposed to meet her. He was utterly clueless about what to get because last time he checked he wasn't an eight-and-a-half-year-old girl. But these problems seemed trivial compared with the fact that today, after a week in hospital, his dad was due home and Adam had no idea where home would be. While his mum had been a near-permanent fixture at his dad's bedside there had been no mention of future plans and Adam knew better than to ask.

Climbing out of bed Adam determined to get as much of a head start on the day as possible. His dad would be discharged at midday and before going to the hospital he would at the very least need to do a shop, get the spare room ready and (given that his cleaning lady was on holiday in Turkey for a fortnight) run the Hoover around the place so that it would meet minimum hygiene standards required for a recuperating pensioner.

His head still buzzing with things that needed to be done Adam left his bedroom dressed only in his boxer shorts and was crossing the landing for a shower when he heard the front-door bell. He really couldn't be bothered putting on clothes when he was already so close to his destination, but recalling that a few nights earlier he had ordered a bunch of CDs for his dad as a welcome-home present Adam resigned himself to a deeper relationship with the postman and made his way downstairs.

'You're not the postman,' said Adam, protecting his modesty behind the front door, as he peered through the gap and came face to face with Russell.

'Well spotted,' said Russell with a grin. 'Whoever claimed you weren't a genius, bruv, was obviously wrong. So are you going to invite me in or not?'

Adam pulled the door open, sat down on the stairs and observed his brother. 'What's going on?'

'Well, apart from the fact that I thought it might be a good idea to come round here and help you sort the place out ready for Dad's arrival I've got some news.'

'Which is?'

'We're not cursed.'

'Who's not cursed?'

'We Bachelors. Do you remember we were talking about it the night Dad went into hospital? I was saying that I thought maybe we were cursed for ever to screw up relationships and you said you thought it was more a case of us never knowing what's good for us.'

'I'll have to take your word for it, Russ, it was three or four in the morning at the time.'

'Anyway, I've been thinking and I've finally come to a conclusion.'

'Which is?'

'That we're late starters.'

Adam couldn't help but smile. 'Late starters? I'm thirty-eight, mate. If I get any later than this I'll be collecting my pension before I'm even ready to have kids!'

'No, I'm serious,' said Russell. 'Just give me a minute and I'll explain. We're not cursed and we're not any more stupid or thoughtless than the next man. What we are . . . in fact what we've always been is late starters in the sense that we just take a lot longer to get where we're supposed to than most.'

'And your proof for that would be what? Luke and Cass getting back together?'

'In part, yes.'

'And?'

'Me and Angie.'

'Are you saying she's taken you back?'

'Not in so many words. Basically I went to see her last night and we talked . . . and we talked . . . and then we talked some more and though she hasn't exactly said that we're getting back together she hasn't exactly ruled it out either. Don't get me wrong, she's still angry with me – and believe me if there's one person you don't want to be on the wrong side of it's Angie – and I know I've still got a long way to go before she'll trust me again but that's fine. I'm prepared to put in the time even if I have to live at Mum and Dad's until I'm your age. But what I feel – and I know you're going to think this is cheesy – is that there's hope. Me and Angie have got hope; Luke and Cass have got it too and do you know what? As bleak as the outlook has been this year there's still hope for Mum and Dad too.'

'That's all good,' said Adam. 'And cheesy though it is I can see it might be true but why are you telling me all this?'

'Because you've got hope too.'

Adam shook his head. 'Nice idea, Russ, but I don't think so. Any hope I had ran out some time ago and do you know what? That's fine. I'm chuffed you and Luke have got your happy endings and no one wants Mum and Dad back together more than me but everything that's happened has taught me this: I'm living my happy ending right now. My life's great as it is and I don't actually need anyone else on a regular basis to give it meaning . . . or depth . . . or whatever you want to call it. I am what I am.'

Russell didn't respond. He simply smiled to himself and offered to make Adam a coffee. 'Two sugars, is it?'

'Yeah,' nodded Adam, eyeing his brother suspiciously. 'Two sugars it is.'

It was just coming up to midday as Adam and Russell pulled into the hospital car park. Adam dialled Luke's number.

'Hey bruv, it's me,' said Adam. 'Are you here yet?'

'Mum and I are just about to get in the lift to go up to the ward. Where are you?'

'Just pulled up. Look, I know this is going to be tricky to answer with her standing there but has she said anything to you about her plans yet?'

'Not a word.'

'I suppose that's that then. I'll see you in a bit, OK?'

'What did he say?' asked Russell.

'Mum hasn't said a word about Dad going home.'

'She'll take him back, just you wait and see.'

'And you know this how?'

'I'm telling you, Ad, you can be as cynical as you like but it's all about hope these days. It's the order of the day, mate.'

Adam and Russell made their way over to the main entrance, and up to the fourth floor where they were buzzed through to the ward by an all-female group of nurses coming out the other way.

'He's all ready for you,' said one of the nurses who Adam had spoken to several times before and who had clearly taken something of a shine to him. 'He looks like a new man. The sparkle is definitely back in those big brown eyes of his.'

'Sounds to me like a job well done. As a sign of my gratitude any time you're over Chorlton way and you're a bit thirsty drop in to BlueBar, mention my name to the staff and the drinks will be on the house.'

'And what if it's just me that happens to be in

Chorlton?' asked the nurse, clearly flirting. 'Will I have your attention to myself for the whole night?'

Adam shook his head. 'I can't say I'm in there much these days.'

The nurse pulled out a pen and paper from the pocket of her uniform and scribbled something down. 'Just in case you're ever at a loose end.' Her friends cackled uncontrollably.

'Thanks,' said Adam graciously.

Adam and Russell continued down the hallway.

'Are you really going to call her?'

Adam shook his head. 'Not in a million years.'

'What? Isn't she your type?'

Adam was tempted to grab his brother in a headlock and rap his knuckles on his skull until he cried for mercy like he used to when they were kids but this being neither the time nor the place, all he did was scowl, screw the paper into a ball and hand it to his brother. 'Come on,' he commanded. 'Let's go.'

Entering Dad's room all Adam's feelings of annoyance towards Russell disappeared. Their father was fully dressed in his own clothes and Mum was standing by his side holding his hand. Adam wasn't sure which was the more shocking sight: his parents' open display of affection or the fact that his dad looked so bloody amazing.

'You look really well, Dad!' said Adam, crossing the room to greet his father. 'I can't believe it! Are you sure it's him, Mum? Are you sure the hospital haven't just made up a replacement out of a few old spare parts?'

'It's the clothes,' explained Dad. 'There's nothing like having your own clothes on to make you feel more like your old self. I tell you son, those hospital gowns are the devil's work: draughty as anything and ugly too. I defy anybody to look well wearing one of those things!'

Once again Adam's eyes were drawn to his parents' clasped hands. He glanced over at Luke and Cassie who were standing on the opposite side of the bed and Cassie grinned back. 'Is everything packed?'

'Your Mum did it all this morning,' said Dad. 'We're packed and ready to go.'

Adam couldn't help himself. 'Go where?'

'Home,' said Mum quietly. 'We're taking your dad back home where he belongs.'

No one said anything. Cassie was visibly struggling with the Bachelor family's muted celebrations and wanted to give vent to the squeals of delight bubbling up inside her. Adam threw a smile of amusement in her direction. She was learning. She was definitely learning. And one day soon she would be fully up to speed with the ways of the Bachelors.

'So what's the plan?' asked Adam, looking over at Luke. 'Will you be OK to take Mum and Dad back in your car? I'll never fit in both of them, plus Dad's stuff, in a million years.'

'Wouldn't matter if you could anyway. You'll be too busy sorting things out to be playing taxi driver.'

'Sorting what out?'

'I think Luke's talking about me,' said a voice from behind him.

Steph was standing in the doorway. He didn't know what to do, say or think. 'What's going on?'

'This is my fault, Ad,' said Russell sheepishly. 'I used your phone to call her this morning while you were in the shower.'

'Listen,' said Dad. 'Why don't we all get off and give your brother some privacy?'

Everyone nodded, said their hellos to Steph and their goodbyes to Adam and within a matter of moments had left the room.

'I'm sorry you've been dragged into all of this, Steph,' said Adam. 'I know Russ meant well but he shouldn't have called.'

'You're right,' said Steph. 'You're absolutely right. Russell shouldn't have called me, you should. Why didn't you tell me what had happened, Adam? Why is it so hard for you to believe that someone would want to be with you at a time like this? Didn't the time we spent together mean anything to you?'

'It meant everything to me. You changed me, Steph. You changed me completely.'

'Then why didn't you let me help you?'

Feeling like he might fall over under the weight of his own body Adam sat down on the edge of the bed. 'I messed things up. You're right, I should've called. I knew you would've been there for me.'

'So why didn't you?'

'Because I couldn't help thinking that maybe what you said was right that first day I asked you out on a date. Maybe I'm not really your type after at all.'

Steph rolled her eyes. 'Adam, that is the biggest load of crap I've ever heard. And I say that as someone who has heard an awful lot of crap in her time. What is it with men and facts? Why are they so resistant to the idea of change? Why can't they see that it's possible to go from finding someone vain, egotistical and full of themselves to adoring that very same person without their entire world falling apart? Just what is wrong with you men?'

'You thought I was vain?'

'Very.'

'And egotistical?'

'Absolutely.'

'And full of myself?'

'Like a bloated windbag in need of the attentions of a good hatpin.'

'And yet you still want to give this a go?'

'I have to. With qualities like that who else would have you? No, Mr Bachelor, you're my type and I'm yours and just for the record I think you ought to know that we are going to be all right.'

Three Months Later

George and Joan Bachelor's
(belated) 40th wedding anniversary
Time: 7.00 p.m. – 1.00 a.m.
Venue: BlueBar, Wilbraham Road, Chorlton

Russell Bachelor

'It tells you a lot about being the youngest member of the Bachelor family,' began Russell, having nervously taken to the stage, 'that when it comes to tasks which no one wants to be the first one to do – for example giving speeches to a room crammed with one hundred and fifty family and friends – more often than not it falls to me to do them. It wasn't even as if I drew the short straw: there were no straws! I got cornered by Adam and told: "Dad's on last, I'm on before him so it's a toss up between you and Luke who goes out there and breaks the ice." As you can see it wasn't so much as a toss-up – that would imply some form of luck at play – nope, I was told that unless I wanted my naked baby photos made into a PowerPoint presentation for the whole world to see I would be going up first . . . and so here I am.

'What have I got to say about Mum and Dad's fortieth that might be worthy of your attention? Not much. Every one of those forty years speaks more eloquently about love than I hope to do. Those years speak about family, about loyalty but above all about hard work and dedication. And it's my greatest wish that Angie and I can have even half the happiness that Mum and Dad have shared over the past decades in our future together. Cheers, Mum and Dad! Happy anniversary!'

Luke Bachelor

'Before I get started the first thing you should know was that I wasn't joking when I told Russell I'd made a PowerPoint presentation of his naked baby photos. It really exists and straight after these speeches it will be making its debut in the basement bar once I've worked out how to hook up my laptop to the projector.

'Anyway, to questions of love . . . because that's what tonight is all about, isn't it? Forty years of love. With one failed marriage under my belt you'd be forgiven for thinking that I'm probably not the best person to be talking on the matter and you might be right. The only thing I seem to have learned about love is that it's a lot easier to get it wrong than to get it right and were I left to my own devices I would have spent the rest of my life getting it wrong time and time again. Thankfully that won't happen for three good reasons: namely my daughter, my parents and the woman I'm going to be marrying the week after next. So often we think of love as being this soft emotion. Strictly for the girls. But true love isn't anything like that – not when it's done right and that's what Megan, my parents and Cassie have all shown me. The only reason I'm standing here is because of their love. And the only reason I know what love is at all is because of them. So here's to love – cheers, Mum and Dad – and thanks for everything!'

Adam Bachelor

'From some of the things that have been said so far you might be forming the impression that we don't take my kid brother Russell all that seriously and you'd be right. But the thing about Russell is, beneath his youth and goofy exterior lies quite a bit of wisdom.

'A little while ago Russell and I had a conversation about whether or not the Bachelor family were cursed! I know! I know! But it was one of *those* conversations. Anyway, having given the matter some thought he turned up at my house proclaiming the good news: we weren't cursed, we were just late starters! I had to laugh. What was he on about? And yet a few months later look at us all: Mum and Dad celebrating their fortieth anniversary; Luke due to get married; Russell finally over whatever caused him to be a major pain in the backside these past few years; Adam Bachelor, bar owner and second best-looking guy in Chorlton, in an all-singing, all-dancing relationship with the single smartest, funniest, most beautiful woman you could ever hope to meet. And it only took me thirty-eight years and a few false starts to find her! Late starters? I was nearly a non-starter! I never thought this love business was for me. But it turns out that Russ was right. And you, Mum, have been telling me forever that it's just about finding the right person. I used to roll my eyes. Well it's true! I finally met her. And tonight, seeing how much my mum and dad still love each other I know that Luke is right: love isn't soft – it's hard like granite, it has to be. So much is expected of it, so much pressure put on it – it has to withstand such a lot. But after forty years of being polished, shaped and honed by life it truly is a thing of beauty. So thanks, Mum and Dad, for showing us not only what love is but how with hard work and real determination just how wonderful it can be. Happy anniversary!'

George Bachelor

'These past few weeks I've spent day and night worrying about what I was going to say tonight and only this morning it dawned on me that all I needed to do was say it. So here goes: I love you, Joan Bachelor. I always have done and I always will. Happy anniversary!'